Hellfire

JOHN CUTTER
HELLFIRE

A VINCE BELLATOR THRILLER

LUME BOOKS

LUME BOOKS

Published in 2023 by Lume Books

ISBN 978-1-83901-527-4

Typeset using Atomik ePublisher from Easypress Technologies

www.lumebooks.co.uk

Dedicated to everyone who believes that heroes are real.

CHAPTER ONE

Vince Bellator had a year and four months of peace.

Now, on a late spring noon, standing in the shallow seawater, Vince dumped a bag of freshly harvested oysters into his dinghy. His young friend Pascual, Lupe's boy, chattered about how Mama would cook the oysters.

Pascual set to smilingly sorting them, as Vince climbed carefully into the dinghy. His wading boots and general bigness made it a bit awkward. He was well over six feet tall and layered in muscle, but there was also the weight he'd put on this year—nearly thirty pounds—from eating Lupe's cooking; too much flan and *capirotada*. Maybe too many margaritas. And, he admitted to himself, he'd been taking it far too easy, at his house on southern Puget Sound.

He had married Dierdre Corlin in March; they'd honeymooned on Kauai, rainy but deeply relaxing, and he had managed to store away his previous life—and all his battle memories—in a locked cabinet of his mind.

It was almost seventeen months after he'd killed Angel Lopez and gutted the Caidos cartel. His investment in the home-based restaurant

1

at the southernmost end of Puget Sound had paid off. His instincts about Lupe Velasquez and Diego Fernandez, his business partners in *El Corazón de México,* had been exactly right. They were both deeply motivated to make the restaurant work, more so now that they'd gotten married themselves. And Lupe was a talented chef.

She was waiting for these oysters for her evening special, *Sopa de Ostiones,* and Vince began to row the dinghy back to the little dock near the home he'd built some years back. He'd done most of the work on the house himself, but he had to admit that the Mexican pastels Diego had added made it an attraction from the sea. Vince was thinking of expanding his dock to let yachts and cabin cruisers tie up so they could visit the restaurant directly from the bay. But then, they already had more customers than they could handle—a great review in the *Seattle Times* had enticed hungry customers from all over Washington State. In its first year, *El Corazon* had become a rousing success.

Watching him row, the boy stared at the tattoo on Vince's forearm. "Vince, is that an Army Rangers tattoo?"

"Yep."

"I want to get a tattoo!" Pascual declared.

"Maybe someday, after you turn eighteen."

"Did that one hurt?"

Vince grimaced as if remembering a terrible memory. "To be honest—it hurt so much that..." He gave out a theatrical sigh. "I cried like a little baby!" Then he looked at Pascual with deadpan seriousness.

Pascual stared. "*You?*" Then he realized.

They both burst into laughter.

"Okay, it stung a little," Vince said. "Tattoos can be pretty, or just cool, but the problem is that they fade. Over some years they get

2

blurry, and they look like a bruise or something. I don't recommend it. But when you're grown up, you'll do what you want with your skin. Just never get one on your face."

Superro, Pascual's chihuahua, was running excitedly back and forth on the dock as Vince drew up behind his cabin cruiser. Pascual moored the dinghy with a deftness Diego had taught him.

"*Que pasa*, Superro!" Vince called out as he tossed the bag of oysters onto the dock and started up the wooden stairs to the dock. The dog yipped in response.

Pascual climbed onto the dock, yelling at Superro to come back with the oyster gripped in his jaws. The chihuahua ran teasingly away, trying to get Pascual to play with him.

Vince smiled, seeing Dierdre coming down to meet them. Dierdre, the former FBI agent—*his wife!* His slender, lithely muscular, beautiful wife. Vince could hardly believe it, even now. She'd puzzled him recently by dyeing her honey-brown hair jet-black. Her newly-black hair was cut short and spiky, and she was wearing close fitting red jeans, a black turtleneck, and dark-red sneakers.

Dierdre was walking toward him from the house, smiling—but was there something else in her eyes? He hadn't seen that look in a while…

"Everything okay?" he asked, taking both her hands as she walked up. She let him draw her a little closer.

"Richie Chang is here," she said, in a low voice.

"Agent Chang," he muttered, looking at the house. Richie Chang was her former investigative partner at the FBI.

"And he's got a guy with him. Says you know him. Name of Tighe."

"Tighe! About fifty, small, looking like he's about to laugh but never does?"

"That's him."

Vince grunted. "Shit. Oscar Tighe. He's CIA."

She grimaced. "You want me to tell them to fuck off? I could say you're out fishing. And before they see you, you really could go fishing!"

"I'd love that, but… better not." Vince wanted no more dealings with the feds, and he'd definitely have got on the cruiser and taken a fishing trip, if he had been alone here. But he had to think about protecting Dierdre and Lupe and Pascual and Diego and… yeah, even the waitress, Nilla.

"Due diligence. They could be here to warn me about something." It wasn't as if he didn't have plenty of enemies out there. "Tighe owes me at least one favor. The prick."

"You didn't have any of our customers killed, did you Tighe?" Dierdre asked, only half joking, as they settled in a booth for lunch.

The restaurant's dining room was an extension they'd built the year before, but the booths and dark wall panels had been brought from an old restaurant and repurposed here. The decorations were mostly color photos of *rótulos,* Mexican food-cart and street-stall advertising: hand-painted with delightfully garish hues and wildly cartoonish lettering.

There was a full crowd for lunch; some from Harstine Island, some from surrounding towns, some from Seattle and Portland. Vince, Dierdre, Chang and Tighe sat in a booth at the window overlooking the water. Today, it had been reserved for certain customers who'd planned to fly in from Los Angeles, but had canceled just this morning.

"Customers… killed?" Tighe said, with an exaggerated look of innocence. The CIA officer was an imp-like little man, going gray, wearing a blue satin New York Yankees jacket, designer jeans, loafers.

4

He had hooded, darting gray eyes, and a thick drink-ruddy nose. His rather girlish lips were nearly always warped into a half-smile.

"The customers who were supposed to have this lunch reservation today," Dierdre said. "Who mysteriously canceled a few hours ago. Right before *you* got the reservation."

"Now if they canceled, how could they be dead?"

"You just waterboard them or something?" Vince asked, waving for Nilla to come over.

"We paid them a ridiculous amount of money to cancel," Tighe admitted.

Nilla sashayed to the table and took their orders. She was a sylphic bottle-blonde with long straight hair and bangs. One of her front teeth was significantly longer than the other. She had big brown eyes that always seemed mystified. She wore an elegant yet simple black couture skirt that Dierdre had bought for her, with sulfur-colored leggings and a Mexican blouse.

A little over a year and a half before, Vince had come upon Nilla as she was set upon by a couple of bikers; he'd dealt with the bikers, and to get her off the streets he'd brought her here and given her a job. Dierdre had semi-adopted her.

"Hey, Dierdre," she said after she scribbled down their orders. "I got that lingerie you recommended. It's really tight in my cooch, though."

Dierdre rolled her eyes. "Didn't Lupe remind you about the difference between waitress talk and Nilla talk?"

"Oh, sorry. I'm so fucked—so messed up today. I went out with Charlie last night."

"You drink too much?" Vince asked.

"No—that's the problem. He wouldn't let me drink and I couldn't get relaxed! But I let him kiss me. I'll get your soup started."

Unruffled, she vanished into the kitchen, and Richie Chang cleared his throat. "Uh… Vince… Something's come up…"

The FBI agent wore a gray suit, white shirt, blue tie. He kept shifting uncomfortably in his seat and stealing glances at Dierdre. Vince had always suspected him of being unrequitedly in love with her. Richie tented his fingers and said, "Maybe we should just launch in—"

"No, you shouldn't," Vince interrupted. The appearance of both the CIA and the FBI at his restaurant had assassinated his good mood. "I'm hungry," he said. "I had one scone for breakfast. I worked three hours in the woodshop with Diego and two hours in the water harvesting oysters. And if you keep talking, it's going to ruin my brunch. Just tell me this," he leaned closer to Richie and lowered his voice, "is anyone here in danger of being attacked today?"

"Well, no. Not that we know of."

"Then we're eating lunch first."

So they did. Tighe said the oyster soup was "Phenomenal! Just incredibly good…"

"You should tell Lupe that, Mr. Tighe," Dierdre said. "She's the artistic genius around here."

As they finished, Vince swallowed some of his flan and pointed a finger at Tighe. "You better fucking tip everyone here big, or I'll turn you upside down and shake the money out."

Tighe gave that twisted little smile again and said, "You hear that, Richie? He's still the same guy. Thinks he can start a restaurant and retire, but—"

"*Thinks?*" Vince shook his head. "I did it!"

"I get it," Tighe said. "I wish I could do it myself. Wonderful wife, wonderful business, wonderful place to live. But these are tough times in this country, Vince. Just exactly when a guy like you is needed."

"You are still full of shit, I see, Napoleon," Vince told him. He and Tighe knew each other from back in the day. Vince had been in Delta Force, interfacing with the Agency on black ops missions in Afghanistan and Iraq and Syria. Tighe was nicknamed Napoleon by the men fighting alongside Vince, because of his little-guy complex. Always in your face and pushing too hard. And sometimes so insistent on a mission's timetable, it got good men killed. Tighe had insisted that two Blackhawk helis go up in bad weather, and one of them was blown by a sandstorm into a power pole. Six men electrocuted.

As if reading that memory on Vince's face, Tighe put down his spoon and said, "Vince, I've grown up. I'm not going to push anyone into anything. But *this* we really need you for."

"Tighe, how many soldiers in the armed forces of this country now? Because last I looked it was more than one million, three hundred thousand on active duty. I'm betting you can find somebody to do the job."

"Sounds like it to me," Dierdre said.

"This job is in Chinese waters," Tighe said, barely loud enough to be heard. "A very quiet op."

"Then get Delta Force. They can spec ops it."

Tighe glanced around. They were in an alcove, with no other tables nearby, and the room was noisy with conversations. No one could likely hear them. But he leaned close to Vince and said, in a low voice, "It's not that kind of situation. It's like... it has to be *infiltrated*. And we think if it's more than one guy, it'll go south. And he's got to be the guy who can do the most with what he's given. That's your forte, Vince. Maybe you haven't sunk a ship before—"

7

"*Ship?*" Vince said. "Jesus." He shook his head. "Hold on." He got up, then turned to Dierdre. "You want a drink?"

She shook her head. "Kind of early, Vince…"

"Not today, it isn't," Vince said. He looked at the feds. "You two knuckleheads?"

"Coffee for me," Chang said.

"Bourbon up," Tighe said.

Vince went to the bar and made his own double-shot Bloody Mary as he chatted with Maria the bartender. He poured a double Old Ezra for Tighe, put the drinks on a tray with a cup of coffee for Richie Chang, and carried it to the table himself.

"Hey, I woulda got that for you!" Nilla yelled across the room.

He blew her a kiss and she blushed.

"Whatever it is, doesn't matter," Dierdre was saying, when Vince sat down. "He's done enough. It's a miracle he lived through it all— overseas and over here!"

Tighe took a long pull at his bourbon and shuddered. "You know the name Pavel Krupin, Vince?"

Vince nodded. He'd been lightly briefed on Krupin; glimpsed him at the Caidos drug compound out in the desert. A Russian operative dealing with a Mexican cartel on US soil. "What about him?"

"He knows about you too, man," Tighe said. "You took down one of his operations. Russian intel had *plans* for the Caidos."

"You saying… he's following up with me?"

"I'm saying it's possible he will. The smart thing would be to get out ahead of it. That's all part of… our proposal."

Vince shrugged. "Not interested."

"Look, this comes straight from…"

"Happy birthday to you!" It was Nilla, with Pascual, both of them singing, carrying a flan to a nearby table. On the flan was a lit birthday candle, and the people at the table were clapping and singing.

Tighe looked around and shook his head. "Let's finish our drinks. Maybe go down to the water. Like on your cabin cruiser, discuss it there. There are documents you have to see. Just you, me, and Agent Chang."

Vince drank his Bloody Mary and thought about telling Tighe to go straight to hell. He didn't want any more missions—except the mission of living his life to the fullest with his wife. He didn't regret having taken lives for a good cause, but he didn't want to take any more. Not without dire necessity.

Trouble is, the name Pavel Krupin snagged in Vince's mind. He had thought about Krupin before, after the Caidos mission, and the possibility that he might send someone here.

Vince decided it wouldn't hurt to hear them out. "Let's talk in the cruiser."

Vince opened the little port window. It was stuffy in the cabin cruiser, with three men in the small space. The briny smell of seawater wafted in, along with the resinous tang of the pines and junipers that thronged the island.

He sat on the fold-down bed-seat; the other two men sat on the padded bench across from him. Tighe looked comfortable, but, hunched forward, Richie seemed tense.

"Nice set up in here," Tighe said, looking around. "Fishing, playing. Whatever."

"Why'd you bring up Krupin's name?" Vince asked.

Tighe pooched his lips and tilted his head. "We-ell, he's been making inquiries about you. He knows you're the guy who wrecked his deal with the cartel. Our man inside says the cartel was going to provide supply ships, and women, and protection for a major SVR operation. That's a lot to lose. They had to scramble to make a deal with the Chinese."

"The Chinese are in this too?"

"I'll come to that."

"It's been more than a year since I took out the Caidos. If Krupin took it personally, why hasn't he made a move?"

"Because he's a top man in Russian intel and they have their sources. He knows we keep an eye on you. He doesn't want his men fighting Homeland Security and maybe the goddamn National Guard. He wants no ruckus. But he'll wait for his opportunity. You shouldn't give him the breathing room."

"I'm not interested in stirring up a hornets' nest any more than Krupin is."

Richie Chang gave a small snort of impatience. "What matters is… he's involved in an operation that's poisoning this country with disinformation and undermining us with cyberwarfare hacking. Ransomware, infrastructure sabotage, every electronic weapon they have. Most of the cyberattacks and the disinfo now come from a ship in the East China Sea. They're using unidentified satellites to transmit this toxic stuff. There's chatter they plan to target our infrastructure."

"That's an IT problem!" Vince snorted. "What am *I* gonna to do about it?"

Tighe shook his head. "We're not asking you to be a hacker, Vince—just to stop the operation at its source. Up close and personal. And it's more than just a hacking operation. It's bigger than that…"

"This ship story sounds like disinformation itself. Russian cyberwarfare originates in mainland Russia."

"*Used* to. A few years ago, we found a way to shut most of that down. I can't talk about how. We had a cyberwar breakthrough. And we threatened their banking structure if they rebuilt it in Russia. So, the Russians hid their cyberwar base of operations elsewhere. We can't use our cyber teams to get at it, not where it is now. The Russians got chummy with the Chinese back when they were up to their knees in mud and blood in Ukraine. They're moving their hostile cyber operations out of Russia, and they're sharing some of them with China. So, there are Chinese hackers involved, too. The People's Republic lets Russian intel operate out of a ship, under cover of a kind of floating bordello, in Chinese waters."

"Then the President should go public with it."

"She's playing it cagey—she doesn't want the Russians or the Chinese realizing we're aware of the operation. Their base is on a ship called *Cupid's Cruise*—and we want it physically taken out. I won't lie to you—"

"Wait, you won't lie to me?" Vince pretended puzzlement. "I thought you were still with the CIA?"

Tighe closed his eyes for a long moment. Then he licked his lips and went on. "It's a big job and as dangerous as anything you've ever done—maybe more. That ship with its stupid name is defended like Fort Knox. And there are other, well… *nuances* to the mission. Some important details that…" Tighe scowled. "Are you *laughing* at me right now?"

It was more of a dry chortle. "You want me to go to China and *sink a ship*! You're out of your goddamn mind!"

"Vince," said Richie, gently. "For a while last year, when the press found out where you lived, they came around here all the time, like paparazzi, trying to get pictures of you and Dierdre, trying to get an interview with the guy who was pardoned for the killings at the Lincoln Memorial—"

"'Pardoned for the killings'?" Vince stared at Richie. "The men I killed were domestic terrorists, Richie," Vince said. "Nazis! They were engaging in mass murder!"

Tighe nodded. "This time, the Russian regime is the new vector of fascism."

"Thing is, Vince," Chang went on, "all those reporters just went away one day. You think that was magic?"

Vince shrugged. "I figured the feds had intervened somehow."

"The President herself intervened! She didn't want all that attention on you. She had a hunch we'd need you for this. What you did at the Memorial was necessary—but it was crazy illegal. She pardoned you and Dierdre. You both owe her for that."

"I'm not the President's attack dog," Vince said. "I owe my loyalty to my wife and the people here who depend on me." A thought struck him. "Wait—are you saying that the reporters will come back if I don't take this mission?"

Richie cleared his throat. "Protecting you from all that isn't easy. That protection could go away."

Vince's fists clenched. He didn't like being squeezed this way. "Listen. If I have to, I'll turn the business completely over to Lupe and I'll leave the country with Dierdre. I'll go into hiding. I'm not going to be browbeaten like that."

"It's not about making nice with the President," Tighe said, waving his hand dismissively. "It's about—*this nation*. It's under disinformation attack, and cyberattack, twenty-four seven. And it's about the fact that a guy like Krupin never forgives, never forgets. He'll find you, and Dierdre. Sooner or later, Vince, Krupin will even the score. You really do need to get out ahead of this. And hey—you can be back in a month."

"Or my wife could be a widow in a month." But Tighe was

starting to get through to him. "I'm going to need you to brief me in as much depth as you can today, and then…" Vince let out a long breath, that became a soft growl. And then he said, "I'll think it over."

CHAPTER TWO

Jim Greenwald decided that someone had to make an example of this woman. It wasn't so much that she had stolen money from him. It was what she had left him with.

Heroin withdrawal. The sickness. A bad one.

He was sweating, his muscles were knotting, his stomach was churning, his skin felt too tight, and his whole body ached. Every time the ship shifted a little in the rising tide and restless seas, he felt a rush of nausea.

His usual dope source was Leng, but the ship's authorized dealer had left for a buy in Macao.

Bad timing. Greenwald had to see Krupin tomorrow.

Greenwald crossed his stateroom to the medicine cabinet. He looked, and found that the codeine was still there. There were two pills. Exactly two. Maybe they would get him through.

He swallowed one and chewed up the other, then washed out his mouth, looking at himself in the medicine cabinet mirror. He'd gotten fatter since coming here; he had chipmunk cheeks now, and there were blue rings under his eyes. His thinning gray-brown hair was pasted to his head with sweat.

How had he gotten here? Not just to this ship. But under the thumb of the Russian GUR.

He'd been making sweet money—he'd had a founder's share of an app, ChatBrat, but they'd pushed him out of the corporation when he tried to open ChatBrat to his radical-right anti-government friends. Then one of his friends had been arrested at the January 6 thing in DC and jailed for sedition, and then his wife left him, and his occasional OxyContin binges became a weekly thing and then every day…

The Russians, knowing his politics, had approached him to join their cyberwar team. "You want to bring down the American government? Let us help you. We're looking for a new control center…"

The ship had been Greenwald's idea. He'd pitched it in a fever of excitement. "You buy an old hulk, like a freighter or an old cruise ship, and you take it to Chinese waters—they're your allies now, right? We can set up there, radically disrupt the body politic of America. It'll be a major step forward for libertarianism! It'll create its own reality in media, and it'll have the best hackers available. I lucked into a lot of data on cyber defense infrastructure…"

Which is when the Russians bought the *Cupid's Cruise*, arranged for him to come to Macao, and set him up on the ship, in his own stateroom. They didn't seem bothered at all that he was an opiate addict.

And here he was.

Greenwald washed the sweat away and went to find Lorvec. Because the girl must pay for what she'd done.

By the time he got down the passageway to the ladder—a nautical term that didn't make sense to him, since it was a metal stairway and not a ladder—Greenwald was feeling a little better, the codeine taking the edge off his withdrawal. It was hotter out

15

here, and humid; there was no air conditioning in the passages. The steel ceiling sometimes dripped with moisture. It was veined with rust and bits of fallen paint littered the passageway deck. The stateroom doors had their own rusty edges. The reek of the bilge wasn't bad on this deck, but it still smelled of oil run-off and cooking grease.

By the time he got down to Lorvec's deck, Greenwald was a little out of breath. He spent most of his waking time at his workstation in his stateroom, supervising the bots and the disinfo team, and his wind was even more depleted than usual.

There were twelve decks on the former cruise ship; he was on deck ten; Lorvec was on nine. He went down the ladder well to nine, walked back to stateroom thirty, steeled his determination, and knocked.

He was always nervous, meeting with Lorvec.

Lorvec opened the door, scowling. He was built, as Greenwald's dad would have said, "like a brick shithouse." The Russian was almost bald, with a big chunk of a face, a short neck, eyes the color of glossy black limo paint. He wore a cammie t-shirt and cammie sweatpants. He smelled like cheap cologne and sweat.

"What you want?" he demanded.

"Something needs to be taken care of. A couple of things. I need them sorted out, so I can get back to work."

"Why you don't call first?"

"Easier to explain in person. Can I come in?"

"No, you stink. The dope, it makes you forget the shower."

"You do know that I own this ship, don't you? A little respect wouldn't hurt—"

"You *own* this ship? Central owns you. Central owns this ship. You have good life here. Shut up. What you want?"

16

Central. Russian intelligence administration. Greenwald sighed. "The girl who goes by Empress. Her name's Bae Quon. She stole from me. Money and... other things. She was doing her job and I went to the bathroom for a second and when I came back, she was gone with my cash and—"

"So? Find her and beat her."

Greenwald shook his head. "She has to be an example for everyone! A really tough example, out in the open! I need some respect here! They all need to know they can't do that."

Jim Greenwald had been troubled by women for a long time. His wife dumped him; the women he'd met sneered at him. Now, the prostitutes stole from him. He had to send a message.

So, Greenwald waited as Lorvec whistled a Russian pop song to himself, which meant he was thinking it over. "Okay," Lorvec said at last, "I am so bored today, we do this."

"She's in three-nineteen."

Lorvec turned and called into the room. "Artyom!"

Wearing a swimming suit and flip flops and white bathrobe, a frosty glass of vodka in one hand, Lorvec's assistant came to the door. He was a pale man, stocky and muscular, his right jaw deeply marked with a scar, his dull blue eyes red from staying up all night. There was a Russian eagle tattooed on his left forearm. Lorvec spoke to him in Russian and Artyom nodded and went back into the room.

He came out with two guns—the black Grach Yarygin automatic pistols that Moscow Central's enforcers carried—and plastic wrist-ties.

Greenwald was sorry he hadn't brought his Glock, or his AR15. Just for appearances' sake.

Taking one of the pistols, Lorvec said, "Greenwald, we go. You show me the berth."

Lorvec had the master key to all the berths. They found "Empress" in her bunk, nodding dopily in her underwear, high on Greenwald's heroin. The half empty baggy was lying on the metal deck beside her. A song by Beyonce played from two small Bluetooth speakers on a little shelf near her feet.

Greenwald picked up the dope bag, folded it neatly, put it in his pocket. The Chinese girl didn't look up till Lorvec took hold of her upper arm and dragged her from the bunk. She squawked and looked around with dope-pinned eyes and struggled to get away till Lorvec back-handed her. Then, she went flailing back into the bulkhead.

Greenwald only followed this peripherally. He was looking for his money. He found it under her bunk mattress.

Artyom yanked the stunned girl's arms behind her, closed the ties on her wrists, dragged her to her feet. She looked around, a little blood running from her cut lip. "Jim!" she said, spotting Greenwald. "I did not! I did not! Please Jim!"

Artyom and Lorvec each took an elbow and steered the girl into the passageway. Greenwald lingered behind, took some of the heroin between two fingers and snorted it. The relief was immediate.

He put the baggy in a pocket and followed Lorvec, Artyom and the stumbling girl toward the aft. Lorvec's free hand was using his walkie-talkie to call the main deck guards. Ordering preparations and an announcement. Greenwald imagined their preparations and he felt sick and pleased at once.

Then came the announcement, repeated over the public address system in Chinese-Cantonese, Macao-Portuguese, and English. The announcer was Zau, who knew five languages and just enough Russian. Most of the crew and the girls spoke some English, left over from working the casinos in Macao, which were thronged by

Americans and Brits, along with Chinese gamblers. The girls had been drawn from Macao jails, where they'd landed for failing to pay the necessary bribes to be prostitutes, or for drug crimes or theft. The Chinese government had gotten them transferred here. It was part of the ship's cover, and provided additional privileges for crew and guards.

There was a single working elevator on the *Cupid's Cruise,* other than the freight lift at the other end of the ship. They took the glass-sided passenger elevator to the main deck, with Bae weeping the whole time, imploring him, "Jim, Jim, you know I did not steal! It was Sasha! She did it!"

They came out into the sea breeze, under patchy clouds. Gulls screamed and the choppy waves glittered with whitecaps. The ship cruised continuously slowly twenty miles south, twenty miles north, a couple miles out to sea from Macao. It never docked. Supply ships made deliveries, and took people back and forth. The only "customers" were occasional Russian oligarchs, or young Chinese heirs on motor yachts wanting anonymous sex and drug parties. All part of the cover.

The ship heeled slightly as they intersected a current. It wasn't too rough out here today, Greenwald thought. He was mostly over his seasickness, but sometimes, when a storm came along, he spent hours on the floor beside the stateroom toilet.

Bae babbled in Chinese now. Occasionally she struggled pitifully to get away. Greenwald wondered, absently, why he didn't feel anything about Bae right now. No pity. He knew what it was like to be a drug addict, like her, after all. Shouldn't he feel sympathy for her?

But he didn't feel much of anything. He was never a bleeding heart—hell, he was a libertarian—but when something like this happened, he used to feel bad.

Not anymore.

Artyom seemed annoyed by the girl's struggling and struck her with the butt of his gun. She slumped, groaning, and they dragged her along like a rice sack.

A few minutes more and they reached the stern, where a crowd of crewmembers and women, some of the women in the sexy garments of their trade, had been brought out to the curved rail. A few ship's "officers" were here, and half a dozen "security guards", wearing off-the-rack security guard uniforms. They were actually armed thugs from the Russian GDR, all of them armed with CS/LS7 submachine guns, provided by the Chinese, and Russian Grach automatic pistols.

Greenwald looked around for Pavel Krupin, and didn't see him. Which was a relief. Krupin made him even more nervous than Lorvec did.

The ship slowed, then came to a halt in the sea. An electric winch was set up about fifty steps from the stern, and a cable from the winch stretched to the rail and drooped over it. The cable's end was formed into a loop.

A rope had been tied to the loop.

Two crewmembers, wearing the red *Cupid's Cruise* livery of the ship, were dumping bloody bits of meat, from the kitchens, over the side and into the water.

Greenwald had heard that Great White sharks had been seen following the ship. He walked to the railing, looked over—and saw them, four at least, churning the water, their dorsal fins quite prominent. Drawn close by the bloody meat.

Then he saw Zau step out onto the next higher deck. A small man with a high forehead, Zau was wearing an officer's white uniform with pressed shorts. He called down to the crowd, speaking first in Cantonese, as Bae was dragged up to the railing. She was recovering consciousness, looking around frantically, as Zau repeated his declamation in English. "This girl has stolen from the owner of this ship! No stealing is allowed here! And this time it merits the death penalty! This disrespect for leadership cannot be tolerated! You see what will happen!"

Now, Bae was screaming as they fastened her ankles with the rope on the cable loop. Artyom crouched by her, a buck knife in hand, and slashed her face and her shoulders deeply. She shrieked—and then they forced her over the rail.

Greenwald could not help but look as she was lowered, headfirst, sixty feet down to the water, wriggling on the line like a fish, blood from the slashes dripping thickly into the seawater. Some Russian sentries watching at the rails hooted and laughed and clapped.

"Christ," Greenwald muttered. The Russians were young agents in training. Brutality was part of the training.

So they laughed and clapped as the sharks jumped at the girl. "*Jiiiiiim!*" Bae screamed.

"Shut up," Greenwald muttered. "Shut up."

The first shark missed her, but another leapt and its snapping teeth caught the top of her head, tearing her scalp off as another one leaped up and caught her face in its jaws, and...

Greenwald felt something at that.

He turned away, suddenly having inexplicable trouble breathing. Okay, so he could still feel, sometimes.

He saw the girls back away from the rail, some of them hugging one another, many weeping.

One hand massaging the dope packet in his pocket, Greenwald walked shakily back toward the elevator. He needed alone time. He needed his dope. Everything would be fine when he got a good hit into him. Then he wouldn't see the picture in his mind's eye anymore, that shark tearing Bae's face away, a face he'd kissed the night before...

It was two in the morning when Vince joined Dierdre in bed. She was sitting up, wearing her short nightie, reading *Lincoln in the Bardo* by George Saunders. Vince had taken a shower and came in wearing nothing but a towel.

Looking at her book, he said, "The bardo?" Vince knew it to be a Tibetan term for a phase of the afterlife. He'd wondered if there really were bardos—and if he'd been to one. He'd had a dream once, in which he seemed to be conversing with Jack Sullivan, in a kind of unearthly realm that took the form of a battle in Vietnam.

Vince sat down beside her on the bed. "You thinking about the afterlife?"

"Saunders made this up," Dierdre said, setting the book on her bedside table. "But I sometimes think that if you do go on another mission, the next time I'll see you will be in a place like... a bardo." She shrugged. "If the afterlife exists. You're getting water from that towel on the bed."

"Is that a ploy to get me to take off the towel?"

"Do I need a ploy for that?"

"No." He took it off and tossed it onto a chair. "I'm hearing about water on the bed. Getting disapproving looks when I have a drink with lunch. You're really starting to be like... a wife."

"Oh, yes? Is that a complaint, mister?"

"You know..." He eased close to her and took her hand in his. "No. It isn't. I like that you feel like a wife, that you're just being a... what did Aretha Franklin call it?"

"A 'natural woman'?"

"Yeah."

"So there was *doubt* that I was a natural woman?"

He laughed. "That's like a wife, too—a guy says the wrong thing and can't seem to say the right thing for the rest of the night."

"I thought you'd never been married before me."

"Never have. But I've been around a lot of couples, and I remember my parents. Mom was just like that. And she was crazy about my dad, and he was crazy about her. Dierdre—you can say anything you damn please."

He bent over and kissed her, and she made as if to resist the kiss for a second or two, and then she put her arms around his neck, and pulled him closer and spoke into his ear. "The problem isn't what you're saying, Vincent Bellator, it's that you're talking at all right now. Shut up and get busy."

A good long while later, they lay in a bed that seemed almost to steam around them, and she asked him to get up and make them drinks. They had their drinks, and then…

A good while after *that*, almost exhausted, they lay in each other's arms and looked at the half moon through the open window. Outside, a nightbird trilled, and Dierdre said, "I love it at this house, with you. The woods and the water down below and *El Corazon* and… just us living life here, Vince."

He suspected this was her making an indirect stab at asking if he'd made up his mind about the mission yet. As if to say: Isn't it time for *a home* in your life—instead of picking up another gun?

Vince said, "I feel the same way about being here with you, honey."

"You were a long time out on that boat with Richie and Tighe."

"They brought out the briefing papers. Laptops. Pictures of the target ship. More on Krupin. The set-up for infil. Plans of the ship.

23

Timetables. Stats about the target's defenses. The whole shebang."

"Did they leave?"

"Yes, they went into town. They have rooms somewhere."

"But you'll see them tomorrow?"

"I will."

"Do you know…?"

"I've… had Pavel Krupin at the back of my mind for a good long time now. I wondered if he might be a threat to us. To everything here. It appears he does plan to go after me; somehow, someday. And that means he'll come after you, too."

"Can you tell me about the mission?"

"I am absolutely not supposed to do that. So, I will."

He told her everything he knew, and added, "Russia has made a mistake, if they've really moved their whole disinformation and cyberattack program onto that ship. They think it's a moving target, and it'll never be attacked because of the Chinese. But… if we can take it out…"

She closed her eyes, squeezed them shut like someone suffering from a headache. Then, in a carefully controlled voice, she said, "I guess you have to do it, Vince. So many conspiracy theories and flat-out lies spread through information warfare. Even QAnon— the Russians don't seem to have created that bullshit but they take advantage of it. And they push buttons on people to get them to go all anti-government… through intermediaries, fake websites, operatives… constantly trying to destabilize America…"

Vince smiled. She didn't want him to go, but she'd forced herself to see all sides of the issue. She had made up her mind to support him in his decision. "Seems like Dierdre Corlin, FBI agent, is still in there somewhere," he said, kissing her forehead.

"Hey, I'm Dierdre *Bellator*, restaurateur! But there's a reason I served in the military, and the FBI. That reason, that feeling—it's still there, inside me."

He nodded. "Yeah. It's kind of hard to escape, isn't it? I have to take the mission, Dierdre. I wish I didn't."

"I know." Her voice was hoarse, and he pulled her close. "I know, Vince…"

CHAPTER THREE

Carrying his scant luggage, Vince descended from the private jet, stepping onto the tarmac at the Ninoy Aquino International Airport, outside Manila. It was a hot and muggy early evening, and he was feeling jet lagged. *Am I getting old?* he wondered.

He wore a light linen suit without a tie, brogues that were hurting his feet, and he carried a midsized suitcase with nothing important in it at all. The weapons would come later.

A white SUV pulled up, and a Filipino man of about fifty, wearing a red and blue Hawaiian shirt, got out, smiled at him and said, "Mr. Bellator?"

"That would be me, yes."

"I'm Jerry Timbol, the embassy sent me."

Vince nodded. He knew that "the embassy" meant the CIA. He'd seen Timbol's picture and recognized his name from the pre-flight briefing.

"Any other luggage, sir?"

"No other luggage. Call me Vince, man. Okay I call you Jerry?"

"Yes sir—I mean, yeah… Vince."

"Let's take half an hour, stop at a food truck, get something to eat, and some coffee. Is Tighe here yet?"

"Yes sir, Vince—came in on military transport this morning."

"The Agency gives me the private jet, makes Tighe take a transport bird. I like it."

Jerry made a motion as if to take the luggage and Vince said, "Don't bother. Just get me to the food. I'm buying, if you're hungry." Vince carried the luggage to the SUV.

Jerry drove them to the Quiapo market in the old district and they ate spicy chicken and fried quail's eggs with *halo-halo* for dessert. From there, they drove to the embassy, Vince wishing Dierdre was here with him. He'd gotten to know parts of Asia pretty well as an Army Ranger. He'd been stationed for a while in South Korea, taking part in training exercises for a big operation that never came about: an invasion of North Korea, to be carried out alongside the South Koreans. But the President of the time had lost his nerve—understandably scared off by the possibility of the invasion leading to all-out war with North Korea's allies, the People's Republic of China. Invasion canceled.

Furloughed after the cancellation, Vince had flown across southeast Asia, visiting Japan and Thailand, Vietnam and the Philippines. Just exploring. He'd been planning to bring Dierdre to Japan next year. He wondered if he'd live long enough to do that.

While he and Jerry waited for the meeting in an American embassy anteroom, Vince phoned Dierdre.

"Hey!" she said, sounding a little sleepy.

"You asleep?"

"Not yet. Couldn't sleep much last two nights. Sorry—don't mean to guilt-trip you."

"Hey I'm guilt-tripping myself. I miss you already."

"You miss my disapproving glances?"

27

"Most of all."

She laughed. "Oh, shut up. No, don't shut up…"

"Dierdre—they promised me you guys would have protection, till this is over. Are they there?"

"Yes. I just wish they were a little more discreet. Hide their guns better. There are three eight-hour shifts. And guess what—it's run by the Secret Service. I don't think I'm going to leave you alone with the President. She's obviously really into you."

Vince laughed. "I'm in a waiting room with some other people, so I'm not saying the mushy stuff. But I'm thinking it."

"I'm thinking it too. Vince, be careful. Be careful as all hell. Be as careful as an ice- skating elephant."

"That something your dad used to say?"

"My grandma."

"I'll take it to heart. Here's Tighe. Looks as jet lagged as I am. They made us go separately and he had to hitch a troop carrier. Not so comfortable."

"Serves him right. Call me when you can, big guy. But remember— elephant. Ice."

"Count on it."

They hung up, and he and Jerry Timbol followed Tighe to the second-level briefing.

The table in the stuffy conference room had just one file on it, one laptop, and a manual on bilge pump repair. Tighe handed him the manual. "That's for you, tough dude. Can you use a wrench for anything besides busting heads?"

It was a dusty warehouse, windows painted over, most of the concrete floor empty. An interior room had been recently constructed at one end, and that was where the intel's undisclosed armory was located. Armory seven for East Asian black ops was run by a guy named Mel Melburn. There was a friendly sound to "Mel" but to Vince, Melburn seemed about as friendly as a wild hawk eyeing a birder too close to its nest. He was a man with beetling black eyebrows, pinched lips, a big beak of a nose and thick, gray-flecked curly black hair; he wore cammie coveralls and there was an old Colt police revolver in a military-police holster on his hip. Vince stood at the counter, pointing at what he wanted arrayed on the rack behind.

"That HK416, with a strap, red dot sight... standard rounds... These flashbangs..." Vince said. Despite the term, the red dot sight didn't use a laser for marking. Vince was more comfortable without the laser—he was old school.

Melburn set the gear out on the counter for closer check-over.

"...that Para Commando knife... this SIG Sauer, with the 21 round extended mag..."

As Vince made his selection from the armory, he remembered the last thing Tighe had said at the briefing. *"If you're captured, we're not going to be able to negotiate a release, Vince. We're going to disavow you. We'll say it looks like you decided to go after Pavel Krupin personally. Which is almost true anyway, if I understand your motivation for taking this mission on."*

"This M110 sniper rifle... this .410 shotgun pistol, standard cartridges for that and I'll need incendiary shells too... Four frag grenades..."

"Just know, we won't be able to exchange for you, if the Russians take you to Moscow for a... well, whatever they call a debriefing there. And if you get in trouble, we won't be able to send in any back-up..."

"You're saying I'm a throwaway."

"I'm afraid so. If you're compromised, we'll deny, deny, deny, whatever you tell them."

"Only four grenades?" Melburn asked, almost emotionlessly. Maybe *slightly* surprised.

"Grenades aren't precise," Vince said, taking the SIG apart so he could look down its barrel. "It's indoor combat, mostly."

Melburn frowned, seeing him look through the gun barrel of the SIG Sauer. "You worried I'll give you dirty guns?"

"Just habit," Vince said. "Get a feel for the gear." He glanced over the pistol's parts, put them back together. "I'll take a suppressor for the SIG."

Melburn handed it over. "You sure you want the M110 sniper? Kind of out of date. We got the M2010 here, with the smart scope."

"Smart scopes are for people who can't aim." But Vince grinned—and Melburn almost smiled back. Vince knew in some conditions a smart scope would be a life saver. "Truth is, I'm not checked out on them. But I would like a thermal scope, with a Picatinny mounter."

"Here you are." He set the gear on the counter. "You need to do a target-shoot for anything? It's at another location."

"Won't be necessary."

"You know those .410 incendiary rounds have no lethal efficiency except close to point blank?"

"I do know that. They're for... tactical purposes."

Melburn nodded. "You want to check out the detonators?"

"Anything new? Like—more recent than six years?"

"Nope. But we have EPX-1. Kicks ass."

"I've used it. Just make sure I have enough to sink a ship."

"You put it where it needs to go, it'll sink that vessel. But you'll need several transponders in a metal ship to be sure your signal can reach the detonator."

Vince set the SIG Sauer down on the counter. "I'll need an ammo belt too, as multicarry as possible."

"That's assumed."

"I can't take any of this aboard the vessel with me. How am I getting the gear where I need it?"

"Going to be tricky, since you're being infiltrated, deep cover. Jerry has a plan to get it to you. He's got a man in place on one of the delivery ships. The goods will be hidden under a crate of canned goods. You'll have to get to them in the hold." He took a large manila envelope out from under the counter. "The cobbler sent this over. Passport, details of your identity legend, some randomized papers…"

"What's my name?"

"As a temporary contractor on the *Cupid's Cruise*, your name is…" He drew out the paperwork and scanned it. "Graf. Hans Graf." He shoved the papers back in the envelope and handed it to Vince. "You can still tell them you're not taking the job, you know. You're not in the Agency, you're not in the Rangers or Delta Force anymore. No obligation."

Vince looked at him, curious as to what had brought on this familiarity. "You know about the mission?"

"I picked up enough. Had to, to lay out the right hardware for you to select from. You know, even if you neutralize every target, it won't stop the problem. They'll just rebuild the system."

Vince nodded. "It'll give us a chance to breathe—and set up better protections." And with luck, it would take Pavel Krupin out of play. He took the envelope, waved goodbye with it, and said, "See you if I see you."

As Vince walked off, he heard Melburn say, "Good luck, Bellator." Softly adding, "God help you."

Greenwald fidgeted in the chair on the balcony of Krupin's ocean view suite, two levels above the main deck. Wearing sunglasses and shorts, watching the waves rise and fall, he was waiting for Krupin.

Greenwald felt kind of sick this morning, but suspected that was just nerves. He'd done his morning dope. It was a challenge, figuring how much heroin was too much for functionality—the balance between staying cogent and keeping from being dope sick. Small hits scattered through the day worked well enough, but there was real danger of a buildup, over the day, leading to nodding out at a meeting or even an overdose.

He tensed as the sliding door came open. "Ah, Mr. James Greenwald!" said Krupin cheerily, coming out in a linen suit and a straw sunhat. He was carrying a small envelope in one hand, a drink in the other. "I am having a spicy vodka, today—an eye opener you Americans say, yes? You will have one, Jim?"

"No, not today, Pavel, thank you."

"Pity. Well… in this envelope is a flash drive." He handed the envelope to Greenwald. "Another expression of yours: 'guard this with your life'… now is not just an expression!"

Greenwald took it, looked in the envelope at the flash drive, and wondered why he'd bothered. It was just a flash drive. "And what is on it, Pavel?"

"Ahhh! You want to change America, correct?" Krupin's English, overall, was very good. He had studied at Oxford as a young man.

"Yes! There are too many regulations, too many laws. I mean, some are needed, but not that many! It shouldn't be a *state*, just a series of small areas of ownership, which—"

"This is your libertarian idea, I believe?" Krupin interrupted.

"It is that, yes. Some of it."

Krupin sipped from his eye opener. "But to change such a big, powerful thing as the American state, Jim, you need complete upheaval, wouldn't you agree? That is why you came to us! Now this," Krupin nodded toward the flash drive envelope, "will be your upheaval. America will change—radically. We call it Operation *Sesennyaya Slava*; Spring Glory, in English. That is the cyberattack procedure for seven key areas of America's... what is the word... its *infrastructure*. Attacks on refineries. Most will go wrong, some will explode. Attacks on power plants including nuclear plants for biggest populations, including District of Columbia..." He paused to sigh in contentment at the prospect, and went on: "Attacks on communications, including satellites. Attacks on aviation controls, attacks on national radar protections, attacks on banking, attacks on electric grids. But all done with cyberwar, *all at once across the USA!* All the same day! No power, no money from banks, no payments for your work in most businesses, power plants and refineries burning down, passenger planes crashing... We predict, of course, rioting and anarchy. So many people with guns—what will they do with them? Ho-ho!" He reached over and gave Greenwald a comradely slap on the shoulder. "Everything you wanted, Jim. *Upheaval!* America upside-down! Then maybe you and your... your *libertarians*... will take over, yes? So—why do you stare at me with mouth open?"

"Hm? Oh sorry. It's just a lot to... to uh..."

"You said chaos would be a chance for your libertarian society."

"But it needs preparation. I mean, we'd have to organize, me and the others... and we're a minority, but maybe..." Something occurred to Greenwald. "Pavel, with communications down, does that include the internet?"

"Oh yes!"

"And cell phones?"

"Not all cell phones. Many of them. Our own people have a special system."

"But when does this happen?"

"In about nine days, if you do your job."

"Nine days! How are we… How are people like me… to organize? We need time to communicate, to plan!"

Krupin shook his head. "You cannot. You will *not* communicate with your fellow libertarians or anyone else. No. Not until it's all done. You only communicate with me and Lorvec and your crew. Use intercom. But there is a plan. When the time is right, to use hypersonic missiles to destroy America's defenses. Radar and other systems will be down, thanks to the cyber offensive. Then, after a time of chaos, we will move our troops in."

"A Russian takeover of the USA? But Russia is a *state*, with a central authority…"

"Not so libertarian?" Krupin tilted his head and mimicked a sad sigh. Then he laughed. "You are truly a silly man! You cannot have a state without a state, Jim! Now, your part is to distribute these data to your teams, and prepare for a general attack. Like you did when we took down the power grid, in the south part of Texas, remember?"

"Yes, that was successful… they never realized…" Greenwald was feeling dazed. Clearly Krupin was only mocking him when he said the libertarians would take over during the coming chaos. Operation Spring Glory was *preliminary to invasion*.

But he had no choice. If he refused, he'd be killed. And there were others who would simply take over from him. The Russians had many excellent coders and hackers to choose from. They had wanted him because he understood America from the inside out, being American, and because, with his help, their little experiment in interfering with Texas infrastructure had worked so well. And here he was, already in place.

He told himself, *Jim, it's best to be on the winning side.* He would have to let go of his libertarian dream. The Russians would have a good position for him, after their takeover. Krupin had said as much before.

"Are you committed to this, Jim?" Krupin asked, watching him closely.

"Yes." He swallowed hard. "Yes, I am."

Krupin reached over and snatched Greenwald's sunglasses from his nose. He said, coldly and clearly, watching Greenwald's eyes. "Tell me again. *Are you committed to this, Jim?*"

Greenwald looked Krupin in the eyes. "Yes!"

"I hope so." Krupin stood up. He tossed Greenwald's sunglasses back to him. "Now, get up and go to your room and begin work! It will take some days before it is all in place. You must start immediately."

Greenwald licked his lips. He fumblingly put on his sunglasses, got up, clutching the flash drive with him as if it were something precious and fragile, which indeed it was. He went to the door and stopped for a moment as Krupin added one thing more.

"And Jim… if you fail me, well, I will simply replace you. But not until I have had a morning's amusement. I'm sorry to have missed the punishment of the girl who was stealing from you. But you could make up for that, Jim. You could be the next to hang head-down, to feed the sharks, as everyone watches, and claps."

Greenwald could see it quite clearly in his mind's eye. His stomach lurched.

He swallowed hard and nodded. "I understand."

Then, Jim Greenwald hurried across Krupin's suite to the door for the passageway. Hands shaking, he opened it, stepped through, closed the hatch behind him, and almost ran down the passageway, trying very hard not to throw up before he got back to his stateroom.

CHAPTER FOUR

The Chinese guard with the CS/LS7 submachine gun was standing on the freighter's deck, by a gray metal lectern. He wore brown and yellow desert-style cammies and a billed officer's cap. His weapon was on a leather strap over one shoulder.

Vince had some Cantonese and Mandarin, but not enough to fully grasp most of what the two men on the gangway ahead of him were saying to the guard. Something about wishing to buy someone? Maybe buy someone *back?*

Waiting to go aboard the small freighter, Vince stood on the gangway in the hot afternoon sun, sweating, wearing greasy mechanic's coveralls, a toolbox at his feet. He had a little sling-backpack over one shoulder, with some clothes and toiletries in it, because the repair work he was supposedly doing would last three or four days.

He was Hans Graf, an itinerant German maintenance man, specializing in ship drainage. Waiting to come aboard the freighter, he ran German grammar and slang over in his mind. *Hallöchen! Was geht? Knall auf Fall? Ich verstehe nur Bahnhof...*

Verdammt.

Vince hoped he didn't have to use extensive German today. He wasn't fluent and there could be a German aboard the cruise ship. The briefing had said there were people from various countries, even the USA, working aboard the *Cupid's Cruise*. If the Russians were suspicious of him, they'd call someone with fluent German over for a talk, and Vince's cover would fall to pieces. He'd have to fight his way out of here. And he had no weapons on him.

Germany. Memories of Gisela came, unbidden. As a young infantryman, Vince had been stationed in Germany for nearly a year before being accepted into the Army Rangers. He'd had a torrid relationship with a delightfully oversexed young woman, Gisela, who taught English to the soldiers. On a month-long furlough from the Rangers, he'd gone back to Germany to see how Gisela was. Married, with two young kids, is how she was. So he'd practiced his German on another girl in Heidelberg.

Now, the guy with the CS/LS7 pointed it at the two Asian men and told them to get lost, and they turned away in disappointment. They looked Filipino. Maybe some girl's father and brother, Vince thought, trying to get her off the cruise ship. They blurred when they passed on his left. Vince's left eye was temporarily out of order because of the faked blindness: the eye had a scleral shell over it. The prosthetic cover, made of some soft, sheer synthetic, was cupped over his left eye. It made his left eye look dead and exotropic, as if glazed over in blindness and misaligned. It was a key feature of his disguise, but it did blur his vision in that eye and was distractingly uncomfortable.

Another disguise feature was the false tattooing; a German heraldic eagle, in red and blue, covered his right cheek. Damned realistic, even made to look slightly time-faded. It wasn't a real tattoo, but neither would it come off in a shower. Maybe after thirty showers. The CIA disguise specialist had shown him a lotion that would remove it. He had other false tattoos; blue inks of barbed wire winding around his arms, and a heart disguising the Army Rangers ink on his forearm. His hair was now reddish brown, and cut to little more than stubble. He had grown a small beard and mustache, also dyed. He didn't look much like Vince Bellator. He was pretty sure that if Dierdre saw him, she'd think, "That gnarly guy looks slightly like Vince."

The final disguise feature was his thumb print. Last available intel said that, when admitting anyone to the ship, the security team took a right-hand thumb print and ran it through a vast database; Russian hackers had copied it from European Union Identities Systems, American TSA, Interpol and other sources. Hans Graf was there—the real one had done time in prison for smuggling. Vince had a fake thumbprint, matching Graf's, glued on very cunningly. If the fake one worked, he should come up in their systems as "Hans Graf, born in 1985 in Berlin", which was four years before the Berlin Wall had come down. Graf's father had been Klaus Graf, a Stasi officer. East German intelligence, controlled by the KGB. Might make the Russians more comfortable around him.

The real Hans Graf was probably dead now. He had been a maintenance engineer on German passenger ships in the early 2000s. Then he'd disappeared during a visit to Bangkok, likely killed by a gang. But the CIA had arranged for "Graf" to turn up again. This "Graf" had gone through some backstreet craziness but was now sober and sane, and looking for work in ship maintenance. That was the cover story, anyway.

Vince's mission could go sideways right here; it could all end on this gangway. He had to successfully pretend to be Hans Graf, because *Cupid's Cruise* needed a man to fix the pumps on troublesome bilge wells. *Cupid's Cruise* was an old vessel, purchased by a shell company controlled by the Russian M.I.D/SVR, just before the ship was about to be stripped and recycled. Now the ship was operated by Russian military intelligence, the GUR.

The guard with the CS/LS7 impatiently gestured for Vince to step up. Vince nodded and walked up to him. The guard scowled at the face tattoo and the warped eye. Speaking Cantonese, the guard asked his name.

Vince pretended not to understand. "I only speak English and German," he said, adding just a little German accent to his English. "If you're asking who I am, my name is Hans Graf."

He passed over the Hans Graf passport—a work of art, complete with a beer stain—and the work order papers.

The guard said, "Drainage engineer?", while looking at the work order. He grunted and looked at an open laptop on the lectern. He nodded, handed the papers and passport back. "Wait."

The guard turned and shouted, and another Chinese guard, the CS/LS7 on a strap over his shoulder, came out of a hatch and walked up to Vince. This one was smoking a cigarette, squinting at him through the smoke. "Put the tools and the bag down, and put your hands up," the cigarette smoker said, with perfect English. He seemed to have been raised in America.

For a second, Vince hesitated. Was this an arrest or just a weapons check? If it was going to be an arrest, now was the time to make a move—knock cigarette guy down, take the CS/LS7, kill them both, and escape.

But he'd been warned they would check him for weapons, and the guard didn't seem threatening. So, Vince relaxed and let the guy pat him down.

"That's a damned big tool kit you got there," the guard said, eyeing the long metal box.

"Big pipes to work on," Vince said. "Need big tools."

The guard opened the toolbox and went through it carefully, finding nothing but long wrenches, screwdrivers, sealants, a metal cutter. Tools. But, taking the tools out, the guard frowned at the bottom of the box and said, "That a compartment under there?"

"Yeah," Vince said. He reached down, tugged a metal flap, and the false bottom came up. It was empty but for a flask of whiskey. "Not easy to get a drink sometimes... you know?"

The guard nodded. "I know." He closed the bottom of the box and went through Vince's sling-pack. He found the small, cheap, outdated cell phone. Nothing on it but a couple of messages in German from an overseas number, talking about money owed by Herr Hans Graf. There was a grimy sticker crookedly placed on the back of the phone: a glossy advertisement for a Bangkok strip club. It was just there to enhance his cover.

"Ha!" said the cigarette smoking guard, tapping the sticker with a forefinger. "I went to that strip club, man!" Seeming satisfied, he tossed the phone into the bag and nodded at the other guard. "He's okay."

"Take him to the others," the first guard said, in Cantonese.

Vince felt a little easier. It seemed he had passed muster... so far.

"Get your stuff," the cigarette guard told him, "and go aboard ahead of me."

The small freighter was even rustier than the cruise ship. The deck was porous with oxidation spots. Walking up to the prow, Vince joined six men in civilian clothes, gathered with their duffels, talking to one another in Russian. Probably getting some R-and-R time ashore. Krupin and Lorvec weren't among them.

The freighter was already underway, its engine rumbling; diesel fumes wafted as it began to churn toward the *Cupid's Cruise*.

41

Vince put his toolbox down and clasped the forward railing, watching as the distant form of the old cruise ship, out in the China Sea, came more and more into definition. The freighter was angling northeast to close course with *Cupid's Cruise*.

The Agency had considered a subaquatic infiltration, with Vince scuba-diving to the ship. He would have sunk the ship from below, using plastic explosives—careful placement could make it look like the explosion of a faulty old engine—but there were people aboard who could not be considered combatants. Nine women had been forced into "service" as prostitutes; there were three cooks, five galley assistants, and a motorman to keep the engines going. That motorman, a man named Morris Henley, seemed to have come with the ship. Non-combatant. And sinking the ship that way would let too many of the enemy get away; experts on cyberwarfare that the NSA and CIA wanted neutralized.

The *Cupid's Cruise* had a small crew, largely overseen by a captain, a chief engineer and a second engineer—basically a bosun's mate. But Agency files designated them all as ex-Russian Navy, very much armed and loyal to Krupin. Combatants. Some of the ship's protective cadre of soldiers doubled as crewmen and stewards. The ship's motorman was an unknown quantity. There were fewer than twenty armed Chinese aboard; they were considered to be working with the Russians, an arrangement between Chinese and Russian intelligence. Which made them hostile, armed Chinese combatants.

Tighe maintained that all but one of the cyberwar and misinformation staff were trained specialists in a division of the Russian GUR. That made them combatants, too. They were continually attacking the USA not only through hacking, but with dangerous misinformation, and they were loyal to Krupin. Some of their disinformation had created fits of social chaos in America. They'd helped to spread

42

election-related lies, the "replacement theory" bullshit, and endless QAnon falsehoods. As far as Vince was concerned, the whole disinformation staff was a good target. The one non-Russian on the disinfo team was an American traitor, James Greenwald. As far as Vince was concerned, Greenwald could go to prison or die on the ship.

The galley staff and the "women of pleasure" had to be—somehow—safely evacuated before Vince could finish the job. It was Vince who insisted on that. There was a sketchy plan for making evacuation happen, but it included hardly any help from the CIA. Vince was mostly on his own to prevent anyone connecting the fate of this ship with the USA. A great deal of improvisation was called for, and Vince had a rep in special ops for effective improvisation as needed.

The CIA assessment stated there were no children aboard. But American intel had been wrong about that before, when a bombing run against ISIS had gone ahead, supposedly putting no non-combatants at risk, and it turned out a daycare was bombed along with the terrorists. Vince wanted no errors of that kind.

His first task was to get past Krupin's security. Maybe the bad eye and the tattoo had been a mistake. Might lead them to stare at him too much, ask too many questions. Blandness might have been better. But then, Krupin and Lorvec would probably recognize Vince without the disguise. And there was no time for plastic surgery. The chatter had it that the Russians planned a big cyberwar move—and soon. No one this side of Krupin and Moscow knew what that move would be.

Lurching and shuddering, the old freighter chugged its way to the rendezvous with the cruise ship. *Cupid's Cruise* was a medium-sized, mostly white cruise ship of twelve decks. It was rusty and outdated now, its paint flaking, but with certain amenities and some features that appealed to wealthy, decadent young males—except they had to be completely vetted by Moscow Central.

As the freighter neared the cruise ship, Vince noticed that *Cupid's Cruise* was written in shocking pink on the prow. It looked as though the ship's name had been painted on within the last year. But his gaze was drawn to chromium shining high up on the vessel's topmost deck: a new set of antennae and transmission disks. They looked like standard cruise ship equipment—but these transmitters were actually far more powerful, actively trading data with satellites controlled by the Russian military and dozens of other receptors.

Most of the ship's gold trim had flaked off. Rust drip stains looked almost like cherry flavoring on the tiered layer-cake of the vessel. Vince smiled grimly. A cake layered with killers, liars, spies and prostitutes—although the women were victims of human trafficking. He noticed a blue glint, at the lido deck. An Olympic-sized swimming pool. He could make out sunning recliners and waterslides.

The *Cupid's Cruise* slowed and ceased headway. The freighter drew up close behind the cruise ship as a winch was swung out to raise cargo from the open hold. The Chinese guard with the cigarette had lit another, and squinting against the smoke rising from the corner of his mouth, he told Vince, "Down to midship, there's a launch. Get aboard."

The others knew the drill and were already filing off in that direction. Vince nodded to the guard and carried his toolbox and pack to the launch, which would take him to the next stage of the mission.

Not for the first time, he pondered the odds of coming out of this alive. Intel said there were almost a hundred armed men protecting Russian and Chinese interests on the old cruise ship. Ninety-seven, to be precise. That wasn't counting Krupin and Lorvec, both dangerous men. Vince's chances of survival seemed slim to none.

He thought about Dierdre. She figured prominently in his will. She'd inherit his money, his land, the house, the restaurant, everything but the profit participation owed to their partners, Lupe and Diego. If he got himself killed out here, what would Dierdre do? Sell out, and move away? Maybe try to get back into law enforcement?

Vince hoped not. He hoped she'd stay on Harstine Island, in the house he'd built with his own hands, and find someone else to share her life with.

A chill went through him as he walked up to the launch boat. He still had a chance to blow off this mission. Tell the guards he was sick. He could say he had the latest covid. They'd send him back to the mainland.

He smiled bitterly at the thought, heaved his toolbox and sling pack into the launch, and climbed in with the other men, for the trip to the rusty hell that was *Cupid's Cruise*.

Then the launch was lowered to the sea, and there was no turning back.

CHAPTER FIVE

Vince watched with his one good eye as the mass murderer at the white-metal desk put on reading glasses to look at Hans Graf's papers. The mass murderer was wearing a white officer's uniform, so that if another vessel happened to pass fairly closely when he was outside, he would look normal on the deck of a cruise ship. In fact, he looked like some character actor from the old TV show, *The Love Boat*. The incongruity was striking.

Vince was standing before the desk, waiting patiently to be accepted as a workman on the *Cupid's Cruise*. The ship creaked under his feet as the murderer peered at the paperwork.

The mass murderer was Boris Lorvec. He had killed seven college professors in Russia. The professors had been privily discussing how democracy could be returned to the motherland—which would mean overthrowing the ruling regime. The professors thought they had been sufficiently discreet. They had not. Lorvec used a hand grenade, and a Russian army assault rifle. Such a weapon was now leaning against the metal wall of the ship's office, behind Lorvec, and Vince wondered if thatRP-16 was the exact same weapon. Quite possibly.

Lorvec had also used an RP-16 to kill an entire family in Ukraine. It was all in the Boris Lorvec file, which Vince had read in preparation for this mission.

Lorvec cleared his throat, looked up at Vince, grimaced, and said, "You can work with bad eye?"

"*Ja*, yes, *da* sir!" Vince said earnestly, bobbing his head. "Only one bad eye! Simple job, takes strong muscles, knowing valves, knowing pipes. One time I was working on just such a ship as this in Caribbean Sea—or was in Mediterranean? Yes. Mediterranean. So then, I am getting a pain in this eye too!" He pointed at his good eye. "Ha, what am I to do! Well, it was only—"

"Shut up," said Lorvec wearily.

"*Da* sir!"

"Do you speak Russian?"

"No."

"Then do not try to."

Vince said, "Yes I will not!"

Lorvec blinked. He leaned back, apparently trying to make up his mind about this Hans Graf. But the Agency had seen to it that every call from *Cupid's Cruise* to hire a drainage engineer had gone unanswered—except one. "Graf" had answered, saying he was referred by one of the companies they had called. Likely Lorvec would conclude he was stuck with Hans Graf.

Vince's left eye was itching—it had gone from minor irritation to maddening. And if Lorvec noticed this drainage engineer was having trouble with his eye, the Russian might look at it too closely.

Lorvec grunted, making up his mind. "Put your thumb here." Lorvec tapped the glass inset into the top of the white metal desk. "Press down. Roll."

Vince reached out and pressed his thumb on the glass inset, rolled it around on the glass inset. A laser from under the glass read the thumb print. If the fake thumbprint failed, Vince could grab the laptop on the desk, smash its corner into Lorvec's head, giving him time to dash around the desk and grab the assault rifle.

But by then he'd have been shot down by the Russian guard standing behind him. So that wouldn't work.

Lorvec was looking at the read-out on the laptop screen. "Yes, yes, Hans Graf, German—so, your father was in the Stasi?"

Vince straightened up. "Yes sir! My father was very valuable to *Russland*—ah, to Russia, sir! Always I have pride in him!"

"This file says you're not good for much but fixing pipes and smuggling." Lorvec pointed at him. "We don't need smuggler. Fix pipes good! Is bad smell on this ship!"

"Immediately, right away I set to work!"

Lorvec asked a question in Russian of the guard behind Vince. There came an answer in the affirmative. The guard came forward and put Graf's mobile phone on the desk. "He has searched you and your goods and found only this," said Lorvec. "This I will keep. No calls from the ship while you are here. Don't try to borrow phone—no one here has such device. Calls out from ship, not allowed."

"Eh," said Vince, shrugging, "that is *einfach!* Me, I have no one to call, only bill collector." The phone was incapable of making a long-distance call, anyway. It was just for show, so Hans would seem like a normal guy equipped with a shitty cell phone. The CIA's source was a Chinese soldier who'd served on the ship and defected to the US Embassy in Macao. He was firm that because of Krupin's acute security concerns, only three cell phones were allowed on the ship. Krupin's, Lorvec's, and the captain's. The radio room's traffic was fanatically monitored.

"This man will show you where you sleep. Here is a blueprint of levels and plumbing." He pushed a paper across to Hans Graf, who humbly accepted it. "Go! Your eye is making me sick."

"Sometimes I wear eyepatch," Vince said.

"Good, put on eyepatch!"

They had given Hans Graf an employee's berth, hardly big enough for a man of Vince's size to stand up in. But it was a relief to get the scleral shell off his eye. The drops in his medical kit cleansed it and eliminated bacteria. His liberated eye was a little blurry for a few minutes, as Vince sat on the bunk, thinking.

If all had gone well, Vince's weapons were hidden under a false bottom in a crate laded with the ship's supplies. He was supposed to look for a crate marked in Chinese ideograms—which he had memorized—meaning "soy beans and pickled vegetables for our friends."

He had to get to the crate as soon as possible. If someone unloaded it, the false bottom might be spotted. And he couldn't be sure when he might need his ordnance.

Vince sat up and looked at the map of the ship and its plans, deck by deck. It was in English, as the ship had once been owned by an American company. Storage holds were on subdecks, under deck one. Subdeck one was storage; two was the engine room. Would the gun crate be down on a subdeck, with the food supplies? But he saw the main galley marked on deck four, next to passenger dining room four. There was a room behind the galley marked as storage too. It could be that food crates were taken there. He could pretend he needed to look at the pipes in the galley—

"Hey!" Someone was banging at the metal door. It sounded like they were using the butt of a gun. "Open up!"

"Who is this, out there?" Vince called, in Graf's poor English.

"I am Yan! Lorvec sent me to take you for bilge wells!"

"*Ja*, yes, I come!" Vince figured the guard was there to keep watch on him, more than to show him the way.

He went to the little room's sink, looked in the mirror and painstakingly put in the scleral cover, cursing under his breath as Yan banged on the door again.

The scleral shell in place, Vince pocketed his eyepatch and the ship's plans, picked up his tool kit and opened the door. A scowling, heavyset Chinese guard stood there wearing the white and gold livery of the ship, an CS/LS7 over one shoulder. The guard gestured impatiently. "Walk ahead down there! I show where to go!"

"*Ja*, sure!"

Fifteen minutes of going down ship's ladders and following passageways. Vince's eye was already irritated, itching, giving him twinges of pain.

Someone's brilliant disguise concept might just cause the failure of the whole mission.

Yan unlocked a hatch, and they went down another ladder… and now they were in a sub-deck. The rumble and vibration of the engine came through the bulkheads. They entered a utility passage, with just enough room to walk in without Vince banging his head. A short walk, lit by caged utility lights dangling from the overhead, and they reached a holding tank for the bilge wells.

The cover over the tank was missing. Vince carefully leaned over for a look. The deep tank was two-thirds full of a red-brown ooze. A strong, distinctive conglomeration of smells arose: oil runoff, rust, seawater, sewage, chlorine, rotting food-grease.

"It stink!" Yan said. "You fix!"

"Yes, *ja*, certainly I will. A pump is not working. *Ich wer die pumpe finden.*"

Vince put down his toolbox, took out a hefty, fourteen-inch wrench and looked around for something to adjust. He would pretend to do the work—maybe even do some of it, if he could find pump controls—until the guard got bored watching him and decided he was just another workman doing his job.

His disguised eye was still itching. Maybe he'd got some dust under the scleral shell. Unconsciously, he rubbed it—something he was not supposed to do. The light seemed to shift.

"Your eye!" Yan said. "That... there is something over it! Not real eye!"

"Yes, *ja*, it's—medical. Necessary. Doctor give me such."

"Move your hand off! Let me see!" The guard drew the CS/LS7 off his shoulder and swung it at Vince.

Vince shrugged—then sidestepped so the muzzle of the CS/LS7 wasn't pointed at him, simultaneously swinging the wrench. The big wrench crunched into the guard's skull. Yan staggered and tipped into the bilge tank. He squeezed off a short burst as he fell, bullets ricocheting in the bilge tank. One zipped past Vince's head.

"Shit!" he muttered. There was a splash, and the metallic ringing from the ricochets fading away. Vince looked over the rim of the tank, saw the guard floating face-down. Bubbles rushed from his mouth. The body twitched, then fell still.

"Only ninety-six more to go," Vince said softly.

Hefting the wrench, Vince went to the level's hatch. He waited, watching and listening. Time passed.

No one seemed to be responding to the gunshots. They'd been muffled by the tank and the engine noise. No one had raised the alarm. But what would happen when they realized that Yan was missing?

Could be Yan's absence would go unnoticed for hours. It would be assumed the guard was still watching the plumber. There might be time to get to the weapons in the crate—and cook up some cover.

Vince took out the fake eye and looked at it. The damned thing didn't seem to be working as a disguise.

He tossed it into the bilge tank. Then he put on the black eyepatch, and with toolbox in one hand and wrench in the other, Vince strolled off toward the ladder that led to the upper levels.

"Leng's not coming back?" Greenwald shook his head. "Do *not* tell me that."

He was standing in front of Lorvec's little white metal desk. Lorvec looked at him over the half-glasses he wore to work on the laptop. His expression emanated a faint amusement, tinged with disgust.

Lorvec shrugged. "Leng is dead. Someone killed him in Macao. Bad drug deal."

Shifting his feet, his hands clenching, sweat running down the back of his neck, Greenwald said. "But there are a lot of people on the ship suffering from opiate addiction—about eight of the girls you picked up are addicts. Well, seven now…" One having been fed to sharks. "Now me—I'm not a major user of… you know… but I do have that back problem and it's very distracting and I've got serious work to do."

"Yes, yes, some pharmaceuticals are coming tomorrow."

"Tomorrow!"

Lorvec offered another shrug. "Drink vodka. Find someone can sell you pills. You will last till the morning. Now go, I am busy."

Lorvec turned to the laptop and began tapping on the Cyrillic keyboard.

Greenwald wanted to scream at him, *How am I to do my job in this miserable condition?*

He knew that Krupin expected him to work at least twelve-hour days till the cyberattack on the USA was fully set up. How could he do that, writhing in the pain of being dope sick?

But Greenwald turned away, thinking, *Maybe Gosog has some pills...*

Ilya Gosog was on the lido deck. The sun was going down, but it was still warm outside. In the middle of the pool, floating on an inflated plastic lounger, was Gosog, wearing only a bathing suit. His legs were skinny, pale, and his knees knobby; his globular white belly shone in the overarching lights set up for evening swims. Luxuriation like this was sometimes assigned to Russian operatives because it could be observed by satellite and flyovers, and reinforce the cover myth of *Cupid's Cruise*. Instagram images of wealthy young men vacationing on the ship were sent out during the occasional weekends when offspring of Russian oligarchs, or billionaire Chinese entrepreneurs, came aboard for a few days of lightly supervised partying. They were not, of course, allowed on deck seven, which was primarily occupied by hackers and misinformation squads. Tourists who looked up *Cupid's Cruise* to book a berth were told the whole ship was "booked for three years in advance".

To Greenwald, Gosog's belly looked like a fleshy beach ball. On a floating tray beside the Russian agent was an icy pitcher filled with what was likely vodka martinis. Two of the ship's working girls, topless, lay on *chaise longues* by the pool, speaking Tagalog in low voices.

There was a sort of class system among the prostitutes on board, and the escorts were at the top of the pyramid. They were allowed leisure time outside, and told that money was being put into a bank account for them.

The sea was becoming restless in the evening winds, and Greenwald was afraid he might vomit into the pristine blue of the pool as he walked up to its edge. "Ah, Gosog, bro. Can we talk?"

"What is it, Greenwald?" said Gosog, almost groaning the words. "I am good here. So good. Do not want to go anywhere, do talk to anyone. This is very pleasing assignment for me. I was made for such assignment. Very important to do. Keep cover strong. Go away."

"Sure, but... can I buy some meds off you? You know what I need. Leng's not coming back."

"Yes, murdered by drug men, maybe by CIA, who knows? Very troublesome. But I am not concerned for that. I am on special assignment. Go away."

"Right, but I'm *sick*, man. You know? You have some oxy, right?"

"Hey, keep your voice down, I don't want these girls around here bothering me for drug. Go away."

"Sure, but maybe later—"

"Greenwald!"

He sighed. "I know. 'Go away'."

A few decks below was Carolyn, the only American girl on board. She didn't like him, but she sometimes had OxyContin and if he offered her enough money...

Greenwald turned and shuffled to the nearest stairway. *Keep moving. Don't stop or it'll just wash over you, and you'll be retching and crying like a whipped dog, right out in the open. You don't want that.*

He went down two "ladders" and almost flew down the passageway to Carolyn's berth. He pounded on the metal door.

There was muffled cussing, then Carolyn opened the door. A willowy, green-eyed woman, she had messy Day-Glo purple hair—except where it had grown out while she'd been here—and purple eye shadow, a little smeared from the night before. Her breasts were too large and perfect to be anything but surgically enhanced. She wore shorts and a tank top, and she held an empty long-neck beer bottle by the neck, as if she was prepared to use it for a weapon.

He stepped back and said, "Carolyn, I have two hundred dollars on me, if you can give three oxy for tonight. My source was killed in Macao and—"

"Leng is dead? Good!"

"Carolyn, seriously—I'm not well. I think I have dengue or something."

"You're dope sick and you deserve it!" She started to slam the door, but he yelled, "I can get another two hundred!"

She stopped closing the door and gave him a wicked look. "Oh well, let me think about this. Do I want to help you—a guy who's part of the upper echelon of shitheads and fuckwads who kidnapped me from a jail, where at least I had a release date, and put me out here to work for nothing, with no release date? And half the time there aren't even condoms!"

"I'll get you off the ship! In fact—I think this whole place will be shut down in a few weeks, because, well, there's a big project that might make it irrelevant. So, uh—they'll probably dump you on the mainland."

"*Dump* me?"

"I mean—I don't know. Maybe they'll... um... I'll make sure they let you go! And... and I'm sorry, but it wasn't my idea to bring you girls here, I have *no say* in all that, and... and I need to get my work done or... or..."

He realized he was babbling.

"You work for Krupin," Jill said. "Why don't you ask him for your shit? They have an infirmary."

"The infirmary supplies are controlled by Lorvec and he's just…" Greenwald didn't want to explain. But he just couldn't beg Krupin or Lorvec for it. He didn't want the Russians to start thinking about how out-of-control his dope habit was. The Russian Federation's SVR—the *Sluzhba vneshney razvedki Rossiyskoy Federatsii*—preferred their puppets to have some important weakness, like drug addiction, to give the spymasters a hold over them. But if they decided an asset was too far gone, the asset was neutralized. If Krupin decided Greenwald's dope sickness was a threat to Operation Spring Glory, he'd simply elevate one of his men to take his place—and fresh chunks of Greenwald would be fed to the sharks.

Greenwald took a deep breath. "Look, Carolyn, *have* you got any oxy? If so, I can come up with more money!"

"Oh, *do* come in!" she chirped. Someone behind her laughed.

Carolyn opened the door and waved him in. There were two bunks, and a stocky Filipino girl was lolling on the other one, wearing tights and a plunging top. She had bobbed black hair, mischievous dark-brown eyes, and seemed to have trouble not laughing at him. Greenwald thought he could smell hashish in the room. One of the boy oligarchs had brought a quantity aboard, on a cover-party weekend. Hashish did Greenwald no good. Opium would have been at least soothing. But no one ever seemed to have opium on this damned ship, he thought, though here they were, in the South China Sea.

The Filipino girl tittered, staring at him. Greenwald made himself give her a friendly nod.

"That's Jill," Carolyn said, going to the medicine cabinet.

Greenwald felt a draft. The glass was missing from the berth's porthole. "What happened to the porthole?" he asked, wiping sweat from his forehead with a trembling hand. A little sea-scented breeze came through and it felt good on his face.

"Busted out by a drunken sailor," Jill said.

Greenwald was fixedly watching Carolyn bringing the OxyContin over. There were only a few caps in the bottle. He stared at it. Here was a measure of relief, at least for the night. Just enough to get him through.

She rattled the bottle at him. "My last three pills! I don't take 'em much 'cause I don't want to end up like you."

He fished desperately in his pocket for his money, came up with the two hundred American, waved it at her. "Take it!"

He reached for the bottle, but she jerked it out of reach. "Oh wait! You're not just part of the outfit that kidnapped me—*you* are the guy who got my friend Bae fed to the sharks!"

"Ohhh!" gasped Jill. "Is this the guy? I did not know."

"He's the guy! Lorvec made it happen because Greenwald complained."

Greenwald shook the money at her. "No! Well, I mean... I didn't tell him to do *that*—"

"You got her fed alive to the sharks," Carolyn said. "And now you're in hell. Where you belong."

And with that, she turned to the porthole—and tossed the pill bottle out of the window. There was no deck outside that window. It was straight down to the sea.

"All gone, asshole!"

"Oh-ah-haaaaa-*haaaaa!*" Jill yelled, delighted. "All gone!" She doubled up with laughter.

Greenwald stuffed the money back in his pocket and spun about, stalked to the door. The beer bottle smashed against it, just missing his head.

"That's right, run!" Carolyn screamed.

He scrabbled at the door, fury rising up in him. "You are going to be so goddamn sorry!"

"I don't fucking care!" she raged. "I'd rather feed the sharks than let these scumbags touch me anymore! Get the fuck out!"

He rushed out the door, grinding his teeth, hearing the laughter follow him down the passageway. He hissed, "Those two are going to pay…"

CHAPTER SIX

The galley staff believed in Hans Graf. They fed him. They welcomed him to their galley. They were even relieved to see him—everyone was bothered by the increasing smell from the bilges—and they took Vince's word for it when he said a pipe in the food storage cooler might be part of the problem.

Having eaten rather good dim sum and wonton, served to him by the middle-aged pepper-pot-shaped lady cook, and having diplomatically evaded her surprisingly explicit sexual invitation to take a break in her berth where she kept "a very, very good bottle of *baijiu*", Vince opened a panel in the wall of the walk-in cooler.

It was artificially cold in here; he could see his breath. Alone in the steel-walled room, he used a screwdriver and box-ended wrenches to expose a pipe that was near the crate marked with the code ideograms.

Crouching between the wall and the big, five-by-five crate, Vince ran a hand along the crate's wooden base. In the space above the support boards, he found the loose wooden cover. He flicked it free with a fingernail and reached inside, locating a small metal wheel with teeth. *Bingo.* He turned the cog five to the right, feeling it click, and then three to the—

"Hey, pipe man," said a white-coated Chinese-American cook, coming in. *Luke Wu* was written on his nametag. "You need help to move stuff out of your way?"

"Nein, nah, *das ist gut!*" Vince said, hastily returning to the exposed pipe. He picked up his wrench and banged the pipe, as if listening for a blockage. "Can you tell me, how many galley workers on this ship? So many people to feed! Too much for you, *ja?*"

"Not so many aboard, Hans." Luke was picking out packages of freeze-dried veggies from another crate. "Not the usual cruise ship. Just for Russian rich guys and shit. Whores and all that. Lotta guys here working on computers, too. I figure they're sending porn out there. I don't want to know any more than that and neither do you!"

"*Ja*, enough to know how to fix pipes and get paid!"

"Exactly, man. I'd like to get paid and get ashore myself. They keep promising. Anyway yeah, we only got eight people working this galley. Still, there's a lot of work for us."

Eight in the galley. That confirmed the CIA's report, which gave Vince more confidence in its overall accuracy. "That door, I can open from inside?"

"Yeah, that red lever opens it from in here."

"Then you close, *ja?* Delicate work. Not for interrupting!"

"You got it. I'll tell the others. Later on."

Luke carried his vegetable packages out, closing and latching the door behind him. Vince turned back to the crate. He felt for the cog. Three to the left.... click, click...

Click. Silently, the side of the big crate extruded a hidden drawer. There, in foam rubber pockets, were the SIG Sauer, the .410 shotgun pistol, the HK416 assault carbine, the disassembled assault rifle, four frag grenades, four flashbangs, and the combat knife.

"Hello, my beauties," Vince murmured, relieved to have the weapons at hand. The guns were already loaded, and additional ammo would be layered under the foam rubber with the plastic explosives. There was the ammo belt too, full of rounds. And…

Where was it? He looked through his supplies, over and over. Nope. No satellite phone. Tighe had assured him that it would be included.

Let it go, he told himself. *For now.*

He turned to his toolbox, quickly emptied it out. He opened the false bottom, took out the whiskey flask and looked at it longingly. He was cold and stressed. He could use a drink. And this was exactly the time when he should not take one. Sighing, he stuck the flask in a pocket of his coveralls. It might be useful for diplomacy, somewhere along the line.

The false bottom in his toolbox had room for the HK416 and the .410 pistol. He set the HK in place, along with its loaded magazine and two extra mags. The shotgun pistol had one round in it already and there was just room in the toolbox for five more rounds, two of them incendiary.

Vince quickly closed the false bottom, covered it with tools, tossed the knife in there as if it were part of the tool kit. It looked out of place, so he rubbed oil and grease onto the blade from the other tools, to make it look like an old knife he used as a prying and trimming tool.

Then Vince removed the SIG Sauer automatic pistol from the foam rubber. He unbuttoned his coveralls part way, and stuck the loaded pistol in the cloth holster beneath his rib cage. He put an extra magazine, fully loaded, in the little loop under the pocket, and buttoned his coveralls back up.

Now there was the problem of the sniper rifle. He couldn't carry it at the moment and couldn't take the chance of leaving it in the crate. He took it out, quickly assembled it, and tucked it in the bulkhead, under the pipe. He laid two the grenades and two of the flashbangs there next to it, along with most of the remaining ammunition, half the EXP-1 plastic explosive and its small wireless detonators.

As fast as he could, with cold-numbed fingers, Vince replaced the metal plate on the bulkhead and the screws that held it in place. He put two grenades and the two flashbangs in the false bottom of his tool chest, next to a flattish brick of plastic explosive. Then he closed the secret drawer under the crate and stood up, stretching, wishing he could risk bringing more ammo with him just now…

He was still pondering the non-combatants. Civilians. Eight personnel in this galley would need evacuation. There were nine party girls—it had been ten, but he'd heard in the kitchen that one had been "killed by sharks". No one seemed to want to discuss how that had happened, exactly.

Eating his meal, he'd casually remarked that he was worried about children on the ship; he had seen bilge tanks unsecured, and if kids wandered into that area they could be drowned.

"No children, not one," the cook told him. So, it was not an issue.

Vince was determined to see to it that every civilian was evacuated from the ship when the time came. Because *Cupid's Cruise* needed to be blown all to hell, its shattered decks and charred bulkheads sunk—and every Russian operative aboard sent to the bottom of the sea along with them.

Vince was walking down a passageway, carrying his toolbox, whistling an old German tune. He was heading for a ladder to the engine room, when he saw two armed Russian guards coming his way. Apart from the submachine guns they carried, they looked like ill-tempered cruise ship officers, white outfits and all. The duo glared at him, then one used the butt of his SMG to rap loudly on the door of the berth to Vince's left. The door opened and the guards shoved their way in.

A woman yelped. The door clanged shut, but not before Vince heard a snarl, a slap, a woman screaming...

He sighed. He really should ignore it and move on. He wasn't ready to make a direct move against the ship's thugs—yet. But he did need to make some kind of contact with the women on board. He had to gain their trust, get them to work with him so he could get them safely free of the ship.

But really. it was all about a woman being beaten. Not something he tolerated.

Vince set down the toolbox, took the wrench in his left hand, the knife in his right. He banged on the door with his wrench. "Emergency plumber! Ship maintenance! Engineer! Fix pipes!" he shouted. Then he hid the knife behind his back.

The door opened a few inches as a guard peeked through. Vince could hear a woman cursing and sobbing, inside. The guard, a lantern-jawed man, his face red and sweat matting his blond hair, snapped, "Not now, come back later!"

"Krupin sent me! Just one quick look, then I go! One pipe only! Krupin said this room!"

"Krupin?" The guard looked dubious, muttered something in Russian, then shrugged and opened the metal door. "Be quick!"

Trying to smile like a humble workman, Vince stepped through and took in the scene at a glance. The lantern-jawed guard on the right, submachine gun in hand; a taller one with bloodied fists on the left, near the two women. His CS/LS7 submachine gun was leaning against the bulkhead behind him. Two women were huddled on the aft bunk, both with bloodied, split lips; the purple-haired one had blood running from her nose. He remembered her from the CIA report: Carolyn Han, a favorite of the escaped Russian. Half Asian. Born in Chicago. Escort girl from the USA in Macao, caught up in a drug raid. Secretly purchased from a prison warden by the GUR.

The other woman looked Filipino. Vince didn't know her, but he saw that her blouse was torn, and someone had bitten her on the shoulder. It was bleeding.

Vince's hand tightened on his knife. He couldn't use a gun, not in this situation, in a small metal-walled room. Even if he placed his shots perfectly, the guy holding the SMG could squeeze off a shot as he died. The ricochets could get one of the women, and the noise might bring more Russian gunnies.

"You!" the guard by the door snapped, "Show me your hand!" He nodded toward Vince's right hand, still hidden behind him.

"This hand?" Vince asked, as he whipped the knife around to stab hard into the guard's left temple, using his strength and skill to stab through the thin bone at that point, slashing deeply into the man's brain.

The guard's fingers didn't work anymore; the strings had been cut. He crumpled to the floor without firing a shot, even as Vince stepped left, jerking the knife free and swinging the big wrench with his left hand and smashing it into the back of the taller guard's head as the man lunged toward his submachine gun.

The wrench cracked home, and the guard went to his knees, groaning, but closing his fingers around the CS/LS7. Vince was still moving, pivoting left, bringing the knife around and cutting through the guard's spine just below the skull.

The Russian thug fell forward, the gun clattering with him.

Only ninety-four to go, Vince thought.

Closing the door, he said casually, "I was hoping that way of doing it would minimize clean-up. Not so much blood, really."

There was no reply from the women. He turned to see them staring at him, mouths agape, and still cringing back, not sure if they were his next targets.

"Oh, ladies, sorry... I should explain. I'm—I'm not actually a plumber."

"No kidding," Carolyn said, in a whisper.

"You two okay? I mean, no broken bones?"

"They would've have gotten around to that," Carolyn said. "Nothing broken yet."

"No bones break," the other woman said. "But this..." She rubbed blood from her mouth with the back of her hand. "Greenwald, he did that. He paid them!"

Vince reached up and pulled off his eyepatch. "Feels good to get that thing off. I'm stuck with the tattoo for a few weeks. Looks pretty real, but it's not."

"You—you're American," Carolyn said, relaxing a little.

"Yeah. Born in Texas. I'm a west coast guy now."

"I figure you're one of those special ops guys," she said, looking at the two dead men. "But there's one thing you don't really do well, man."

"What's that?"

"A German accent."

Vince grinned. "Yeah. I'm not a thespian. But I figured, the Russians and the Chinese soldiers aren't going to be experts on Germanized English, and this was the identity on offer so..." He shrugged.

"And just who the hell *are* you?" Carolyn asked, getting off the bunk. She went to the sink and began washing blood from her face.

"My name is Vince. That'll have to do."

She wiped her face with a towel and said, "I'm Carolyn. And that's Jill. You have some agenda here, mister. I don't think you're here for pussy."

"No ma'am, I am not. I can't really tell you who sent me here, but… I do have a mission. Just know that I'm not going to hurt you. In fact, I'm going to do my best to help you."

"Oooh!" Jill said. "Can I keep him, Carolyn?"

Carolyn looked at Vince skeptically. "Face tattoos and all?"

Jill squinted at Vince. "I don't think they're real."

Vince nodded. "You have a good eye."

Carolyn snorted. "I need a goddamn drink. Fat chance around here. You gotta blow someone for a drink."

"Actually," Vince said, "you don't." He took the flask of Scotch out of his pocket. "Just a pint, but it's all yours, ladies."

"Oh!" gasped Jill. "You see? He is the perfect man! Ask him if he has any diamonds in his pocket!"

Greenwald had scored exactly three codeines. Not oxycodone, just codeine. Weak shit. He couldn't take them all at once. He had a night to get through.

On one codeine, he was just able to function in the meeting with Krupin and Feske. But he was still stewing in his own misery. The sun was down, and it was chilly now, but the dope sickness made Greenwald feel as if he was being slowly cooked alive.

They sat in the living room of Krupin's suite—Greenwald, Feske and Krupin, ranged around a table with three laptops, a bottle of flavored vodka, and glasses. Greenwald hadn't touched his drink—he knew if he mixed alcohol with codeine, he'd get crazy and probably lose his temper.

"Here are the charts and probability data," said Feske, smugly, projecting the information onto the screen.

Heggie Feske, former Russian sleeper agent, had gone to MIT under the name of Bill Thurston. He had no detectable accent when he spoke English. He'd insinuated his way onto the staff at DARPA for a while, till the feds sniffed him out and he had to skedaddle. The Russians had brought him here to use computer wizardry against the Americans. And now Greenwald was stuck with him. This tanned, slimly muscular and fox-faced man, in yoga pants and sleeveless shirt, was always condescending when he spoke to Jim Greenwald. He was forever hinting that Greenwald was an empty suit. Figuratively—Greenwald wore shorts and a red silk shirt today. Feske always carried a Grach Yarygin pistol, the show-off. Even now, it was on a belt over his yoga pants. Absurd.

The data was projected on a screen for them all to see; the lists of firewalls penetrated, the array of American electrical grids that would go down; the nuclear power plants that were to be disrupted, possibly destroyed; the vital American satellites that would be hacked and then crashed into oil refineries and chemical plants.

The blueprint for sabotage of the entire American infrastructure.

"And there it is, that's the lay-out for the first wave of attacks," said Feske.

"Ahh," Krupin said, lighting a Gauloise. Greenwald had never seen a Russian willingly smoking a Russian cigarette.

Tobacco smoke made him feel a little sicker than he already was. "This is all pie in the sky until we mount some feel-out runs," Greenwald pointed out.

"Isn't that what we've been doing for a year already?" asked Feske, pretending to be puzzled. Condescending as ever.

Greenwald shook his head impatiently. "Only a percentage of the firewalls have been—"

"Silence!" Krupin barked. "Can we do it, or can we not?"

Greenwald had to admit that most of it probably would work. He hated to give Feske the satisfaction. Moreover, he had found himself dragging his feet on this whole thing, and he wasn't sure why. He didn't want to think about why.

The winning team, he told himself. *Be on the winning team. That's all that matters.*

Seeing Greenwald's hesitation, Feske turned eagerly to Krupin. "We can do it, sir! Even if some of the attacks fail, most of them will go through. The power grids will go down. Most communications. Hospitals, cops, armed forces, satellites—almost no communication. Cell phones, gone! Then the explosions start."

"How many casualties the first two days?" Krupin asked, smiling in anticipation.

"Oh, I would think at least three hundred thousand dead. The fires this will start alone…"

Krupin looked at Greenwald. "Well? You say nothing?"

Greenwald clasped his hands together to keep them from shaking and then said, "Oh, I think we have to go ahead on schedule. We could even do it sooner. Just don't expect the USA to be *completely* crippled. Backup systems—"

"Are almost non-existent," Feske snorted.

Greenwald almost hit him. *Keep yourself under control or you'll be replaced by Feske*, he told himself. "We don't know that," he said, forcing himself to speak steadily.

"And anyway," Feske went smoothly on, "all we need is to get their defenses down long enough for the intervention troops to come in."

A hundred sixty freighter vessels, apparently ordinary maritime commerce, would be hiding 200,000 heavily armed troops that would be deposited on American shores as missiles took out most

American defenses and paratroopers dropped "like the petals of ten thousand Russian lotuses," as Krupin said, upon Washington DC.

Greenwald turned to Krupin. "I need to make some… some computer models, launch some multi-systems tests, just to be sure. We have to be certain we can keep their ICBMs down. I should get started right now."

Anything to get out of this room.

Krupin nodded impatiently. "Go!"

Greenwald stood up, nodded to Krupin, turned to go—

And suddenly Krupin said, "Jim!"

Greenwald turned nervously back to him. "Yes, Pavel?"

"You know you're being monitored, yes? Any message you send through our systems will be seen and scrutinized."

Greenwald feigned bafflement. "I don't understand, Pavel."

"The USA is your native country. Maybe you change your mind… and warn someone?"

Greenwald lifted his chin. "I am an anti-statist libertarian! I have no native state! I now choose only *one sta*te over all others. The Russian Federation!"

Krupin grunted. "Had better be. Best you forget anti-statism—completely! Russia is your state… or your next state is Hell. You understand that much?"

Greenwald nodded. "Completely. My loyalty is to you, and the SVR—the entire Russian Federation! Have you promised me a comfortable home on the Black Sea?"

Krupin nodded. "Certainly."

"And a good living?"

"Yes."

"And a great career serving the Motherland?"

"That is what we offer."

"My mind is completely made up!"

This was such a lie that it almost caught in Greenwald's throat; it nearly made him gag. His mind was far from made up. But he managed to say it with conviction.

"If he did tell anyone," Feske chuckled, "no one would listen. He would sound like one of our conspiracy theorists!"

"Quiet, Feske!" Krupin snapped. He turned to Greenwald. "Jim, you are at the center of this because you know American systems better than anyone else, and because you have a great talent. But be sure you make *no* mistakes."

Greenwald nodded. He needed to convince Krupin he was loyal. "Let's do it sooner—in four days!"

"Ah!" Krupin nodded. "Yes. If it can be done! Now go—see to it!"

Greenwald hurried out. But it worried him that Feske was still there with Krupin. What was Feske saying about him?

"These bodies are starting to stink," said Jill.

"Yeah," Vince said. "That's why I'm standing by the porthole. Nice clean breeze."

The two dead Russians were side by side in the middle of the floor. Vince had stanched their wounds with paper towels and plumber's tape from his toolbox, to get them to stop bleeding—there was some bleeding even after death—so there would be less liquid gore to clean up. He'd already wiped up most of the floor himself.

"Getting dark enough outside," he said. "Almost time to get rid of these guys."

"You really think we can get them out of here and dump them without getting caught?" Carolyn asked.

She was sitting on a bunk beside Jill, drinking the last of the Scotch from a coffee cup. Vince expected her or Jill to show some drunkenness, but none was apparent except sometimes Jill giggled for no special reason.

"I think we can probably figure something out," Vince said. "It doesn't seem like these guys reported where they were going when they came here. No one's shown up looking for them."

"They each had a hundred bucks in their pocket," Carolyn said. She and Jill had appropriated the money. "Greenwald had two hundred bucks with him. He must've paid these guys a hundred each to punish us. So yeah, they didn't tell anyone. The rules say they can't mess with us unless it's on Lorvec's say-so."

"I was... instructed," Vince said slowly, thinking it through as he spoke, "on how to release the lifeboats. The big ones. Suppose I was able to put the bodies in one of those, and release it? Make it look like the missing men just deserted. Them and another guy I had to deal with... His body will have to stay where it is..."

Jill got round-eyed. "How many these assholes you kill?"

"Just one other, so far. Guy named Yan."

"Oh, I knew him! What a dick! Bad breath, too!"

Vince nodded. "But, uh—I need to keep a low profile a while longer."

Carolyn looked at him askance. "And when you *don't* have to keep a low profile? What's that going to be like?"

"Very... busy. You won't be aboard. I'm getting all the civilians safely off, before."

"Before what?"

Vince shook his head. "Cannot talk about that. But I'm going to give you a cover story. Can't talk about *that* yet, either."

Vince realized that he was taking a big chance on these two women. He scarcely knew them. He was going by gut instinct. But he could be wrong. They could decide to blow his cover to the Russians, maybe make a deal of some kind...

"He's going to get us off the ship, Carolyn!" Jill said. She jumped up and threw herself into Vince's arms. "Yeah! *Kahanga-hanga* big man! Thank you!"

Vince laughed and detached her gently from him. "You're welcome—in advance."

Carolyn smiled, then grimaced because it hurt her split lip. "Ow. Yeah, that's fucking awesome if you can pull it off. And *if* we don't have to float endlessly in the ocean like refugees… and die out there of thirst and…"

Vince shook his head. "No, we're going to arrange something. And you're not going to be turned over to any cops, either. You're gonna be given passports and a way to get where you want to go."

"Really?" Carolyn's face lit up.

We're going to arrange something else. The CIA's "something else". But he didn't know if he trusted the Agency. Percolating in the back of his mind was a hunch that maybe he couldn't trust Tighe.

Oscar Tighe might not want anyone from this ship to survive. Including Vince Bellator.

At the briefings, Tighe kept repeating that it was vital no one connected the fate of this ship with the USA. And he seemed nervous about keeping that secret.

He'd promised Vince a satellite phone, but it wasn't in the crate.

Paranoia, Vince told himself. *Don't go there or you'll get bent out of shape. Got to keep chill and focused.*

Then Carolyn looked with narrowed eyes and said, "Aren't you kinda too good to be true?"

Jill shook her head. "He's been exactly what he is."

Carolyn looked at her. "What the hell does that mean?"

Jill shrugged. "He's the real thing, girl." She eyed Vince. "You married, big guy?"

Vince nodded. "I am. I took off the ring because Hans Graf isn't married."

"That what you're going by, 'Hans Graf'?" Jill giggled. "I used to go by Venus Gold."

Vince smiled. "Listen, Venus—both of you—don't tell anybody else yet about my plans for you. Because that's too many people; someone might be tempted to make a deal with the Russians."

The two women nodded as one, as if they understood perfectly what he meant. Not trusting people was standard for them. They were making an exception for the guy who had killed the assholes who seemed about to beat them to death.

"Within two or three days we'll tell everyone who's getting off the boat," Vince went on. "Just not yet. Right now, I've got a plan to get these dead sons of bitches to a lifeboat... Going to need your help. You allowed to go on deck?"

"Not unless there's a special deck party," Carolyn l said. "But we do sometimes, when we can get away with it. What do you have in mind?"

CHAPTER SEVEN

It was a cloudy, starless, humid night out on the sundeck. The sea hissed and shushed, and a veering breeze soughed through the railings.

The sundeck went all the way around the boat. It was guarded by four sentries: one Chinese and three Russian. One at a time they strolled along the deck in their white faux uniforms, ambling through the glow of the gooseneck lamps extending from the bulkhead; strolling into shadow, into light again; trailing cigarette smoke, stopping to chat when they reached the end of their postings. Then each turning back…

They had no clue. Not yet. That's how it looked to Vince. He was observing them from further aft on the deck, where he was pretending to inspect the deck-drainage nozzle. Near him was one of the davits that winched lifeboats up and down. The lifeboats were large, roofed boats, each with room to seat eight people comfortably and more, uncomfortably.

A guard walked past, muttered something in Russian at Hans Graf, probably "get those stinking pipes fixed", and kept going.

Vince said, "*Ja*, sure."

He glanced up and down the deck. Right now, there was only one guard patrolling this particular deck. The Russian guard walked up beside the hatchway where Jill was hiding in the shadows. She stepped out and exposed her breasts and hissed something. He exclaimed, and stepped in with her...

That should keep him busy for a while.

Leaving his toolbox on the deck, Vince hurried to the door opposite him. Carolyn was just inside, standing by the door to a storage room for deck chairs and deck-cleaning gear and extra blankets for cruise guests. She opened the door, and moved to keep watch in the passageway as he pulled the big awkward bundle out.

The corpses were wrapped in blankets, which were taped closed. Vince picked up the dead-weight and raised it onto his shoulder, then carried it onto the deck—still no one in sight. He crossed to the rail and dumped the dead men over onto the nearest lifeboat roof, about eight feet down. Then he vaulted over, came down with a thump on the roof of the lifeboat, opened its top hatch and slipped the bodies through.

The theory was that a rumor and an absent lifeboat might explain the three missing guards. *Deserters*. The ship was only ever a couple miles from shore. Easy enough to take a lifeboat to the Chinese mainland. That might at least create enough doubt that a general alarm wouldn't be raised.

Vince climbed the ladder to the railing. Saw a guard coming from his right. He ducked down and heard the man muttering, then calling to the guard who was supposed to be coming his way.

Couldn't be helped, Vince thought.

He waited till the guard had passed, then climbed over the rail, quietly took the combat knife from his toolbox, stepped up behind the guard and clapped his left hand over the man's mouth. As the

Russian struggled, Vince flipped the knife to a downward-cut position in his hand, and hooked it under the man's right arm, around the guard's torso, stabbing through the ribs to the heart. Ten seconds of struggle, five of dying. Then the guard went limp.

No time for the lifeboat. Vince carried the body to the rail, forward from the row of lifeboats, and threw the dead man over. He watched the body drop into the sea. Vince hoped no one was looking out of the wrong porthole.

For the moment the sundeck was clear. Another guard would be along soon—and would see the telltale blood-spill.

Vince sprinted to the doorway where Jill was entertaining her guest—and found the guy crumpled in a corner, dead, his throat cut. She straightened up from him, a bloody buck-knife in hand. "I wanted to see if I could kill a real soldier! Easy, when their pants are down and they're not paying attention to anything but—"

"Jill!" He put a finger over his lips, and she fell silent.

He peered out from the shadowy hatch and saw another guard coming from the prow.

Vince sighed.

"Step out and summon that next guy, will you? But let *me* take care of him."

She went out, called to the guard. The Russian hurried up—and Vince knocked him cold with the butt of his knife. Then he checked the external deck—it was clear. He picked up the unconscious guard and laid him atop the one with his throat cut. Then he picked them both up, using his legs for most of the weight.

"Oooh, you're strong, big man!" Jill whispered.

"I guess I *better* be, around here," he grunted, shifting to improve his grip on the two dead men.

"Poor Vince! Are you *grumbling*?"

"Hell yeah." He checked to see if the way was clear, then carried the men to the railing. He chucked them both over with one heave. A pause—then a double splash. The unconscious man would drown—so Vince hoped.

Only ninety-two more.

He returned to Jill. "There's a puddle of blood here, you realize, and some splashed on the deck back there."

"This one is my fault. I'll clean it up."

"You should leave the killing to me, Jill."

"But I hate the Russians!"

"There's such a thing as time and place and... never mind. Find the mop... I've got to release that boat."

He had to hurry before another guard came along, so ran down to the lifeboat release. There was a control unit for the lifeboat davits in a metal box mounted against the rail. It was locked; but it wasn't much of a lock. He put the knife back in his toolbox—*don't forget to clean the blood off, first chance*—and took out a large screwdriver. He snapped the lock on the metal box with the screwdriver and main strength, opened the cover and hit the emergency release button for the specific boat. The lower clamps released, the davits swung the boat out, and lowered it to a position not far over the waves. He hit the release button again. The boat dropped into the sea.... and drifted away on the wake of the cruise ship, vanishing into the night.

Maybe someone would notice it passing the stern, maybe not. If they saw it, maybe they'd go after it... maybe not.

Vince always tried to leave nothing to luck. But sometimes you just had to get lucky.

He used a rag from his toolbox to clean up the blood from the man he'd stabbed. There wasn't much. He'd managed a pretty clean kill. Then he tossed the rag overboard and picked up the toolbox. He had to get down to the engine room now.

Time to resume being Hans Graf.

Jim Greenwald felt like some beached sea mammal, dying slowly from dehydration, shriveling up on the sand.

A man resting on his bunk shouldn't feel like that, he thought. *Got to get to a medical rehab, sometime, somewhere.* But nothing like rehab was to be found on *Cupid's Cruise*. And Krupin wasn't going to let Greenwald off the ship. Not for a long time.

The withdrawal was coming back hard, but he was putting off taking the next codeine. He had two left, to last until morning. If he took two at once, would it get him through? Unlikely. Impossible to know if the OxyContin would be coming in the morning as Lorvec had promised. Maybe he could break into the infirmary.

Sure. And get yourself tossed in the ship's brig—or even over the side.

Greenwald turned on his back, hoping a change of position would bring some relief.

It didn't.

His mind was as tormented as his body. He had tried to find the two guards he'd set on Carolyn and Jill, to call them off. After he'd cooled off, Greenwald realized he didn't want those women hurt. Especially after what had happened to Bae. But he couldn't find the guards, and the women were missing from the berth. Where had they gone? Were they shark food?

Then, the visions of mass destruction across the USA returned. He could imagine the scene as the American house of cards collapsed. He saw cities burning as desperate rioters swept through, after the entire country had lost its electricity, its air conditioning. Water supplies suddenly very limited. He visualized the burning, exploded refineries, and Russian missiles sweeping past the downed radar—the impacts, the swelling fireballs, the screams of thousands of dying people...

As an "objectivist", Greenwald told himself that his philosophy advocated putting oneself first; it embraced survival of the fittest. Those who couldn't survive must perish, that was nature's way. The strong would take their rightful place.

But was *he* among the strong? He wasn't strong enough to kick heroin. Not so far. But now he had to be strong enough to face the new reality he was helping bring about.

He had wanted truly radical change in the USA. How would it come without violence? It wouldn't. But this was invasion of America— instead of the usual bombing raids at the start of an invasion, this one would use thousands of cyberwar raids, launched all at once. The physical invasion would come only after the opening salvo of the cyberwar.

Jim Greenwald would flourish, would he not, after the USA fell to Russia? If Krupin was to be believed, yes. But Krupin was a master of misdirection. Maybe they would just kill him, or keep him handy in some jail cell in case he was needed.

Get up, he told himself. *Take half a pill and get back to coding. The only reason they have you here, really, is that you managed to collect the world's biggest database on the faults in cybernetic firewalls protecting American infrastructure. Use that database as Krupin told you to, or die.*

Groaning, he got out of the bunk, and staggered to his PC. Chewing half a codeine, he logged on, and started work...

And came to a grinding halt. Because the apocalyptic images were still flooding his mind. The burning refineries, the missiles sweeping past the downed radar, the impacts, the swelling fireballs, the screams of thousands of dying people...

He mustn't think about it. Survival is all.

But it was hard to ignore all the consequences when you weren't numb.

Hands shaking, Greenwald took another half-pill. And then he surprised himself by bursting into tears.

Patch over his left eye, toolbox toted with his right hand, Vince sauntered into the engine room, trying to look like he belonged.

Located on the bottom platform not far over the keel, the high-ceilinged chamber was big as a medium-sized factory. The two hulking diesel engines, cased in grease-blotched chrome-steel, rumbled on either side of the utility aisle close to the stern. Farther forward, the four turbines hummed. The air was heavy with diesel fumes and motor heat.

The floor was a steel grate, with a shallow bilge under it to catch leaks, diesel runoff and condensation, all of which would be flushed to the tanks. The old mechanisms had their leaks, and black fluid perpetually swirled under the steel grate.

Up above, along a catwalk to starboard, were the windows of the engine control room. A muscular, shirtless black man in overalls and grimy boots sat on the top step of the steel stairs to the catwalk. He was smoking a cigarette, directly under a sign that said *NO SMOKING*. He looked about sixty; his hair, worn in an afro, was speckled white; his face seamed from work in a harsh environment.

Vince gave a casual salute and walked toward him. The man watched emotionlessly as Vince climbed the stairs.

"Greetings!" said Hans Graf, pausing a few steps down from the top. "I am drainage engineer Graf! You are Motorman Henley?"

The motorman said, "Right enough, I'm Morris Henley." He had an Australian accent; his voice was raspy from smoking. "You say you're a drainage engineer, mate? Which kind of bilge pumps you checked out on?"

"What kind?"

"Model. Brand."

"Oh—every model, sure, *ja*. Every brand."

"Such as?"

"Well, you know, mostly German brands…"

"Uh-huh. How much pressure per square inch you get in Germany on a bilge pump?"

"*Ach*, we have metrical system."

"Square centimeter then."

"Well… this is not a specialty of mine… I mean, to remember this, so many years since school…"

"Take off that fucking eyepatch."

"What?" Vince was disconcerted.

"I'm betting the eye under there works just fine. You know, you got a shitty German accent."

Vince snorted. He hoped Morris wasn't friendly with the Russians. He'd hate to have to kill him. "Carolyn was just giving me shit about my German accent," Vince said, abandoning his cover.

"You fool the Russians?"

"So far."

"You met Krupin?"

"Not yet."

"You won't fool him, mate. You'd best do the Harry, next chance."

"Do the Harry?"

"Run! Get the fuck off the ship, man. Krupin catches you… what are you, a reporter? Doing an undercover?"

"Nope. You know what the real agenda of this ship is?"

"Some kind of disinformation thing, I take it. I had a smoking buddy who worked on that deck. Haven't seen him for a while."

"They treat you right?" Vince asked.

Morris looked at him coldly. "What makes you ask?"

"I'm not working for them, if that's what you're thinking. They catch me, they'll do their best to kill me."

"You tell me yours, I'll tell you mine," Morris said, flicking his cigarette butt down through the floor grate. It seemed a reckless thing to do. Supposedly there was a scum of flammable oil down there? It seemed the motorman was past caring.

Vince said, "Let me ask—are you on this ship voluntarily?"

"No, bloody *hell* no. But they know that already. And they know I'm not best pleased about the sitch."

Vince made up his mind about Morris. "Okay. I'm here to do several things. Primary mission is to get non-combatants off the ship. Second is to kill every combatant on the ship. Just the combatants. Not civilians. Third thing is to blow the ship to little bitty pieces."

Morris sat back and raised his eyebrows. "So—you got a death wish."

Vince grinned. "Some might say."

"How many of you are there?"

"Basically..." Vince pretended he was going to count them on his fingers. "Let's see... one." He shrugged. "Me."

"There's almost a hundred guards. And all the officers are armed."

"I see an old Royal Australian Navy tattoo on your arm, there."

"What of it?"

"These tats aren't mine. They can be removed, with some work. Under this one on my arm, I've got US Army Rangers ink."

"You claim you're American special ops?"

"I retired. Certain people took me out of retirement. There's more than disinformation going on in this ship."

"Meaning you're, what, CIA?"

"Used to be Delta Force. Still have some of those connections."

"For some reason, I think I believe you. Maybe because there's no boast in you when you say it. It's like you're talking about your ute."

"My what?"

"Your *car*, mate. Telling me about your car. Anyway—even if I believe you, so what? You're still insane. You can't take down all those men."

"If I have to, I'll blow up the ship with them on it and me too. But I'd rather get the ship way out to sea before I do that. We don't want the blast seen from shore. So that means taking control of the ship to move it out to sea. And keeping control of it. Which will mean killing a good many of the bastards before the ship's neutralized."

"*We* don't want it seen, you say? We?"

Vince shrugged at that. "Me, then."

"What's your name?"

"It's... Vince."

"Vince? Delta Force, Rangers...and Vince. I read an article about a guy...that barmy shit in Washington DC...you're not the Vince Bellator that killed all them neo-Nazis?"

Vince didn't want to lie to Morris. But he didn't want to confirm his last name either. He just looked calmly back at the motorman.

"Crikey!" Morris stood up and glared at Vince. "Take off the eyepatch, now!"

Vince sighed, and took it off, stuffed it in a pocket.

"You *could* be him, under that stupid German ink. But..." Morris shook his head. "Wait—I heard some guards are missing. You?"

Vince nodded. "Hoping Krupin thinks they deserted. Made sure they're missing a lifeboat too."

"I've planned to steal one of those fucking things for a year. But they watch me close, if I leave here. And there are deck sentries all day and night. Then too, I reckon I'm worried if I jump ship, they might take it out on my family. My sons and my grandkids. I want off this tub, but…"

Vince said, "I hear you."

"You really think you could get me off this shit-bucket?"

"I think so."

"How about the bad consequences for my family?"

"If Krupin and the others here are dead, how can they punish you? The GRU will think you went down with the ship, if they think about you at all."

"If you really think you could… oh, but…" He shook his head. "Hard to believe it could be done, mate."

"How'd you end up here, Morris?"

Morris sighed. "After four stretches in the navy, I worked for Gold Edge Cruises going on twenty-four years. I was about to retire, and they paid me to caretake this old hulk till they could sell it for parts. I figured, why not? Then Krupin's shell company bought it, and they hired me to work as motorman till they could bring in another guy. But they couldn't find anyone else willing to do the job who under-stood these outdated turbines. So, they said: Morris, you're staying. I said no, I'm leaving. They showed me how people *leave* when they've displeased Krupin. They made me watch when a galley assistant was skinned and tossed to the sharks."

"Jesus," Vince muttered.

"They set a guard on me in here… and all the other guards were alerted that I wasn't to go on deck, except for visits to the lido for a swim and then they keep two guards on me. And they keep one on me down here all the time. I'm a prisoner here, Vince. They claim they'll let me go after some big project they have coming up."

"What big project is that?"

"No notion. Anyway, not a prayer they're letting me go. From what I've gleaned, this vessel is a top-secret Russian intel operation. I feel like a traitor, working here. Keep trying to figure out how to sabotage the thing without getting killed for it. Lately thinking of seeing if I can get control of the Azipod—"

"What's an Azipod?"

"It's a thruster, mate, a kind of rudder combined with propellers. It's on a pod that swivels when the control room steers the ship. The Finns developed 'em. They got the early model on this rust bucket. Now see, there's a hydraulic steering motor on the upper unit of the Azipod, that's inside the hull. I think I can muck with the steering motor, take control of the ship's direction, send it to run aground. That might wreck it—which will make me feel some better, and it might give me a chance to escape. But the shore's about three kilometers off, and before it got here the buggers'd come down here and see what's up. And then there's my family to think of. So my problem, mate, is—"

Vince raised a hand. "Wait, hold on, rewind a sec, Morris—you mentioned a *guard* that's posted down here. Where is he now?"

"I am right here," said a voice behind Vince. The English was clear, but with a Chinese accent.

Vince turned, and saw a chunky, crookedly smiling Chinese guard, perhaps forty, wearing a grimy white uniform. The noise of the engines had covered his approach. And the guard had his submachine gun pointed right at Vince.

CHAPTER EIGHT

"Take it easy, Hiya!" Morris said hastily, standing up. "He's on our side!"

The Chinese guard frowned but lowered the submachine gun. "What makes you believe so?"

"He's against the Russians, and he's going to get us out of here! He's gonna scuttle this damned rust box, Hiya. And I for one will do a fucking hornpipe when I see it go down!"

"Your relationship with your friend here calls for some explanation, Morris," Vince said.

"How about you crack open that bottle of *baijiu* you've been saving, Hiya," Morris said, grinning. "I'll tell you his side, you can tell him yours."

"Your name is Hiya?" Vince asked the man.

The guard shrugged. "If you want. It's *Hàoyǔ*. But because my friend Morris here has damage in the brain from inhaling diesel fumes, he calls me Hiya."

"Oh, so I'm brain-damaged!" Morris said, mocking outrage. "Who beats you in chess, ya wankin' womba!"

"Only because I let you win, you Aussie bugger!" Hiya responded. "You bloody derro!"

"You wristy bogan!"

"Apparently," Vince said, "you guys have been together a while now—Hiya seems to have learned a passel of Aussie insults."

"I know them all now!" Hiya said proudly. "Me and this wanker have been stuck together for more than a year!"

"Truth is, we're good friends," said Morris. "But cussing this drongo out keeps me sane."

"Drongo!" exclaimed Hiya. "You can get stuffed ya fuckwit! And you're a *ben dan* too!"

"Now you've gone to the Chinese insults! Well, you're a *gou pi*!"

"What! Call me a dog fart! Why you bludger!"

Vince laughed. "Okay, enough. Let's crack that *baijiu*. It's been a long day."

They were in the motor control room overlooking the engine deck. There were several half-broken swivel chairs between panels of monitors and readings systems, along with a folding card table where a chess board was set up. Vince, Morris and Hiya sat around the chess board, drinking.

One good shot of *baijiu* was enough for Vince. "How much alcohol's in this stuff?"

"Oh, this one's only about ninety proof," said Morris, pouring himself another.

"Christ," said Vince. "You can use it for fuel if you run out of diesel. How do they fuel this ship if it never docks?"

"It's set up to be refueled at sea," Morris said. "Gets tricky when it's choppy out. They spill a lot of fuel. But Krupin's security protocol says *Cupid's Cruise* never docks, not ever."

Hiya drank some *baijiu* and looked at Vince with amazement. "The crazy man who shoots Nazis from a helicopter in Washington," he said. "Here you are, in person. It was on the news in Beijing, to show us how chaotic America is, but I remember admiring your nerve. It is hard to feel sympathy for Nazis."

Morris looked at Vince quizzically. "You mind telling me, mate, if you ever thought about going into a different line of work? I mean, besides just killing buggers that need killing?"

Vince chuckled—a sad sound, even to his own ears. "I did go into a different line of work. For a year and a half. And then I was dragged away from it. But you know—my dad was an experienced combat vet. When I told him I was joining the Rangers, he warned me I'd either get tired of the whole thing after a few years, or I'd go a little..." He tapped his forehead. "I got tired of it *and* I went a little nuts. Both! Started plotting when I would get away from special ops. Dreamed about another career. Maybe go into construction. I built my own house, you know. Two stories."

"All alone?" Hiya asked, looking surprised.

"Ninety per cent. That's something I'm proud of. Proud of serving my country, too—but I did my part. Yet here I am, 'killing buggers' again. You know what my dad went into after the military? He became a flower farmer."

Morris laughed. "You're taking the piss!"

"Not kidding. Organic flower farming. Did well at it too. He was as badass as they come—but he loved flowers."

Vince felt emotion tugging at him, thinking of his parents. He cleared his throat and said, "Look, after you leave the ship, if you guys tell anyone, and I mean *anyone at all*, who I am, and what I was here for... it'll be a disaster. It could lead to a war."

Morris blinked at that. "Then I hope you have a damned good reason for this mission, mate."

"I've said too much already. But if you want off this ship, I need you guys to trust me. Even afterwards. You can't tell anyone about me."

"I won't mention you, I swear it," Morris said.

Hiya nodded. "I too have no wish to cause a war."

"We want people to believe the ship is going to blow up as a result of an accident in the fuel line. That'll be the story, anyway. You can help us, Morris, by confirming that. You can say you warned the captain, and that no one would listen to you about the risks."

Morris nodded gravely. "That's what I'll say."

"Gentlemen—can we shake hands on this?"

Feeling the weight of responsibility, they shook hands all around.

"With the age of this ship," Hiya said, "no one will be surprised if it suffers a fatal accident."

"Where'd you learn your English, Hiya?" Vince asked.

"Beijing University,and Hong Kong. I wanted to go into science, ecological studies, but the university said I was too radical."

"What made them think you were radical?"

"I was against coal-powered generators! Air pollution is choking China. So, the Ministry of Human Resources told me to shut up and pushed me into PLA."

Vince nodded sympathetically. The People's Liberation Army. "What kind of duty they give you?"

Hiya grimaced. "They sent me to help guard an internment camp for the Uighurs. The camp treated the Uighurs so badly; it is… simply not my nature to do such things to people. I spoke up, said some changes were needed and…" He shrugged. "They punished me by sending me here. Some PLA soldiers, with very good behavior, they get shore leave. Not me! I am 'the one who criticized the People's Republic'. I always wanted to defect—maybe go to the USA."

"The USA!" Morris jeered. "They're all mad buggers there! Nothing personal, Vince. But Australia's the place!"

"Not such a good place for your ancestors," Hiya observed. "Very hard for aborigines."

"All that's changed," Morris said. "Mostly, anyway. Believe me, mate, when we get off this bloody ship you got to come with me to Sydney! I'll show you a time!"

"Yes, that sounds good." Hiya sipped some liquor, shuddered, then looked pointedly at Vince. "You must understand, the Chinese guards on board know very little about the operation here. They were put here to keep an eye on the Russians. When the Russians invaded Ukraine, they had to become friendlier with China. The intelligence services got friendly, too. Our Ministry of State Security, they send some disinformation to the USA, and some cyberattacks. The Russians make a deal with the People's Republic to allow this ship in our territory, but... China doesn't trust Russians so much. So, we are here to watch the Russians. My people working here, they're trapped too. Some get a little shore leave, and what of it? They cannot go home."

"You hear anything about a big project coming up?" Vince asked. "Something special happening on the cyberwarfare deck?"

Hiya shrugged. "They tell us almost nothing."

"How many Chinese guards here?"

"No so many as Russian. Sixteen. But I heard one man has gone missing. That idiot Yan. Probably got drunk and fell overboard."

Vince decided to hold off on telling Hiya about Yan's fate. "Your compatriots—they'll kill me if they're told to."

"Some would kill *me* if they were told to, also. But you know, Vince—I would not kill them unless in self-defense. And even then, it would be hard for me. I will help you all I can. You do what you must, but I do not want to kill my countrymen. They just go where they are told."

"If I was in your place I'd feel the same way," Vince said. This complicated an already complex situation. He'd have to try to disarm the Chinese aboard instead of killing them. Give them a chance to escape the ship. Tighe wouldn't be pleased.

Vince regarded himself as being at war with the Russians. He was no fan of the People's Liberation Army, either. But the Agency file had presented the Russians aboard as all hardened killers, many of them having worked in interrogation in Ukraine, and in other dirty corners of intelligence. The background of the Chinese guards had been listed as unknown—except for their CO, Commander Mun. Mun had a background in anti-American intelligence. He was known for his brutality. Vince figured him as fair game. And it occurred to Vince that Mun might make a useful pawn.

Vince picked up a pawn from the chess set, contemplated it, and said, "Gentlemen, I have a plan. I'll try to go easy on the Chinese aboard. I'll try to get them ashore. But every Russian on board is going down. And so is this ship."

"How can you alone sink the ship?" Hiya asked.

"I have plastic explosives. They're well hidden. Enough to do the job if carefully placed."

Morris whistled. "Bloody hell!"

"You men are going to deboard on a lifeboat well before that happens," Vince said. "Right now, Morris, I need to understand this hydraulic steering motor you mentioned…"

In some ways, Jim Greenwald was feeling better when he reported for the meeting with Krupin and Feske. In other ways, not so much. Greenwald had gotten a supply of OxyContin that morning, provided by Lorvec's supplier, so he wasn't sick. But visions of America's destruction were still haunting him.

Fuck all that, he told himself as he got some coffee from Krupin's silver samovar. *Just keep your head down, your nose to the grindstone, and get through this. And hope Krupin doesn't have you killed when it's over.*

Greenwald took a seat, and the first projection from Feske's laptop had just lit up the wall when Lorvec came in, looking grave.

He addressed Krupin in Russian; Krupin answered in the same language. Then said, "Lorvec, tell Greenwald what you've told me. Maybe he's heard something. I'd like to know who spread this rumor…"

Lorvec said, "Jim, sentries are missing, five of them. And a lifeboat. There is a rumor. One of the girls said she heard the two sentries speak in English to a Chinese guard, Yan is his name. He was suggesting Yan go with them, there's room for one more…"

"Have you heard anything about this, Jim?" Krupin asked.

"I haven't," Greenwald said. "But…"

"Yes?"

"A few weeks back a couple sentries bitched to me about their assignment to this ship. The tedium, I think. Hardly ever going ashore, that kind of thing."

"Which sentries were complaining?" Krupin asked sharply.

"Ah, I don't recall." Greenwald didn't want to get anyone punished. The nightmare of Bae's death had been more than enough. "I don't know the names of most of them anyway, to be honest… They were Russian, that's all I know."

"We will speak of this again," Krupin said, pointedly. "Later maybe you will remember more. If the missing men are deserters, they must be found and punished."

"What else could it be but desertion?" Greenwald asked.

"That is exactly what I am wondering," Krupin said. "Let us resume work now. We have moved up the attack and we must be ready."

"If I'd known it was so easy to launch those lifeboats, I'd be on the shore already!" Carolyn declared.

"Yeah, for some reason the guards forgot to mention that to you," Vince said dryly.

They were in Carolyn and Jill's berth, the two women seated on Jill's bunk. Jill was wearing silk pajamas, Carolyn shorts and a blouse.

Vince was leaning against the bulkhead, one foot on his toolbox, looking out of the broken porthole at the sea. He'd breakfasted with the cooks in the galley, trying not to talk much. His Hans Graf cover was wearing thin.

"You ladies spread the rumor?" he asked.

Both women nodded. "I do just what you say, Vince," Jill said.

"Oh yeah? I didn't tell you to kill that guard last night."

"You didn't tell me not to!" she said, grinning.

"Jill here came out of Sampaloc," Carolyn said, shrugging.

Vince nodded. That was the most dangerous neighborhood in Manila. Likely that killing wasn't Jill's first rodeo.

"I just want to please you, big guy," Jill said, pouting.

"Oh shit, Jill," Carolyn said, laughing softly.

Jill scowled at her. "Why don't you leave me and Vince alone for a little while so we can talk? You got a swimming pool day, you can go there."

"Oh, so you can put the make on Vince? Fine, if that's what—" She started to get up.

Vince put both hands up like a traffic director requiring full stop. "Carolyn, please stay here!" He turned to Jill. "Look, if I wasn't married—how could I resist you?" What was the expression the kids used? "Um… you're *fire*, girl!"

"I am?"

"Sure! But I'm a big believer in oaths. Including the marriage vow."

Jill's pout was now a real one. "Men, men, men, all around me all the time, and I don't want to go to bed with any of them! Finally, one I want in the bed, and he's married and he believes in *vows!*" She swore in Tagalog and threw her pillow at him.

Vince caught the pillow and threw it back. "After this is over, you can find another line of work, and find a guy worth being with. It'll happen."

"Fuck that. Maybe I go to a convent."

Carolyn barked a laugh. "*You*, in a convent!"

Jill punched her in the shoulder. "Shut up!" But she had to laugh.

Vince lowered his voice. "Listen—you two know a Chinese guard named Hiya? That's not exactly how it's pronounced. He watches the engine room."

"Yeah, I know him," Jill said. "He smells like diesel. Nice man. I kinda like him."

"You two keep this as quiet as death now, but he's on *our side*. I'm telling you this because he's going to help me organize the escape for the girls. And he's going with you. Morris from the engine room, too."

"When?" Carolyn demanded, clasping her hands.

"Not today, but it'll be soon. I promise it'll happen."

"Men *promise* things," Jill sniffed.

"This really will," Vince said. "I have to set it up carefully. If we get you into a lifeboat now, they'll just fire on it or radio for someone to bring you back. I've got to kill a few dozen Russians first."

"Oh, is *that* all," said Carolyn dourly.

"Listen… you know Commander Mun?"

94

Carolyn groaned. "Oh god yeah. I hate that fucker. But he's an officer, so he gets girl privileges, and he picks on me sometimes."

"He got a stateroom?" Vince asked.

"Yeah. I've been there."

"Can you give me directions?"

"You going there now? Pretend to be Hans?"

"Not right this second. But I've got a plan and I'm going to need Mun to make it work. Hiya doesn't know the room number, he's never been to Mun's deck. Says it's all ship's officers there, and a few Russian sentries."

"You going to kill Mun?" Carolyn asked, brightening at the thought.

"I'm going to kidnap him."

Carolyn grunted. "Hell, I've been to his stateroom more times than I want to remember. I could draw you a map."

"That'd be good. I've got paper and pencil in my toolbox. Draw a map, give me the room number. Does he have a sentry outside his room?"

"Yes. And there's some on the deck somewhere. You'd run into them on the way there. If you try to kill all those sentries on that deck, you'll get every soldier on board after you."

"I'll do a workaround."

Vince recalled Hiya mentioning at least half the passageways on *Cupid's Cruise* were no longer used. They were empty, sealed off. Those empty passages might offer a way to get past sentries on the other decks...

"Hey boss, almost done. Did Yan tell you?"

Lorvec looked up from his laptop at Hans Graf. "Eh, it's you!" He grimaced, then seemed to remember something. "*Yan,* you say? Yan is the guard I put on you! He's on the list of..."

"Yes?"

"Never mind! Where did you see him last?"

"He left, first day, hated the stink of bilge! Said he was tired of all this." Vince waved a hand to indicate the ship itself. "Said only officers get women." Vince shrugged. "He resigns, *ja?* I remember another ship I worked, sailor was so *traurig*, so sad, he hang himself from the…" He mimicked someone raising a flag, then acted as if he remembered the word. "The *flagpole!* Another sailor, he…" Vince once more mimicked raising a flag. "Raise up his body very high, leave it dangling like flag *ja?* And then we all laugh! But the captain he is say—"

"Graf!"

"Yes?"

"Shut up!"

"*Ja*, sure, I shut up," Vince said, scratching at the eyepatch as if it were irritating his bad eye.

Lorvec grimaced. "Just… go get your work done."

"I come to tell you, I need electric pipe cutter. My pipe cutter too small, not electric. The Chinese on the freighter, they say I cannot bring my big one. Cook he says there is one in hardware hold, is locked up, I need key—"

"Yes, yes…" Lorvec swore in Russian, then called out, "Artyom!"

A guard came in, carrying a submachine gun. This must be Artyom. "*Da?*"

He spoke in Russian and tossed the guard a ring of keys. Artyom caught it, saluted, then escorted Hans Graf—Vince Bellator, the undercover Delta Force special ops killer—down the passageway, toward the locked storage room. Hans Graf whistled a German pop tune as he went.

Vince reflected that this simple hardware tool, the electric pipe cutter, might be the one thing he'd need to give him a chance to survive on this ship long enough to carry out his mission.

He hoped Artyom didn't get suspicious of him. It would be awkward if he had to kill him. The guard clearly worked closely with Lorvec; he'd be quickly missed. Best not push the envelope by making more guards prematurely disappear.

But Lorvec had seemed to accept Graf's story about Yan. And they all seemed to accept the eyepatch. What seemed to work best was the ludicrous tactic of babbling annoyingly on. It made Lorvec want to spend as little time as possible around Hans Graf. Vince based it on a guy he'd grown up around in Texas, Bubba Dunsmuir. Bubba ended up pumping gas for a living.

Following the guard down a ladder to a lower deck, Vince wondered what Dierdre was doing right now…

Dierdre turned the pages on the accounts book and scribbled another entry. She sighed. She'd wanted to use a bookkeeping program, but Vince and Diego and Lupe had said, *Please don't.* None of them knew how to interpret a bookkeeping program.

It was getting late, almost ten, and Dierdre was tired. The restaurant was just about to close. Diego and Lupe, and Nilla and Maria the bartender were dealing with that. Oh, and the busboy, Ricardo, who had been puzzled when he was told the FBI would have to do a full check on him, fingerprints and all. "But I have a green card!"

That's not it, Ricardo. It has to do with Russian spies, and other enemies of the owner of this restaurant. She hadn't been able to say that to him, so she'd just shrugged and said, "The owner prefers it."

The Secret Service guards had been replaced by a couple of US Marshals in plainclothes, pretending to be contractors. They didn't look much like contractors.

Dierdre put down the pen, looking out the window at the fir trees swaying gently in the night wind. How long would this federal protection set-up go on? She was starting to wonder if they were surveilling her as much as watching out for her.

Her mobile rang. She glanced at it, recognized the area code—a call from Manila!—and snatched it up. "Vince?"

Richie Chang chuckled dryly and said, "Sorry, it's just me, Dierdre."

"Richie! Are there complications over there?"

"I'm not exactly sure. But I'm calling for a reason. At least, I think I am."

"That's way too cryptic, Richie. Any news about Vince?"

"Only that he got aboard the ship."

"This can't be your phone."

"Yeah, I didn't want to use mine. It's Jerry Timbol's. He's with the Agency. He took a real liking to Vince, and he's worried about Tighe. Anyway, he's worried about Tighe's attitude toward Vince."

"Meaning what?"

"Tighe wouldn't let Jerry come to a meeting with a CIA asset, one Ray Ramos. Said it was a 'need to know' restriction. Jerry looked at Ramos's file—he's neutralized a couple guys for the Agency. Invariably shoots people in the back. And Jerry got a look at a file that Tighe copied to Ramos. It was Vince's file. And Tighe's being secretive with me, too. Says there's no need for me here now, I need to go back to the States. But originally, he brought me in because Vince trusts me more than him. So that, and a general change of tone and stuff that's hard to really nail down…"

"Are you suggesting Tighe is thinking of neutralizing Vince, if he survives that ship?"

She could hear Richie take a deep breath. "Uh… maybe. I'm far from concluding that. But here's the thing. When I said I wanted to wait in Manila for Vince to finish the job, I spotted a guy following me. I figure Tighe is having me watched. So why would that be?"

"I can't imagine. Unless he mistrusts you."

"And why should he? The only thing I can think of is Tighe obsessing about the risk that if Vince succeeds, the Chinese and the Russians will figure out who was behind destroying that operation."

"If anyone could find a way to complete the mission without leaving American fingerprints all over it, Vince could."

"I believe that. But does Tighe? The day before he went out to the cruise ship, Tighe kept trying to talk Vince out of saving the civilians on *Cupid's Cruise*."

"That little shit!"

"Yeah. See, this mission is the topper on Tighe's career. If it succeeds, without implicating the USA, he may become CIA Director someday. But if it backfires... I don't know.

I feel like Tighe's not going to take a chance on it. And Vince has told you something about this mission, right?"

"I..." Should she deny it?

"You don't have to say it. You guys are close. You knowing about it might make you a target, too."

That had occurred to her. But it wasn't her own life she was thinking about right now. "You're thinking that they'll arrange to pick Vince and the civilians up, and kill *all* of them?"

"Could be, if Tighe sends Ramos to pick him up. I just don't know. I wondered, did you have any kind of personal backchannel to Vince? Maybe he has a phone hidden, something the Agency doesn't know about?"

"No, Richie, nothing like that. No way to warn him. Oh, God..."

"I'm sorry to dump this on you. It could be a misreading of the situation."

"I'm glad you told me." But Richie's theory had made Dierdre's blood run cold. "I'll think about this. Maybe I can think of some friend of Vince's with connections to the Agency. Find out if the CIA has approved…"

She didn't want to say it.

"Just don't blow it wide open," Richie said, his voice an urgent whisper now. "Don't tell anyone, no matter who, where Vince is or exactly what he's doing. If this comes out wide, it could get me killed. I've gotta go. I'll be in touch."

And with that, he hung up.

Dierdre just sat there, in shock, staring out of the window but no longer seeing the trees. She was seeing Vince, smiling at her. And then she seemed to see his face going blank, the life draining from it—as someone shot him in the back.

CHAPTER NINE

"I am so tired," Hans Graf said, shaking his head as he removed the grid over the air circulator. He was squatting close by the bulkhead. "So tired, *ja.*"

"Finish and get out," said the Russian operator of the radio room. "You make distraction." The radio operator was in the swivel chair behind Vince, looking out the curve of the windows. The sea beyond surged silver and blue. A distant fishing boat was heading in toward shore.

Under the window was a variety of radio panels and microwave transmitter controls. The radio room was one level higher than the bridge. Unseen from here but not far overhead were those big chromium transmitters and receivers Vince had seen on the way to the ship.

"Hurry up and get it done!" said the operator.

"Lorvec say check for mold, I check for mold," said Vince. Humming *99 Luftballons*, Vince took a quarter pound of shaped EPX-1 plastic explosives from under the wrenches and screwdrivers in his toolbox. Blocking the action with his body, he placed the plastic explosive in the ventilator opening, and replaced the grid.

The detonators were ready for his signal. "No mold is here," Vince muttered, tightening the screws on the grid. "*Nein.*"

He picked up the toolbox and, sighing wearily, carried it to the other ventilator grid. He hunkered down, glanced over his shoulder at the radio man, who was muttering in Russian into his headset, looking bored and irritable and not the least interested in Hans Graf. Vince quickly removed the grid, set the explosives in place and closed up. "Detector finds no mold. *Das ist gut.*"

"Yes, good, now get out!" the radioman said.

Vince stood up, gave him a salute, and went to the door. Next stop would be dodgy. The Bridge. There were three men there, the captain and two officers, which meant three times the chance someone would notice something off about this Hans Graf.

As Vince came in, humming the song, the captain turned in his chair and frowned at him. He was a gray-haired man with rheumy blue eyes. He wore a white captain's uniform. "What do you in here? We have no plumbing. Only behind the bridge, in the *komnata.*" The Russian word for restroom.

"Sure," Vince said, "We check for black mold, always, so… I look at your vents, maybe."

"You look at them? No, we have no mold."

"Always hard to see in beginning, *ja*, but sure, okay—I tell everyone, why worry about black mold? Life is too short. Probably not there. Cancer kills us first, no? Or heart attack? Why worry. I will go and I will Krupin you say no."

He turned away and went to the door—and stopped, relieved but not showing it—when the captain said, "Yes, *da*, very well, but no spraying chemicals in here. I have allergy."

The other two officers glanced at Hans Graf; one of them made a remark in Russian and the other laughed as Vince went to the vent and crouched down. He unbuttoned the top of his coveralls, so he could reach in and draw the SIG Sauer if one of these guys decided this "drainage engineer" was a phony. Then he puttered with the vent for a few moments, pretending to examine the back of the grid. Looking with his peripheral vision to be sure the three men weren't watching him, Vince retrieved the plastic explosives from the toolbox and set them in place. This time he put a half-pound in. That should be enough to take out the bridge.

Replacing the grid, and humming, Vince left the bridge and walked out to the little walkway around the con structure of the ship. The wind sang between the narrow upper structures, bringing a strong smell of brine. He was only fifteen feet under the array of transmitters. A small hatch opened to the comm-cable locker under the transmitters. Now it was time to see if he still had the lock-picking skills he'd learned when he'd gone to the CIA's prep school, as part of the liaison between Delta Force and the Agency. He glanced around, saw he was out of sight of the decks and the bridge, and took a particular screwdriver from his toolbox. He unscrewed the grip and took out the lockpicks the Agency had hidden there.

His skills, as it turned out, were rusty. It took him five tries, but at last the lock opened. Vince pulled the hatch aside and stepped into the small maintenance space under the transmitters. He left the hatch open just enough to provide light. The indirect daylight showed him cables and modulating boxes rising from within the deck up through the maintenance hold. He took out a chunk of plastic explosive and glanced past the hatch. No one out there, so far. He reached up, carefully inserted the shaped charge so its blast would carry upward. It would unseat the transmitters and receivers and blow through the cables coming from the radio room.

Vince turned to glance out the hatch—if anyone even reasonably bright caught him in here, the firefight could commence immediately. It would be too hard to explain why a drainage engineer was in this particular maintenance hold.

The coast seemed clear. Carrying his toolbox, he stepped out, carefully closed the hatch, and went to the ladder that would take him down to the passageways. He set up his last detonator transponder on the backside of the comm cable locker. It wasn't until he was inside again, heading down the passageway to the ladders that would get him to the engine room, that he became fully aware of his racing pulse, and thudding heart. It always hit him after the fact.

He forced his mind to the next step.

Have to block the ship's ability to communicate with the land. You think you've got their communications covered? Nope.

The Russian and Chinese soldiers and the staff were not allowed mobile phones, walkie-talkies or satellite phones. There was no WiFi on the ship. There were public address systems and there were intercoms, but nothing that could communicate with the shore or other ships, except the radio room and the few phones Krupin allowed.

Krupin considered everyone's phones and laptops and iPads to be security risks. They were not permitted. Krupin allowed himself two phones, Lorvec one, the captain one. No others. The interdeck com system was good enough for the ship's daily needs. In an emergency, walkie-talkies could be distributed. But that last one Vince had covered—the emergency comms locker, with satphones and walkie-talkies, was near the engine room. Morris and Hiya would dump its contents into the sea tonight. All but three satphones. Vince was going to need them...

Vince knew there was a radio in every lifeboat. Fortunately, the ship did not have the regulation complement of lifeboats. There had been only eight and—thanks to Vince—one lifeboat was now missing. Vince thought he could slip past the deck sentries into the boats and destroy the radios and outboard controls in all the boats. He had to make sure Krupin couldn't access the boats to radio for help. There was a locker full of inflatable boats, but those didn't contain radios.

He also had to get the mobile phones away from Krupin, Lorvec and the captain, the only three men allowed them. His plan to get those phones involved women…

An hour after sunset. Thick clouds. Choppy waves. The heavy air hinting of a coming storm.

Vince was creeping along in darkness.

He was hunched down, moving a few quick steps at a time. An awkward position to move in, but it worked to keep him in the shadows that fell across the deck. The sundeck, without a speck of sun on it now, was splashed at intervals with deck lights. There was the guard going around the corner, onto the open area at the prow. Vince turned his head, saw the shadow cast across a lit area: Another guard coming, still half the ship's length away.

Vaulting over the railing, Vince dropped onto the top of a lifeboat. The thump of his two feet on the boat was too loud for his liking. He hurriedly opened the hatch, slipped through, and waited. No response from overheard. The guard hadn't seen him.

Vince used a penlight brought from his tool chest, keeping it dialed low to search for the radio. The only one he could locate was attached to the navigational panel at the aft of the lifeboat. Vince made sure there weren't any satphones or spare radios in the cabinets under the benches, then he went to the nav panel. He took a screwdriver from his pocket and pried the metal facing open, then bent and twisted and tugged out the radio's innards. He opened a port, tossed them through, and then did the same for the controls of the outboard. Time to move on to the next boat...

"So! You have something special to show me!" Lorvec said, grinning widely as Jill came into his stateroom. "Such a promising message you sent!"

She'd put makeup over her bruises, and was wearing a raincoat and transparent high heels. Carolyn had done Jill's hair and now she looked her best.

Lorvec was wearing only a coffee-stained white bathrobe; he stank of vodka and sweat, as if someone had mixed them in equal amounts to fill a bucket. Jill didn't care. Ignoring the plethora of reeks from her customers was part of her job. Today, though, he was not quite a customer. She was here to make it easier for Vince to kill Lorvec.

Jill just wished she could do it herself. She had often imagined getting hold of one of his steak knives and hiding it near the bed. He liked her to climb on top and pump away, saving him all the work. She could use that opportunity to cut his throat. An appealing idea. Before, she couldn't do it—even though she hated him deeply and profoundly—because every sex worker was admitted to the stateroom by a sentry. Her name was written down on a guest sheet. And more than one sentry saw that sheet. She couldn't kill them all.

But now? Now Vince had a plan. It required careful timing... and the time to kill Lorvec was not yet. Too much chance he would be quickly missed, and if that happened, Vince's next move would be jeopardized.

Jill threw off her raincoat, showing Lorvec her very best black lace lingerie, and the body it scarcely concealed.

106

"Oh ho!" Lorvec said, his eyes lighting up. "This is what you wish to show me! I see it and I want it!"

"And to do my very best work, I want to make us both a glass of vodka—and I will offer a toast to you!"

"A toast! Yes! With vodka martinis!"

"Await me on the bed, you big handsome man!"

He went chuckling to the bed, muttering in Russian, as she went to the steel liquor cabinet, and poured the vodka into martini glasses. Then she took the capsule from where it was tucked into a slit in the hem of her lingerie. Stirring the drinks with one hand, she flicked the capsule open with the other and poured the powder into his drink. Her body blocked his view of the drink mixing. He was behind her, gawking at her *puwet*.

So sad, using up her last sleeping pills like this—she had just one more to use on the captain, later.

Jill made sure the powder was dissolved, came to the bed with the drinks and said, "A toast—to a man like you having two orgasms!"

"Bah! I can have three if you work hard enough!"

"Then we drink to that. But for three orgasms—the whole drink!"

She drank hers down; he gulped his and gasped. "Now, where is your roommate, that girl with hair like grapes? Maybe I have two girls tonight!"

"Carolyn? She is with your boss tonight."

"What? Krupin!" He yawned. "Why... well, next time."

He threw his glass against the bulkhead, smashing it. She smashed hers against the wall, too, and then straddled him...

It wasn't long before Lorvec was sound asleep. Then Jill found his cell phone, in a locker under the bed. She searched thoroughly to see if he had another one hidden. But no.

She donned the raincoat, put the phone in its pocket, and slipped out of the stateroom.

The sentry made a joke about Lorvec making short work of love tonight.

Jill waved at the guard and went to find Vince. She hoped that Carolyn had enjoyed as much luck with Krupin. Then she thought, *how often does Lorvec use his phone when he's on the ship?*

When Lorvec wakes up tomorrow, will he notice it's gone?

Vince would have to worry about that. Right now, she had to get to the captain's cabin. He'd be even easier to drug than Lorvec, and Jill knew where he kept his cell phone.

It was morning, two hours after dawn, but as Vince came down the steel stairs, he was struck by the fact that there was no morning or night in the engine room. It always looked the same in the windowless perpetually lit, diesel-fumy chamber, whatever time of day or night it was.

He hurried down the ladder to the engine room deck, and back aft to the exposed upper section of the Azipod. Vibrations from the enormous undersea propellers, hummed loudly through layers of mechanism and hull. *Whum whum whum whum…*

Gloves slick with fresh grease, Morris stood on an access ledge inside the upper Azipod maintenance pit. Only his head and shoulders showed above the deck. He was turning a wrench, opening a protective cover over the steering mechanism. It was through this device that signals from the bridge ruddered the ship.

"You still think you can get that thing to steer from down here?" Vince asked.

Morris nodded, as he exposed the intricate wiring of the steering mechanism. "But all I can do is lock it into a new course. And I mean it'll be locked, mate. If we're about to run headfirst into a rock, too bad!"

"Long as it's straight out to sea, away from Macao, that'll work fine." With a little luck.

"It's going to take time to set it up. Maybe an hour."

"First chance you get, head us out to sea."

"The instant it changes course for the due east, they're going to blow a gasket on the bridge. They'll call me and demand to know what's up."

"Tell them you don't know. Tell them there's a glitch, wires crossed, short circuit, a hacker—anything to buy time."

"They'll probably send some men down here."

"Talk to them. Stall them."

"They'll stop the engines, though... unless..."

"Unless what?"

"I can override that, down here. I'll just pull out the wires for the bridge's engine controls."

"Good! When I'm back, duck down and I'll take out whoever they've sent."

"What if they sent like six guys?"

"I'll deal with it."

"If you say so, mate."

"Once we're far enough from Macao that no one can see the explosions, I'll blow up the transmitters, the bridge and the radio room. Then we get you and our friends off the ship."

"You got all the plastics here?"

"Yeah. Got all my gear in your control room. Even the sniper rifle. I brought it down in a bundle of pipes. Brought my travel bag, too."

"When are the women coming down?"

109

"I'm going to get them in a few minutes. Then the Chinese guards—if I can make that work."

"How about the kitchen staff? They're just hirelings, stuck here the same way I am."

"I plan to get them out last. I plan to leave the ship with them."

Morris took a deep breath. "It all seems dodgy. But I'm with you all the way, mate."

"Good man. Now, take a break and show me the best place for the plastics to go."

Morris peered up at him nervously. "You sure there's no way those things can go off early? They get a signal to explode—maybe get a stray signal from somewhere else?"

"They're designed to react only to the specific code the detonator sends them."

"But if you set off one set of plastics it won't set off the other? You won't blow me and Hiya to atoms in here?"

"Nope, different detonation codes."

Morris pursed and lips and nodded as if he wanted to believe it. "Come on then." He stuck up his hand and Vince pulled him out of the maintenance pit. "Right. I'll show you the best way to blow this tub to tiny little pieces."

Singing softly in German, weaving as if soused, Vince made his way down the passageway alongside the berths of the "comfort girls"—till he was stopped by a scowling Russian sentry.

"What you do here?" the man asked. "You drunk? You bother the women! You don't have woman privilege! Get back to your deck!"

"Not even that woman?" Vince asked, pointing past the guard.

The guard turned—and as he registered that there was no one at all in the passageway behind him, Vince knocked him cold with the pommel of the combat knife. He didn't want to leave telltale blood on the deck, so he dragged the unconscious man by the collar around a corner, and into a utility closet. There, Vince cut the man's throat and left him to bleed out. Closing the hatch, he returned to the passageway and saw Jill standing over a slumped guard about five berths down.

Sighing with aggravation, Vince loped over to her. "What the hell, Jill," he whispered, looking down at the dead man as Jill wiped her buck knife on the guard's uniform. She'd stabbed him through the heart, and the body was bleeding copiously onto the deck.

She shrugged. "You said we had to kill the sentries in this passage!"

"Keep your voice down. I said *I* had to kill them. You are getting so damned... *stabby*."

She reached up and stroked his cheek. "You just say that to be sweet."

"You know, someday you might meet a Russian who's not a bad guy."

"There are some?"

"Of course there are! There's a whole resistance movement fighting the regime in Russia. Brave people and good people. These guys on the ship, though, are longtime operatives of the regime. But you let me deal with them."

She pouted. "Carolyn says I'm not supposed to kill the Chinese. But I don't like Chinese much, either."

"Lots of good Chinese around. Hiya's Chinese, he's a good man. Even in the People's Republic most people are quite decent—they're just stuck with the system there." This was no time for a discussion. He looked up and down the passageway. Coast clear so far. "Can't worry about this guy's blood. Let's dump him in the berth and we'll tell the women the time's come."

Ten minutes later, Vince was leading a procession of whispering women along the passageway toward the ladders leading to the engine room. Carolyn and Jill were just behind him, trying to keep the others quiet. Some of them giggled.

Hiya met them at the hatch and grinned, waving to the ladies. They'd been briefed about him.

Gathered in Morris's engine control room, the women were sitting on the floor, looking scared but excited.

Hiya volunteered to babysit them. "You're going to hear some explosions soon," he said. "Don't let that scare you. We're leaving here right after. Me and Morris are coming with you... Try to rest..."

"You're not going to entertain us?" Carolyn asked archly. "How about doing a little dance?"

The girls laughed.

Hiya grinned. "Uh, would anyone like to hear a story? Once there was a girl who married a handsome Chinese soldier..."

Down on one knee, Vince was whistling Beethoven's Ninth and using the electric pipe cutter to slice through the welds on the closed door to the starboard passage of deck four. The cutter was a reciprocating metal-cutting saw with an extra-long blade, perfect for the job.

"What is this?" asked Gosog, the pot-bellied Russian officer, striding up. "Why you work here?" Vince had encountered him when he was bringing the bundle of pipes concealing his rifle back from the galley storeroom, and it had been an unnerving encounter. But Gosog had only glanced at the pipes. He'd told him that Lorvec wanted to see him right away. Vince had said "*ja, ja*," but had ignored the request. Now, here he was again, hands on hips, SMG on his shoulder, glaring down at Vince.

"What is this you do now? That deck is closed!"

Vince stopped the pipe cutter. "There is drainage blockage on the deck. There I cure all stink problems on ship!"

"Yes? I spoke to Lorvec—he sent me to find you! You did not go to him!"

"He is meaning *direkt jetzt?* I have just finished cutting through here, *ja*! The door will open. But I will go with you and tell him you made me stop work and let the stink go on…"

"Wait—where is this pipe? Can I see it?"

"Yes, it will be leaking in there! I will show you!"

Vince stood up, opened the door, carried the battery-charge cutter in with him. "This way!" He found a light switch, flicked it. Lights came on sequentially down the dusty, deserted passageway.

Gosog stepped through, and then scowled as Vince closed the door behind them. "Why do you close door?"

Vince started the saw and swung it. With a deft motion of his wrist, he sawed Gosog's head off.

Making a gargling sound, the head fell away, thumping onto the deck and leaving a trail of blood behind as it rolled.

Stepping back to avoid the blood fountaining from the collapsing body, Vince set the saw onto the deck, next to the still-wobbling head. There was just enough charge left in it to cut through the welds on the next hatchway. A small yellow light blinked, showing it was charging. Then, he tugged the submachine gun from the headless body and wiped the blood on it on Gosog's clothes. Have to clean the blood off that saw, too. He was going to need it again.

Whistling Beethoven's Ninth once more, and carrying Mun's submachine gun, Vince hurried off down the passageway. Mun's stateroom was on the deck below, at the far end of the passageway. He could avoid most of the sentries on the deck up here, simply by

113

walking above them. But there were others, down at this end, that he would have to deal with.

Carolyn had made an appointment for a "nooner" with Mun. She wouldn't be showing up. Hopefully, Mun was still waiting in the stateroom...

CHAPTER TEN

"Hello, Oscar," said Dierdre, as she stepped up next to Oscar Tighe at the hotel elevator. "You look surprised to see me."

The CIA officer was tense and pale as he looked up at her; Dierdre was almost a head taller than Tighe. She was wearing the gray and black pantsuit she'd worn as an FBI agent and had a compact but effective .32 automatic pistol in a holster under her coat.

"What the hell is this?" Tighe demanded.

"No law says I can't take a trip to Manila. I just want a word with you about a couple things. You promised to keep me up to speed about Vince. You didn't. You didn't answer my phone calls."

He relaxed a little, she noticed. He'd been afraid she was here for something more than pushing for a briefing. What was he scared of?

The elevator door opened, she stepped in, and put her hand out to keep the door from closing. "Let's talk on the way up, Oscar."

He grunted. "Fine. Just don't ever ambush me like that again."

Tighe stepped into the elevator and pressed the button for the penthouse. The door closed and the elevator rose. "I said I'd keep you as much up to speed as I *could,* Dierdre. But there's nothing I can tell you at this point. You're not cleared. You're not even with the Bureau anymore."

"Kind of a plush hotel for running an agent, isn't it, Oscar? And you're in the penthouse. Posh!"

He glowered at her. "It's got good security. The penthouse is safer."

"Sure it is. I did get some interesting information on Vince's sitch, Oscar."

His eyes narrowed. "From whom?"

"Oh, I interfaced with the CIA when I was in military intel in Iraq. So, I looked up old friends from back then."

"Was it Dipsey Smythe? Or maybe that prick Riggs? Ah—I'll bet it's Carl Westholme!"

"I'm not going to say."

The elevator opened and Tighe stepped up to the door of the penthouse suite. "I suppose I should invite you in for a drink. You must be bushed after the trip."

"I took a red-eye and I'm tired. But I'll get a drink at my own, more modest, digs. You'll invite me in right now because I insist on it."

Tighe gave her a cold look. She gazed steadily back at him. After a moment he shrugged, unlocked the door, and they went in. They were immediately greeted by a spectacular view of Manila from a glass wall stretching the width of the suite.

He picked up a remote from a rosewood coffee table in front of the leather sofa, pressed a button, and oxblood curtains whirred shut over the glass.

"And I was just enjoying your glorious view," Dierdre said lightly. "Such a safe and secure view, too."

"Enough of the snark, Dierdre," he said, going to the suite's bar. He took ice from a canister, put it in a tumbler and poured himself a generous whiskey. "Whatever you heard from your supposed contact at the Agency—if that person exists at all—is bullshit. They couldn't know a thing about the operation. Almost no one is cleared for this. I knew Vince would tell you about it. Which was tantamount to treason, on his part. Because of him, you know more than all but two people at Langley."

"I know that you arranged for a guy like Ray Ramos to be the retriever for Vince."

Tighe pivoted to her, the ice in his glass clinking with the suddenness of the turn. "That's not anything that..." He broke off.

Dierdre smiled and leaned against the counter of his kitchenette. "Not anything that the CIA would know? Because you didn't *tell* anyone at the CIA about Ramos? But... someone did find out. And it got back to me. My contact at Langley was surprised you were using Ramos. Because he's an asset that's only been used to neutralize people. Ramos is a professional murderer, Tighe."

He took a sip of the whiskey, as if he needed time to think. "I wanted someone tough for the job. Vince could be under fire during the extraction."

"Lots of tough people you could have used. But you chose this lowlife who'll do anything for money. From what I hear he'd strangle a baby for a small fee."

"You'll have to leave my team selection to me, Dierdre."

"Here's my theory. You know Vince isn't loose lipped. Back in the day, he was part of a dozen operations that would make the press's hair stand on end, and he never said a word about them. But you also know Vince won't allow innocent bystanders to die in the operation. And you know there are some on the ship. And you want them dead—because you want no witnesses alive to say anything that could point to the Agency being behind this operation. But if you arrange for the non-combatants to die too, maybe when they're being taken off the ship, Vince will come after you. Meaning Vince has to die when they do."

Tighe blinked. He licked his lips and took another drink. Then he shook his head, laughing softly. "Wow. That is truly paranoiac. You should see a doctor."

She reached into her jacket and drew her .32.

"Small gun for a small guy."

His eyes widened. "There are cameras in the lobby of this hotel. The Agency will find out if you—"

She pointed the gun at his head. "Shut up and listen."

He shut up.

"Tighe," she went on, "I actually do not want to kill you. I will, if I have to. I'd rather not. But if Vince dies in this operation, and if there's even the faintest breath, the slightest hint, that you had anything to do with it—I'm just going to go with my gut. And I will shoot you in the nuts. Then I'll let you think for a while, and I'll shoot you between the eyes. I'll be right here, in town, where you can't find me. But I can find *you*. And I'm not here alone."

With that Dierdre backed to the door, holstered the pistol, and left the penthouse.

She took the stairs down.

Vince finished cutting through the weld on the farther door of deck five. He turned off the saw, set it aside, as he heard voices on the other side, in Russian. He'd known that cutting through the weld here would draw the enemy. He was gambling that it was just the sentries on deck four. He drew the SIG Sauer, now equipped with the sound suppressor, and put his left hand on the lever that opened the door.

The men on the other side sounded like they were arguing. Thinly through the little aperture he'd cut under the door—he heard one of them shout, "You, German! Is that you? Come out, hands up! You are not authorized!"

"*Ja*, coming out, hands up!" he shouted.

He opened the door, and immediately shot the two Russian sentries between each man's eyes—placing the two hissing shots in under a second, at almost point-blank range, so close there were burn marks on their foreheads as they fell.

Vince drew his hand back, listening. He heard nothing but ordinary ship's noise. He stepped out, grabbed the nearest body by the collar and dragged it through the hatch. He did the same with the second one, dropping them to one side in the passageway. The blood on the deck, outside, would have to stay. Vince extended the gun through the door, then stepped out into the passageway, glancing left and right.

No one in sight. Ahead was a spiral metal stairway down to the next level. Mun's deck.

Vince crossed to the stairs, descended as quietly as he could, and found himself behind a Russian sentry. A pop from the SIG and the guard fell, shot through the back of the head.

Vince stepped over the body, reached the open passageway for deck four, and stepped out, gun in hand, ready to fire. The Chinese sentry in front of Mun's stateroom gasped and fumbled at his SMG's strap, trying to bring the weapon into play, shouting a warning—Vince aimed carefully, and shot the man through the hand while he was reaching for the gun. The bullet passed through and lodged in the guard's left arm. He yelped in pain and the SMG fell away from him, drooping on its strap.

"Let it drop!" Vince snarled, gesturing with his gun in case the guy didn't know any English.

The guard groaned but let the submachine gun fall to the deck.

Vince strode to the sentry, kicked the SMG away, and said, "Open the door!"

The sentry gulped but shook his head. He was clutching his wounded hand to himself, grimacing with pain.

Vince said, "You're a brave man."

Then he cracked the sentry in the forehead with the butt of his gun, placing the blow with precision. The guard fell, stunned.

Vince knocked on the door with the tip of the suppressor. A handful of seconds passed, with Vince tensely watching the passageway, then the door opened. Commander Mun was wearing a red silk robe, slippers, and nothing else. A chubby man with a froggish look to his face. Mun gaped in surprise at Vince, then at Vince's gun, then at the collapsed sentry.

"She isn't coming," Vince said. "Just me."

Mun looked at him in confusion. "You—the pipes man? The man Graf?"

With his left hand, Vince took off his eyepatch and stuffed it in his pocket, with his right he prodded Mun with the tip of the suppressor and the Chinese commander staggered back, protesting in Mandarin. Vince stepped through, closing the door behind him, keeping Mun covered.

"Who are you, in truth?" Mun demanded.

"I'm the point man for a ship full of pirates, up from Borneo. If you don't want to be tossed overboard when they get here, you'll do what I tell you."

"Strait of Malacca pirates? They never come north!"

"That assumption is why we figured it was safe to do it. Now, don't fuck around." He pointed his gun at Mun's head. "Put on your uniform and do it faster than you've ever done it."

Mun licked his wide lips and nodded frantically and scurried for his uniform. He shrugged out of the robe, exposing his surprisingly large rear. He went to the closet and yanked his pants off a hanger, then did a sort of dance trying to put them on.

"Faster!" Vince said. He didn't want to be trapped in this stateroom. He heard a noise from the passageway, opened the door, and saw the injured sentry getting to his feet. "Stay away from that gun!" Vince said. "Or I'll shoot your commander! Now get in here!" The guard understood enough to comply.

"Faster, Mun!" Vince barked, closing the door. In three minutes, Commander Mun was mussily dressed in his uniform. "Okay you two... Head out. I'm right behind you."

They went out through to the passageway, Mun first. Someone shouted, and Vince stepped out and shot a Russian who was coming from the left. The man spun and fell, shot through the sternum.

Vince tried to remember—was he down to something like eighty-six of the enemy left? He'd lost count.

He turned the gun to Mun and the sentry. "You two, head forward, go to the stairs!"

He got them herded down the passage and up the stairs—the wounded guard groaning, Mun cursing in Mandarin—and through the door to the deck five passageway.

Mun cried out in alarm, seeing the dead men lying inside. Vince closed the door behind them, picked up the pipe-saw, and urged Mun and the sentry down the passageway.

All of a sudden, the entire ship shifted. Vince and the other two staggered, bumping into the bulkhead with the suddenness of the vessel changing course, now bearing due east.

They managed to keep their feet and Vince shouted, "Keep going, faster!"

There it is, Vince thought as he drove his prisoners along. *Morris changed the ship's course.* The engines were still rumbling. He'd cut off the bridge's controls there, too—the captain couldn't stop the ship.

The bridge would be on the intercom to the motorman now, shouting questions. Morris would be pretending puzzlement, suggesting a short circuit in the Azipod, or that somebody had hacked into the controls remotely, or human error in the bridge. Giving them all three of those to chew on—and insisting he'd have it fixed in a few minutes.

Meanwhile, *Cupid's Cruise* chugged at top speed to the open sea.

Commander Mun shrieked as he saw the remains of the guard Vince had beheaded.

"Yeah, you had to be there," Vince said. "It was the expedient move. Turn around, Mun! Look at me!"

Mun turned, quivering with fear. The other guard was goggling at the dead man's head on the floor.

Vince raised the saw. Mun backed away, sobbing. "No, no, no!"

"You notice the blood on the saw blades? No way to treat a good power tool. I don't want to do it again, but I *will* if you don't do exactly what I tell you to, Mun! You understand me?"

"I understand!"

The sentry turned and vomited against the bulkhead. He swayed, seeming dizzy.

Vince hooked a thumb toward the wounded man. "Mun, this man is injured and he's lost blood. You are going to help him get where we're going. Get over here and put your arm around him, help him."

Mun blinked. "Me? I am… I am…" Then he looked at the electric saw in Vince's hand. "Yes. Yes, I will."

* * *

"What is going on down here, Greenwald?" Krupin demanded, coming into the room where Greenwald was working with Feske and Mojin.

They were on the cyberwarfare deck. The hackers and disinfo teams were mostly in separate rooms, workstations cabled together, WiFi being a security problem. The cables ran down the hallway floor, into and out of open doors. Elaborate workstations were set up in each berth. There were a few staterooms on the deck, and Greenwald—who preferred to work in his own stateroom—sometimes came to this one when it was more efficient for the three top hackers to work side by side. Yuri Mojin, a man who hardly ever ate and looked it, was an amphetamine addict getting into one of his semi-psychotic modes, periodically babbling till someone gave him a Xanax. He had matted hair and a thick, gummy beard. He wore a swimming suit, flip-flops and a foul-smelling t-shirt sporting a faded picture of Moby.

"What's going on where?" Greenwald asked mildly. He had done a bit too much Oxy and nothing seemed to matter very much right now. His usual fear of Krupin seemed absurd. Which was itself absurd. He almost laughed at that thought.

Careful or you'll be shark food, he told himself sternly.

"You are nominally in charge down here!" Krupin thundered. "Someone has hacked into our steering system!"

"I *thought* I felt us change direction," Greenwald said. "But surely it's some error in the system, or a crossed wire or…"

"Motorman can't find those things! Maybe someone hacked in! We are headed out to sea! The engine is also not responding—it won't shut down! It had to be someone in this department!"

"Wasn't anyone in this room, sir," Feske said, a little grudgingly. "I'd have known if one of them tried it. And I don't see

123

how it could be done at all from here. It would have to be done at the bridge—"

"They looked at everything, nothing was hacked at the bridge!" Krupin said, bringing a fist down on Greenwald's desk.

"We don't have WiFi here," Feske said. "No way to interface with ship's steering. The transmitters..." He hooked a thumb toward the top decks. "They aren't set up to affect the ship. You saw to that, sir."

"That's so," Greenwald said. "Fear was beginning to stir in him, despite the opiate numbing. "We have nothing that connects to anything but the transmitters and the satellite receptors, Pavel. It was not this department."

"We *could* have!" Mojin burst out, running the words together into *wecouldhave*. "We could build WiFi from parts, we could hack, we could, maybe, redirect the transmitters!" He cackled. "But we *didn't*! We didn't, we did *not*, Komisar Krupin!" He followed that up with something in Russian. He had Russian parents, who were spies in New York, but he'd grown up in the USA.

Krupin stared at Mojin. "He called me *komisar*! And he says he can hack us!"

"He is not to be taken seriously, sir," Feske said, shrugging.

"Is he not?" Krupin pointed at Mojin. "Now—you say it could be done? How? *Who* has done it!"

"Oh nononono!" Mojin said, shaking his head like a maraca. "It wasn't done, truly really wasn't! It would take weeks of setting up some kind of WiFi that could be used to attack the bridge—"

"It wasn't on the bridge! It must be the engine room, but that motorman is no hacker! *You* are!"

"Ah but I'm far more than that," Mojin said, passing a shaking head over his face. "I'm kind of a god, like a god, yeah a god, sort of a god, a total god really."

Krupin stared at him. "Feske, is Mojin useful for Spring Glory?"

"He *has* been useful," Feske said. "Right now, he's gone a week without sleep, he's always on amphetamine—not useful anymore. We don't need him anyway, at this point. We're pretty much there."

"Ohhh, I'm more useful than *seven* of you, Feske!" Mojin crowed.

"I will have no crazy men working in here!" Krupin said. "There are dangerous things happening on this ship." He turned to Greenwald. "You! You know the whores on this ship! That woman Carolyn stole my phone. I have men looking for her—no one can find her!"

"Have they searched the engine room for her?" Fiske suggested. "Something seems to have gone wrong there... Could your phone have been used to interfere in the control signals?"

Krupin stared at him. "The engine room—no, they haven't looked there for her, not yet! I shall send more men there!"

Greenwald cleared his throat. "Maybe she escaped—she was talking once about using one of those inflatable boats and..."

"Maybe she was carried off by a hundred seagulls!" Mojin cackled.

Lorvec came in then, and spoke to Krupin in Russian. Greenwald understood just enough Russian to grasp that someone had been killed. "Someone is dead?"

"Yes," Krupin muttered. His face was red now. "There is a mutiny of some kind aboard! You know nothing about this, Greenwald?"

"Me? No!"

"The women are all gone from their berths and bodies have been found. Sentries." Krupin shook his head.

"I wish I could help, honestly I do," Greenwald said.

"We're going to destroy America," declared Mojin laughing, "but this ship is going crazy on its own!"

Krupin glared at Yuri Mojin, then gave an order to Lorvec in Russian.

Lorvec shrugged, drew an automatic pistol from under his jacket and shot Mojin through the head. Mojin's head jerked back and he slumped off his chair onto the floor, his face a grinning rictus.

Even Feske was startled.

"Holy shit," Greenwald muttered.

"We will have no psychosis in here!" Krupin roared. "We have a mission to complete! But first…" He jabbed a finger at Greenwald. "You! Go to the engine room! Find that fool of a motorman! Examine steering equipment! Find how it was hacked!"

Greenwald wanted to protest that he knew nothing about such engineering intricacies. It was not his bailiwick. And he doubted hacking was the problem. But he didn't want to anger Krupin. Not with bits of Mojin's brain splashed across the floor.

"Yes, sir." Greenwald stood up and, stepping carefully around the spreading pool of blood, hurried out of the stateroom. Feeling like he was in a dream, he rushed toward the aft of the ship, hearing Krupin, behind him, shouting at Feske in Russian.

Arriving at the catwalk over the engine room with Mun and the wounded sentry, Vince saw three Russians with submachine guns on the level below, standing around the maintenance pit of the steering mechanism. They were all glaring at Morris.

"Why you can't fix it?" one of them shouted.

"I'm trying!"

"You are liar! Why you do not stop engines?"

"It isn't responding to engine room controls, Soloyov!"

"Show me the cord to cut! I will stop!"

"It would damage the engine controls to cut any power cables!"

Vince nudged Mun with his gun and the Chinese commander helped his guard along the catwalk toward the door of the engine control room. Keeping an eye on Mun, Vince opened the door, and ushered the two men inside.

The women seemed to be arguing with Hiya, all in hoarse whispers. "I can't do anything about those men down there!" he protested. Then he saw Vince—and Mun. He grinned at the sight of Mun in Vince's custody. "Ah, Commander! Please join us!"

Hurriedly, Vince said, "Everyone, keep your voices low. Carolyn, Jill, help this wounded man. There's a first aid kit under that console. Hiya, grab your weapon and keep it on Mun. Keep him quiet!"

Hiya nodded. "No problem. He picked up his submachine gun and pointed it at Mun, giving him an order in his own language.

Mun sneered at Hiya and said something insulting—his face expressed the substance of it. Hiya, smiling, repeated his instructions. Mun grudgingly obeyed.

"Ha ha ha, it's *Mun*!" Jill was chortling, as Vince went back to the catwalk.

Vince raised his Sig, aimed at the man nearest Morris, and then caught a movement from the corner of his eye. He turned to see someone entering the engine room through a utility door on the lower deck. Plump, balding—that face. *James Greenwald.* He'd been in the Agency's *Cupid's Cruise* files.

Greenwald seemed agitated, unsure of himself, as he walked, then strode, then jogged down the steel aisle between the engine cowling and fuel pipes.

Vince lowered his gun. He wanted Greenwald alive, for now. He had questions for him. If he opened fire on the Russians from up here, Greenwald would run.

"Hey!" Greenwald yelled. "Soloyov!"

The tallest of the three Russians around Morris turned. "Greenwald? Why are you here?"

Vince couldn't go down the main stairway to the floor. He'd be seen that way.

He went out the way he'd come in, at the back of the catwalk, through a doorway, then hurried down a passage to the ladder Greenwald had taken. He hurried down it, reached the engine room deck, and went through the hatch toward the stern.

Greenwald was talking to the Russians—none of them had seen Vince yet. Greenwald was blocking one of the targets and partly blocking another. Vince was about sixty feet away. One of them could turn and notice him, any second now…

Morris was down in the maintenance pit, only head and shoulders up out of the deck. He was at their feet. Vince noticed Morris staring at him, so he pointed at Greenwald's legs and motioned for him to pull on them.

Morris nodded, grabbed Greenwald's ankles and pulled so that, with a yell, Greenwald fell over backwards, flailing. And in under two seconds, Vince aimed and fired three times. Red mist splashed from the skulls of two Russians, the third one spun around and fell, the round hitting him in the shoulder. Vince strode up the aisle, looking for a better shot.

The wounded Russian sat up, fumbled to get his SMG ready to fire. Something silvery gleamed in Morris's hand—he stabbed at the man's leg, driving a big screwdriver deeply in just above the Russian's knee.

The Russian screamed and turned the SMG toward Morris. Vince fired three times, the second shot cleaving the Russian's forehead. The Russian sagged back, dead.

Vince skidded to a stop on the slick metal surface and took a breath. "You're a dangerous man with a screwdriver, Morris," he said.

Morris climbed a short ladder to get out of the work pit. "God, look at this mess…"

"No need to clean it up. You'll be off the ship soon and a few more bodies won't matter. Right now, Commander Mun has to call his men on the intercom."

He turned to Greenwald who was lying on his back, gazing at the ceiling. "There's a whole ecosystem of arthropods living up there in those webs," Greenwald said dreamily.

"What's with him?" Morris asked.

"Heroin," Vince said.

"Sadly, all I've got is OxyContin," Greenwald said, sitting up. "The local generic for it, anyway. But it is quite… numbing. One of these days they'll give me fentanyl instead, and it'll probably kill me." He sat up and blinked at the dead men. "You shot them."

"You want to weep, go ahead, mate," said Morris. "Me, I'm glad to see the bastards gone."

"I have so little feeling, anymore, I'm so numb," Greenwald said. "But I was never fond of the Russians. They just kind of caught me in their web and there I was, waiting to be sucked dry by the spider."

"No one forced you to sign on for them," Vince said. "File on you says you're helping them with cyberwarfare against the US."

"The file on me? You're some sort of spy?"

"No kidding! You've committed treason, Greenwald. I should shoot you now."

"Yes," he said tonelessly. "I expect you should. These dead men here, they look rather peaceful. I'd like to be peaceful."

"I could take you prisoner," Vince growled, "and you'd end up in the peace and quiet of a supermax security prison, because they won't want you to talk to anyone about what happened here. Or maybe some overseas black prison. For life. You'll be debriefed for a long, long time. Without any dope."

Greenwald ground his teeth. "If I help you…"

129

"Help me, and I'll see what I can do. Maybe they'll go a little easier on you. What's the cyberwarfare operation Krupin's got planned?"

Greenwald took a long breath. "You probably won't believe me. You'll think it's too outrageous. You'll think I'm making it up."

"Try me," Vince said. This was taking too long. But he needed to know more about the cyberwarfare deck.

"Operation Spring Glory," Greenwald said, looking at his hands. "I've got dirt under my fingernails somehow. I never do that. It is deplorable."

"You could break a few of his bones, to get him to talk," Morris suggested helpfully.

"Oh no, that won't be necessary," said Greenwald, taking a pill bottle out of a shirt pocket. "But I do have to think this through…"

Vince reached down and snatched the pills from him. "Then you'll have to do it without your dope."

"What? No! That is… it's medicinal!"

Vince chuckled. "I have a wounded man upstairs. I should give it to him."

"No!"

"Then what's Operation Spring Glory?"

Greenwald closed his eyes. "All right. I've lost my taste for this whole affair. I wanted out for a while now. When I realized how far they were taking it. I *thought* it was something I desired. To bring the whole USA down. But… they're not going to just crash it. They're going to *take over*. The Russians—believe it or not—have a plan to invade America."

"What a load of bollocks!" Morris burst out. "The USA is protected by nukes!"

"We developed a firewall penetration that will make all that inoperable. They'll destroy American infrastructure, too… every power grid, every refinery, communications systems, satellites… and a great deal more."

"When does this happen?" Vince said, feeling a chill go through him—because he found that he believed Greenwald.

"When? Oh, as to that…" He laughed coldly. "Well, we had a major breakthrough! It's been moved up. It happens today. In a few hours! May I have my drugs back, please, now?"

And at that point, a phalanx of armed Russians burst through the lower hatch, coming straight at them on the aisle between the engines. And the lead man raised his submachine gun to open fire.

CHAPTER ELEVEN

"Get him under the stairs, Morris!" Vince shouted, as he snapped off a shot with the SIG.

His round hit the closest Russian but not before the man got off an SMG burst. Bullets sang by, struck a bulkhead, ricocheting wickedly. One of the ricochets nicked Vince's left ear and there was a shout of dismay from Greenwald. "I'm hit!"

Vince's first target fell, the second one was firing, bullets strafing off the steel deck—even as Vince dodged to the right, firing as he went, pumping the trigger to enfilade the men lined up in the steel passage between the engines. He heard shouts of pain and fury as he flattened against the engine cowling, out of sight of the oncoming enemy, aware that Morris had half-dragged Greenwald out of the line of fire.

A spray of bullets cracked aft, ricocheting around the engine room. The plastic explosives were well tucked away in here, but it was not impossible one of the blocks of EPX-1 could be struck and ignited. Then the whole engine room would go up. There was diesel fuel in here too, giving off fumes—and those fumes could ignite. Altogether, a dangerous place for a firefight.

Vince heard men running up the aisle toward him, around the corner of the engine case. He stuck his arm out, emptied the rest of the clip down the aisle. Someone yelled. There was loud swearing in Russian. Bullets cracked by.

Vince withdrew his hand and popped the magazine from his pistol, quickly replaced it with a full clip, racked a round, then crouched and opened the small maintenance door in the engine cowling beside him. Underneath, there had been just enough room to store his toolbox against the engine, hidden because now it contained only weapons. He grabbed a flashbang, removed the safety pin and tossed the flash-grenade around the corner as a new group of men started his way. He closed his eyes as the flash went off; the bang made his ears ring. There were yells of consternation from the temporarily blinded Russians. Vince stepped out, tracking his gun to his targets, one-two-three-four, firing four times in two quick heartbeats, with deadly accuracy.

Four men fell dead. One of them was an officer; presumably the idiot responsible for sending the men through this killing ground. Vince was lucky they hadn't tried to come in through the higher entrance, or divided their forces. Probably they were a search squad, not expecting this much resistance.

Vince turned to find Morris and Greenwald huddled under the stairs up to the engine control room. Morris had his bloodied screwdriver in his hand. Greenwald had been shot in the lower thigh of the left leg, and Morris had used Greenwald's belt as a tourniquet.

"Now you got to give me my medicine," Greenwald moaned. "Bullets *hurt*, man!"

"I bet you're already so zonked you hardly feel it," Vince said. He tossed the bottle of pills to Morris. "Give one to the whining traitor here, and one to the wounded Chinese guard, Morris, will you? Then take treason boy to the control room. And tell Hiya that Mun's got to get on the intercom, right now, and call, *only in Chinese*, to his men. They have to meet him at the aft load-in port. They are not to speak to the Russians on the way here. Make it a strong order from Mun! If he doesn't want to do it, tell Jill she can use her knife on him till he does. Once that's been done, Hiya's got to go release the lifeboats manually. He's probably going to have to use that SMG on some Russian sentries."

"Crikey," Morris muttered. "What about the kitchen staff?"

"I'm going to have to go and get them. They'll go with me in the final lifeboat."

"And how are you getting away?"

"I have a plan," Vince said. "No time to explain. There'll be more Russians coming at us and I have to be ready for them."

"I can't get up those stairs," Greenwald said, in a whine. "I got shot in the leg!"

"You'll do it," Vince said, "or Morris is going to shove that big screwdriver up your ass."

"He might like that," Morris said. "I'll stab him in the bollocks instead."

"I'll go," Greenwald said, blanching.

"One more thing," Vince said. "I can't take a chance on them starting their cyberwar transmission. I'm going to blow the bridge, the radio room and the transmitters—right now."

He went back to the toolbox and pulled out the detonator. This model looked almost like a small walkie-talkie. It had a screen that showed a selection of pre-coded explosive receivers. He tapped it to point one, and then hit the *detonate* tab. There was a pregnant hesitation…

Then the ship bucked as a clanging echo went through it, stem to stern. The deck quivered under his feet.

He dialed it to point two and hit the tab. Another massive clang, another reverberation…

Point three, and tab. A final blast, a resonating clang, the ship wobbling from this one enough to make him stagger a little. A sickening wrench in his belly…

Then it was gone. An alarm went off somewhere, and his satphone buzzed.

Vince took the satellite phone from its loop on his belt and answered. "Hiya?"

"Vince?" came the familiar voice. "You set off that blast?"

"Yes. Their radio and all ship hardwired communications are gone. So is the bridge. So is the captain and his officers. Any of that bother you?"

"No, as long as there were none of my people there."

"None that I know of. You take care of the lifeboats?"

"Every one released but the three we need. I had to kill two sentries out here. I was lucky and surprised them. I've never had to kill anyone before."

"It sucks. It's hard at first. The worst part is that it gets easier. Now listen—you got to bring the boat farthest aft over here now. We have to move fast. I got to go, got to set up something that'll slow them down…"

"You sure this place is safe?" Dierdre asked, as they came into the cottage. It smelled of the sea, mold and old cooking.

"Hey," said Richie Chang, "it's a safehouse, isn't it?"

"It's a weird little cottage down near the beach with no cover to run to if things go to shit, is what it is."

"Best I could arrange on short notice," Richie said. "Or the best Jerry Tobol could arrange, anyway."

"My ears are burning," Jerry said, coming in with Dierdre's luggage.

"You really didn't have to carry my luggage in, Jerry. Thank you, but…"

"He used to work at the airport, moving luggage around," Richie said. "He can't seem to let it go."

Jerry laughed. He let the luggage go and it thumped onto the floor of the little one-bedroom house. "I let it go, okay?"

Dierdre smiled. "I got some gin and pomelo at the airport. I hear a GinPom is the cool thing to drink around here. Who wants one?"

There was a brisk wind outside as she made the cocktails, and they sat around chairs overlooking the beach, under a bamboo porch roof, watching the waves lash and the sunset burn itself out.

Dierdre got up, walked to the corner of the house, looked toward the road. No one there. She came back to her seat and said, "I hate to keep being the paranoid one, but that's who I am today."

"I told you," Richie said, "I moved home base, slipped out, lost the guy. You're okay here."

"Does Tighe know where you're staying now?"

"Hell, no."

"What do you think, Jerry?" Dierdre asked.

Jerry shrugged. "I think we don't know for sure what Tighe knows."

Dierdre finished her drink and asked, "Jerry, what's your opinion? You're a homeboy around here. Is Ramos someone we can find?"

"You want to neutralize him?" Jerry asked.

"I don't know," she said. "Maybe just keep him under lock and key somewhere while we find a safe way to get Vince back from that ship."

"You know, *Cupid's Cruise* just changed its route for the first time in a year," Richie said. "It's headed out to sea. In fact, it's gone completely out of Chinese territorial waters."

Richie rattled the ice in his glass. "Has to be Vince's doing."

"The Moscow station in Manila must be freaking out," Dierdre said. "Sending agents out in boats to see what's going on."

"Depends on what Krupin reports on the radio, maybe," Richie said. He finished his cocktail and put it on the sand-gritty deck. "I've got to go. I've got to write up a report, a shitpile of justification for all my time here. Jerry, can you stay here and… uh… just be an extra pair of eyes, tonight? Sofa's a fold-out."

"Sure I can," Jerry said.

Richie stood up. "I'll find out if there's more news on the ship or Vince, but I doubt it. Only one other person at the FBI's been briefed on the mission. The Director. With the President and a couple people at the CIA, and Tighe, that's just a handful of people who know. And we're closer to events here than they are."

"I don't know that much, myself," Jerry said.

"Safer that way. So Tighe says." Richie waved goodbye and circled around the corner of the house, headed for his car.

"I am so beat," Dierdre said. "That flight and… I haven't slept in a while."

"Go and crash," Jerry said. "Get a long rest. I'll keep watch here."

"Thanks, Jerry."

Dierdre went into the bedroom, took off her jacket and shoes, and put her gun and holster on the lamp table. She lay down on the creaking, mildew-smelling bed. *I should really take a shower,* she told herself, *and maybe… maybe…*

Sleep swept over her. There were unsettling dreams of Vince piloting a ship toward an exploding volcano at sea…

And then the sound of a gunshot woke her up.

Diedre got quickly but clumsily out of bed, blinking, the dream still fading as she reflexively unholstered her .32 and swung it toward the door.

She almost shot Jerry Timbol. The twitchily fired round cut past his head and he jumped back from the doorway.

"Jerry! Did I hit you?"

"No!"

"I was asleep and—"

"*Flatten down!*"

She threw herself on the floor just as three bullets, fired in a burst from an Uzi, crashed through the window, pocking the wall exactly where she'd been.

Jerry stepped out and fired several shots from a Glock at the window. More glass shards glittered through the air, and then something fell with a *whumpf* onto the bed. Flames roared hungrily up from the bedclothes.

"Firebomb!" Jerry yelled.

Fully awake now, Dierdre leapt up and bolted through the bedroom door, swinging the gun to face the living room window—and the silhouette of a man. She could see light glimmer along the edge of the Uzi as he raised it.

She fired the .32 four times across the window glass; glass straight at the center of his mass. Glass shattered as he dropped from sight. Flames crackled from the hallway now, and smoke whirled.

"Jerry!"

He called from the open door onto the patio. "Here!"

She ran to the front door, shoved it open hard to get a reaction from the gunman, and stepped back—bullets skittered through, haphazardly fired from a low elevation, digging into the wall to her left. She glanced through the door, saw a man trying to get up—her rounds had struck his Kevlar vest, knocking him off-balance. He swung the Uzi toward her—she ducked back. Smoke curled around her, and she coughed.

Then, two shots from the corner back corner of the cottage. Jerry firing the Glock.

"He's down!" Jerry called.

She stepped out and saw the assassin, quivering on his side, blood bubbling from his mouth. Jerry's shots had grazed the gunman's head and cut through his neck.

"Nice shooting," she said, lowering her gun. She stepped over to the dazed, choking assassin and kicked the Uzi out of his reach. "Is that Ramos?"

"It is," Jerry said.

"The place is on fire. My shoes are burning up in there." Her purse was on the kitchen table. She held her breath, ran into the cottage, grabbed her purse. She had to run out the patio door, the fire was spread too quickly everywhere else. Coughing, hurrying up to Jerry, she said, "You're hit!" There was blood twining down his left arm.

"Yeah, it just grooved my arm, is all, nothing much. Painful though."

"Let's get you to an ER, you need it cleaned and stitched." Her head was throbbing. Fire was roaring at the windows.

"You know what—I say we don't dodge this, Dierdre. Let's make a police report. I have an uncle with the Manila PD. He knows who my employer is. He'll be cool. I'd like this to be on the record—that Ramos tried to kill you. The CIA should know. It might give them second thoughts about Tighe."

"Okay, call your uncle. Ask for an ambulance. And the fire department."

Dierdre took several steps back from the burning cottage. It was going up fast. She'd almost burned up with it.

Watching the flames, she knew that Ramos wasn't the only killer Tighe would have in his database.

"*Think* before you try to bullshit me, Greenwald," Vince growled. He took the HK416 assault carbine from its shoulder strap and pointed it at Greenwald. "The ship's radio, and all its transmitters, are gone. Blown to shit. Is there any way that cyberattack could still be launched from this ship?"

Greenwald was sitting in the corner of the engine control room. Morris was standing to one side of him. The women were down at the load-in port, with Jill keeping watch over Mun, waiting for the Chinese soldiers to along the sundeck and down the ladder. The open load-in gate was not far above the whipping sea.

Greenwald was staring at the pill bottle in Morris's hand. Morris tossed it, as though tossing a coin, over and over.

"The cyberattack?" Greenwald said, dazedly. "My leg hurts…"

"Answer the question," Vince snapped. "*Can a cyberattack still be launched from this ship?*"

"No. Unless…"

"Unless what?"

"Krupin doesn't tell me everything. Maybe he has some backup transmission? Maybe the seven guys left on the cyberwar team could figure a way. The ship's computers are not set up for any internet whatsoever. Cyberwar programs are sent up to satellites and transmitted to the internet from there. Krupin was afraid the ship having its own internet access could lead us to get traced back and hacked by the Americans. And maybe someone would get cold feet and warn the American feds. You destroyed our comms with satellites. You've delayed the attack for sure. But these guys are resourceful, and Krupin will put a lot of pressure on them."

Vince nodded. "Okay. Everyone on that deck'll have to go. On the way to the kitchens…"

"Can I have a capsule now?" Greenwald whimpered. "I really need two, with this hole in my leg."

"Give him one to put a stopper on the whining, Morris," Vince said.

"Shooting him would stop it, too."

"I'm tempted. But he might be useful somewhere else."

Morris handed Greenwald a pill, then glanced at the bank of camera monitors. Mostly, the monitors watched over machinery in the engine room. But one of them monitored the sub-deck passageway to the engine room. He pointed at that screen. "Vince, they're coming! And the ones in the lead are wearing Kevlar vests!"

Vince nodded. "Been expecting them. Probably be another squad coming the other way, from the upper deck."

"They're stopping at the emergency comms locker! Looks like Krupin's hoping to get a call out to his allies."

A Russian officer stepped up to the locker, with three soldiers close by. The Russian officer unlocked the door to the locker, opened it—and the image on the monitor was blotted with smoke and fire. A metallic booming echoed to the control room and the walls shivered.

"Two grenades?" Morris asked.

"One frag wired up to a piece of leftover plastic explosive and three flares taped together. Plus a handful of screws."

"Ouch!"

The smoke cleared, and they saw three bodies bleeding out on the passageway deck—they'd caught grenade fragments in the head; the officer was still alive, protected by his Kevlar, but he was half slumped against the wall, bleeding heavily from his crotch and neck. The uniforms of two of the dying men at his feet were on fire.

"That should give the rest of 'em something to think about," Vince said. With any luck they'd be stalled, concerned about further traps.

Now for the other entrance. Vince had the .410 shotgun pistol

141

and shells in the left pocket of his coveralls, the SIG Sauer on the loop inside, a flashbang and a frag grenade in the cargo pockets. He had strapped on an ammunition belt, loaded up with cartridges and clips, and fitted with the combat knife.

It would have to do for now.

Vince gave Morris the pill bottle. "Give him exactly one. Keep an eye on him; I'll let you know when you're clear for boarding the lifeboat."

"What about me? Which lifeboat am I going in?" Greenwald said.

"If you live, you're going in the last one with me. And if I have anything to say about it, straight to a CIA black-site 'detention center'."

He took the capsule from Morris and swallowed it dry. "You don't mean that."

"I definitely mean that—alternatively, I could toss you overboard, treason boy."

Morris took out his satphone. "You want me to make that call now, Vince?"

"Yeah. You remember what to say?"

"I call Macao port authority, identify myself as a motorman. I say the ship was attacked by pirates from the Strait of Malacca, everyone on the bridge killed. The engine was damaged and I'm afraid it's going to explode. All vessels are warned to stay clear. Then hang up on them."

"They'll try to call you back—don't answer. We want to keep them guessing, long as we can."

Morris nodded. "Got it."

Vince hurried off to the catwalk, the HK416 tucked against his right shoulder, his eyes and ears keen, his heart thumping. His left hand was on the foregrip, his right on the battle grip. His trigger finger was already on the trigger, applying no pressure. The catwalk met the metal stairs part way along two flights; to the right the stairs

142

went down to the engine deck; to the left it went up to a passage to the starboard utility access deck. And that's where the six Russian soldiers were coming from. He saw two of them first, their booted feet showing as they descended. They'd changed their white uniforms for khaki. He watched three of them descend, about forty feet away, a little above the engine control room level. They were looking toward the lower deck—and seemed surprised when Vince stepped into view on the catwalk.

SMGs were swung toward him—too late.

He was already firing the HK416, looking through its red-dot sight, firing the five-five-six standard NATO rounds in three-shot bursts, one burst per man, aiming at their faces—they all had Kevlar vests and helmets. Eyes were splashed into brains as three men fell back and slid lifelessly down a few stairs as cries of consternation echoed from above.

Vince strode toward the stairs, taking the HK416 in one hand, the other fishing a flashbang from his pocket. He removed the safety pin and chucked the flashbang up the stairwell, closing his eyes. He heard the hard bang as it flashed, and men shouting.

Vince opened his eyes, then ran forward, swinging the assault carbine up the stairway, squeezing off two bursts before he even had a target, so that ricochets would create wounds, terror and disorientation to add to the blindness. Then he stepped out, aimed up through the red dot scope. An SMG coughed bullets at him, slicing to his right as he fired. Two men went down; a third was running. He fired at the runner, knocking him forward with the impact on the back of his armor. He could tell by the sound of the bullets' impact on the vest that the Kevlar was hardened with an underlayer of ballistic plates.

Running up the stairs, Vince saw the man getting onto his hands and knees.

"Sorry, no prisoners," Vince said, firing. He didn't have a clear view of a vital spot, and the rounds struck the Russian's groin and rump. The man screamed and fell flat, writhing. Vince now had a clear shot at the back of the target's neck; he put the soldier out of his misery with a shot through the spine and then rushed up the stairs past him. Russian voices from the left…

Vince stepped out, making sure of his targets, five soldiers clustered into a passageway. Two of them in front had Kevlar vests; three men past them didn't, which confirmed there wasn't enough armor to go around. He switched to full-auto and opened fire, aiming low at the men in front, catching them in the legs, knocking them down. Vince threw himself flat as the men behind opened fire. Submachine gun rounds cracked-crack-cracked over his head as he fired another full-auto burst, using up the last of the bullets in his clip.

The three Russians standing seemed to dance backwards and then spin, almost like choreography, before falling, dying. But the others were still alive, lying on their bellies, badly wounded, but trying to bring their weapons into play. Vince ejected his ammo mag, slapped in another, fired, rattling a long burst into them, so the bullets cut into their uplifted faces. They flopped limp.

In a sense, Vince reckoned as he got to his feet, the confined spaces of a ship worked to his advantage against greater numbers—they were crowded into one another, and he was likely to hit some meat with every burst.

He strode up to the dead men, listening for sounds from down the passage—he heard voices, and bootsteps. More of them coming.

Vince moved a couple bodies to half lie on the others, to give himself some cover. Then he lay down flat on his belly, switched the assault carbine's fire to three-shot bursts, planted his elbows on the deck, laid the barrel of his gun along a dead man's shoulder, sighted through the red dot… and waited. The smell of blood, sweat, and fear was in his nostrils,

It was a smell he had become accustomed to, in firefights. He hardly noticed it.

A group of Russians, talking in low voices, trotted along toward Vince, not seeing him yet. The two men in front had vests; those behind didn't. The officer at point cursed, seeing the dead men. He raised a hand for the others to stop, just about twelve steps away—and then his eyes widened as he saw Vince lying amongst the dead, and the muzzle of a gun pointed right at his face.

It was the last thing he ever saw. Vince sent a burst through the offer's forehead, the splashing blood and brains startling the others; freezing them with horror long enough for Vince to track another target. Before the officer had fallen to the deck, Vince was dialed in on the sergeant behind him, sending the rounds right between the target's eyes. The Russian went down, and the others were trying to fire at Vince, but their angle was awkward and he was hard to see, mixed with the dead. Bullets slapped into the corpses to either side of Vince, splashing blood as he returned fire, squeezing off fifteen rounds in five bursts, cutting the four soldiers down.

More blood, more sweat, more fear. More death.

Vince got to his feet, feeling oddly sick to his stomach. Maybe it was laying down with the dead guys. He'd had to do something like it before. In Syria he'd had to crawl over the bodies of friends and enemies to get out of a kill cone of fire…

Putting the memory firmly away, he jumped over bodies and ran till he got to the end of the passage. He listened. Nothing but the sound of the ship motoring blindly to the east.

Vince nodded to himself, decided that the enemy was flummoxed for the moment. He'd bought some more time.

But it wouldn't last. The Russians would find a way to get at him, soon enough.

Turning, Vince loped back down the passage. He had to get to his sniper rifle, and cover the Chinese guards and the women as they got into the lifeboats.

There was only a small window of time to give them a real chance of escape.

And if he didn't do it soon, they might never make it off this floating death trap.

CHAPTER TWELVE

Morris had switched the ship's engines off, and made sure they couldn't be restarted. He'd thoroughly sabotaged the drive system. They couldn't go any farther out to sea without making it too hard for the lifeboats to get to shore. There was still some stored power, which Morris controlled.

Now, the ship was wallowing, rocking in the night-dark waves of the open sea, as Vince attached the first transponder for the detonator on the hull beside the load-in port.

He could hear the women talking, excited and worried, sitting on the deck in the freight hold as they waited for the lifeboat. Now and then he could hear a remark from the Chinese soldiers, sitting in a group across from the women. As per their orders, they'd come without weapons. The last time Vince had checked in on them they'd been staring in bafflement at Hiya and Commander Mun.

Cupid's Cruise was far from the shore now, and the only light was indirect and spotty. The moon had risen over the ocean; there were some lights from decks. Flame glimmered where the bridge had been, though most of the fire from the exploded bridge, radio room and transmitter/receiver center had been put out. The dim silhouette of the topmost decks, the bridge and communications section, was ragged, blackened like the outline of a ruined fortress.

Vince stepped out a little more onto the lowered hatch. It had opened down on its hinges to become a ramp projecting three yards out from the ship's hull. The loading port was meant for bringing freight in, not for loading people into lifeboats. But it was a place Vince could defend. The lifeboats were too exposed to enemy fire. Still, only the awkward angle of fire from above protected him here—and nothing protected him from spume thrown by the waves lashing at the hull close below. Spray shushed up; now and then water splashed onto the ramp, making it slippery.

Vince laid the M110 sniper rifle barrel across the unlit projecting light on the forward side of the hatch. He peered through the rifle's scope, scanning for human shapes along the higher deck rails. There—a couple of sentries, looking his way. The opening freight hatch must have caught their notice. The lights around them put too much glare into his scope. He couldn't hope to hit them precisely enough. The problem was complicated by the wallowing of the ship.

A bullet cracked by, struck the end of the ramp, zinged off. Vince thought he knew who the shooter was; he centered the crosshairs as best he could and squeezed off a round. No clear indication of a hit.

Another shot cracked by, closer this time.

Vince stepped back into the loading port and took his satphone from his back pocket. "Morris, you there?"

"I'm here," came the fuzzing voice on the phone. "What's your situation, mate?"

"Getting some fire from upper decks. You see any sign of them coming on the monitors?"

"Not so far."

"Your engine room give you control over the ship's power source?"

"Yes. All the power comes from the engine."

"What about emergency power?"

"Electricity is stored, so if the engine goes off there's still power for a time. But I can shut that down too if I want."

"You got an electric Coleman in there?"

"There's one in a cabinet, sure."

"Get it and turn it on. When I give you the signal, shut all the ship's power off. I need a blackout for a while. Then we'll turn it back on so Hiya can lower the lifeboats."

"Right."

Vince cut the connection and went into the freight hold. It was a strange sight, two lines of People's Republic soldiers squatting on the deck to one side, glaring at a large group of prostitutes on the other.

"Hey, pirate guy, when are we getting off the ship?" one of the women called.

Only Carolyn and Jill had an inkling of who he really was. And he'd sworn them to secrecy about it. "Soon!" he called, adopting his Hans Graf tone. "*Ja*, soon!"

Hiya was standing over Mun, who was sitting cross-legged, glaring about him. Vince crossed to Hiya, leaned over and whispered in his ear, "Go launch the lifeboat, bring it around the stern, right up to the port. We'll put your people aboard first. You want Mun to get out alive?"

Hiya leaned close and whispered, "Reluctantly I must say yes—I want no part of killing any of my people, unless they force me to. Even him."

"But can we trust him to go to shore? What if he orders the men to go back to another part of the ship?"

"I've told him the ship will be destroyed. He's a coward and he will desert the ship at first opportunity. He will certainly go ashore."

"Okay. Go and get the lifeboat."

Hiya nodded and hurried off. Mun scowled at Vince. "What you are sending him to do?"

"To get the lifeboat. This ship will sink soon. All you have to do is head west, and you'll reach shore."

"You pirates don't take hostages?"

"What we want is the Russians. There are some important men. The Russians will pay a lot of ransom for them. The People's Republic wouldn't make such a deal. Now, you're going to make an intercom call to Krupin." He took Mun by the collar and shoved him toward the intercom box on the wall by the port. "Mun, if you want to live, listen closely. You will tell Krupin that your men are leaving in two lifeboats. They won't be, but tell him that anyway. Tell him there are some going with the women. And tell him that you have a radio and if anyone from the ship fires on those lifeboats, you'll tell your superiors that Russia tried to kill Chinese troops."

Mun licked his lips and nodded.

"Say it all back to me in English," Vince said.

Mun repeated the message. "Okay," Vince said. "Get on the intercom and say it like you mean it."

Mun thumbed the intercom button, got through to Krupin and repeated the demand in English.

Krupin replied, "Very well. But I want to talk to the man who's down there with you, the one who's attacking us. I know he must be close."

Vince shook his head at Mun.

"He is not here," Mun said. "I don't know this man."

Vince stepped up and switched off the intercom. "Okay, that's enough." He gestured for Jill and Carolyn, and they hurried over to him. He handed Jill his SIG Sauer, and said, "*Ja*, you keep him watch on this Commander Mun, *fraulein*."

He grinned as Carolyn rolled his eyes at his German accent. Jill nodded eagerly and loudly said, "I'll shoot Mun if he gives me even a tiny bit of trouble!"

Mun looked appalled at this.

"*Das ist gut, ja!*" Vince said. He drew Carolyn aside. "I'm taking some fire out there—I'm going to switch the ship's lights off so I can use my night vision scope. You see those emergency lanterns, over there? Give one to each group and one to Jill, for when the lights go off."

"Okay. Where'd Hiya go?"

"He's bringing the first boat around. I'm going to cover everyone boarding the lifeboats best I can, but when it's your turn, follow directions closely. It'd be easy to fall into the ocean."

"Why send the Chinese first? I mean, those assholes…" She shook her head in exasperation.

"I figure the Chinese deserting will confuse the Russians; they won't know what's going on exactly. I can't see them firing on it."

"Okay Vince. Be hella fucking careful."

"Hella fucking careful is a good plan."

And don't forget to be as careful as an elephant on ice…

Taking the M110, Vince went to the nearest ladder and climbed. The third deck up was open to the sea. Vince figured the Russians would have men coming down that deck to check out what was going on at the load-in port.

Hiya had told Vince there weren't a lot of munitions aboard. No explosives, not even grenades. Just rifles, submachine guns, pistols, and lots of ammo. Ninety-seven soldiers and trained two trained GUR killers, Krupin and Lorvec, along with the protection of the being in Chinese territorial waters had seemed safe enough.

But they were no longer in Chinese territorial waters, their communication with Russia and China had been eliminated, and they were sixty miles out to sea. By the time their allies figured something was up, due to the sudden cut-off of communication from Krupin, it'd be too late for the Russians or Chinese to assist. The ship would be sunk.

Or else…

Or else Krupin's allies would come out to *Cupid's Cruise* and find that a certain operative, who had been killed, had crippled the vessel. And eventually they'd work out that the dead operative was Vince Bellator. They might well take out their revenge on Diedre Bellator. And they'd blame the United States. And who knew what international horror would arise then?

Seems I've got to win this thing, Vince thought. *Or else.*

It was definitely time to be hella fucking careful.

Now he was just inside the open door to the outside deck, listening. Russian voices carried to him. Vince set his sniper rifle down and laid flat on the deck. Tugging the rifle along he wormed into the doorway and looked down the deck. There they were; at least twelve men with submachine guns. Again, the ones in the lead wore Kevlar. Vince reached for his satellite phone and called Morris's frequency.

"Yeah mate?" Morris answered. "Lights out?"

"Lights out."

He put the phone in his back pocket and waited. Thirty seconds…

And all the lights on the ship flickered and went out. The moon hadn't risen high enough to illuminate the deck here. He could make out the metallic gleams of submachine guns among vaguely human shapes down the deck.

Vince got to his knees, then went to a kneeling rifleman's posture, one knee down, right elbow braced on his cocked knee, facing the approaching enemy. He took the thermal imager from a cargo pocket, attached it to rails in front of the sniper scope, activated it and peered through.

Thermal scope images could be black and white, or could be adjusted to a variety of colors. This one showed the Russians, lit up green by their own body heat against a red background. He remembered an instructor's morbid joke about that color thermal from Rangers' school: "Blood with a slice of lime."

Vince steadied the M110, took a breath, let it slowly out, tracking the scope's crosshairs to a blob of lime-colored light he knew was a man's head, squeezed the trigger. The head jerked and the thermographic image showed blood as a green spurt.

I can see them better than they can see me.

He was already tracking the second soldier—the man threw himself down and fired. Bullets cracked by and Vince dropped the sights to the blob near the deck, and squeezed off a shot, thinking, *Thank God for semi-auto sniper rifles.* Bolt action was too slow.

The enemy fire ceased—and then started again from another source. But they couldn't see him in the darkness. Vince was tracking center-masses now, squeezing the trigger twice, shifting, firing again, shifting, firing again. One figure went down and came up back—Kevlar vest. Vince found the target's head and fired. Back down he went.

Vince fired twice and another went down. But then a bullet hissed by. They'd spotted the muzzle flash.

He threw himself to the left, heard rounds crack where he'd been a moment before as he fell on his side. He crawled back through the doorway, quickly got up, and heard men shouting, running toward him along the deck. He took the .410 from his left-hand pocket. The shotgun pistol was loaded with the incendiary shell. He moved to the other side of the doorway, and waited, listening to their running feet. Someone fired again. Bullets skittered along the deck.

Still Vince waited. They were close now, their voices loud. He could hear their panting breaths. He leaned the rifle against the cornering of the doorway, took the 12-gauge shotgun pistol firmly in both hands and stepped out onto the deck, immediately triggering the .410 at the knot of soldiers coming his way.

The zirconium pellets in the shell ignited the instant they left the muzzle, and a spout of flame rushed into the group of Russians. He caught a glimpse of their faces lit demonic-red by the hellfire of the blast, as they reacted, screaming and flailing. The plume of flame was gone but their clothes and hair were afire and one of them was shrieking and clawing at his sizzling eyes.

The ones in the rear of the group turned and ran.

Vince stuck the .410 in a pocket, scooped up the rifle, brought it instantly to his shoulder and fired, over and over, killing the burning men and nailing the two who'd run... The soldiers fell on their faces, dead before they stopped skidding on the deck.

He squinted through the scope—saw no one alive on the deck. But a bullet careened off the deck near him. He raised the scope, saw the blobby green shapes of three sentries on a higher deck firing down at him over a rail. They had no clear idea where he was in the darkness, but he could see their thermographic outlines.

Vince returned fire, squeezing the trigger five times. The three shapes vanished.

He raised the M110 higher, searching upper decks. There— three decks higher. Two more blobs exactly where men would be who were looking for targets below. And a bullet cracked by him, pinging off the deck.

Vince fired twice more, and they vanished. He was sure he'd gotten one, probably not the other. That one had gone to ground.

Just as well. He needed a witness to tell the others how dangerous it had gotten down here. *"And he has a flamethrower!"* At least, Vince hoped they'd think the incendiary round was a flamethrower. Another tactic to slow them down. As long as he had the initiative, he had a chance of beating them—against all the odds.

He smiled grimly, turning back to the stairs. He paused there to set up another transponder on the metal wall overlooking the deck. It took only a few seconds. It was just a little matchbox sized unit, painted white, so it probably wouldn't be noticed by the Russians.

A crackling sound came from his back pocket. He took the satphone out.

"Hiya?"

"I'm at the loading port! The PLA men are getting into the boat!"

"Good man! Assign someone to run the outboard and come back aboard the ship—unless you've decided to leave with your compatriots."

"They all saw me holding a gun on the commander! They assume I'm one of your imaginary pirates. I can't go home."

"Then you'll get to know Australia really well. I'm coming to the load-in port."

When he got there, he was met by Hiya. "All People's Liberation Army soldiers except Mun are on board, Vince. But it's crowded."

The covered lifeboat wasn't built for so many, and it was low in the water, but Vince was certain it could get them where they needed to go. One of the soldiers was already on the outboard operator's seat, with the engine in a low gear, and seemed impatient to leave. He was yelling something in Mandarin.

"Says 'no room for Mun'," Hiya said.

The PLA commander would be last to board—that was Hiya's doing—and now Mun lumbered nervously toward the slippery ramp. He half-skidded down it, then jumped onto the top of the lifeboat. He clung there, trying to get to a hatch as the outboard operator put it into gear and angled away from the boat, toward shore. The sudden motion almost flung Mun off. The boat moved off as Mun shouted at the PLA soldiers. Vince assumed he was ordering them to pull him into the boat hatch.

Then the boat picked up speed, making it jolt in the water. And Mun fell off.

He floundered about, trying to swim after the lifeboat. A big wave came along and swamped him. He vanished, and never came up again.

"Oh well," said Hiya, shrugging. "I tried. But he was the worst commander in the PLA. They didn't want him on that boat."

Vince nodded. "Yeah. Not a popular guy."

He went to his spotting position at the corner of the loading port and raised the M110 to scan for heat signatures. There were two men defined in blurry green at the topmost intact deck. He centered his scope's dot and fired. One blob of light vanished. Then the other vanished too, all on its own.

He swept the scope along the decks, saw no one set up to fire on his position. He stepped away from the port, into the hold, and said, "Hiya, bring the other boat around."

"On my way!"

Vince called Morris on his satphone. "Tell treason boy he can have another cap of oxy if he'll get his ass down here, bullet in that leg or not. You need help bringing him down?"

"I think we'll manage. What about the lights?"

"Leave it status quo for now. No air conditioning, no electricity for those cyberattack scumbags. Make it harder for them to come at me tonight."

"Got it."

Vince laid the M110 atop a crate and went over to Carolyn and Jill. "Your ride is coming. It'll be crowded, so some of you women will have to sit on some laps and on the floor. Not a long trip to the shore. I think I can arrange for someone to meet you."

"Who?" Carolyn asked.

"Couple of friends. I'm going to make certain demands on your behalf. Morris and Hiya are going with you to the shore. Morris is an old navy man, he'll guide the boat in."

"Oh! I'll sit on Hiya's lap!" Jill declared. "He's nice."

"Hiya will enjoy the trip," Vince said. "Can I have my gun back now?"

Jill pouted. "I wanted a souvenir of you."

He took his black eyepatch out of his pocket, and put it on her, tugging it down over her eye. "I'll trade you that for it."

"Am I a pirate now?"

"More one than I am."

She took the SIG from her pocket and handed it over. "Thanks. Thanks for everything, ladies. I owe you big time. Go on, now. Get the girls over to the port. Not too close till it's time to board the lifeboat."

He went to a quiet corner of the hold, took his satphone from his pocket and called a memorized number.

"Who's this?" came a familiar voice.

"It's Bellator, Tighe."

"What the devil do you think you're doing—"

"Why didn't you put the satellite phone I requested into the crate?"

"Where did you get this number? And that phone?"

"Stop changing the subject, Napoleon. I am pretty sure you want me to die out here. Maybe you'll get your wish. But I do have some intel for you. First, the Russians were about to launch a major cyber-warfare attack on America, including the suppression of our ability to respond with nuclear weapons in the event of an attack. They were going to cripple us and invade. I stopped that from happening. Blew up their comms."

"Kind of hard to believe they could… I mean, what you're talking about…"

"I don't care if you believe it or not. It's called Operation Spring Glory. You'd better warn Homeland Security and the cyber defenses team—anything they can do to shore up defenses, change access modes, put in new firewalls."

"I'll do that. We can't take a chance they haven't got some other way to transmit it. But Bellator, that ship still needs to be sunk."

"Yeah. Theoretically. To cover up our incursion here. I don't *have* to do it."

"You want to turn traitor so close to completing your mission?"

"Is that supposed to work on me, Tighe? Listen to me. Here's some more intel for you: I'm sending nine women to shore in a lifeboat. Along with them are a couple of men who have been critical in making this mission work. Their names are Morris and… well, I can't pronounce the Chinese soldier's name. We call him Hiya. They are the only two men aboard the lifeboat. Satellites should pick the boat out for you. There are two boats. It's the second one you want, says number seventeen on the side. If you want me to finish this mission, then you will see to it that everyone on board gets a passport and a ticket to wherever they want to go. You hear me? Every last one. I'm in touch with these people. I can talk to them through satphone. If for some reason you don't help them to go exactly where they want to go, then I will kill you, Tighe. I'll find you and I'll kill you. Hell, I'll call every ex-Delta Forcer I know and tell them to kill you if they don't hear from me."

That last one was a bluff—and so was the threat that he might decide not to complete the mission. But Tighe didn't know that.

"You there, Tighe?"

"I'm… yes. And I'm sick of having people threaten me. First it was—"

"Yes? Who was it?"

Tighe growled. "Forget it! You have anything *else* to say to me, Bellator?"

"That cell phone you gave me as part of my cover—they have it."

"It doesn't work. It'll fry itself if they try to make it work."

"Then all I have to say to you is—do as I've told you to. Or you won't live to collect your pension."

With that, Vince hung up. A moment later the satphone rang again. It was Hiya. "Vince! I'm under attack at the lifeboats! They're trying to stop me from getting away… I've got to return fire…"

Then the line went dead.

CHAPTER THIRTEEN

Flashlight shining in one hand, sniper rifle in the other, it took Vince ten minutes of running through passages and climbing ladders to the lower port deck. He heard the rattle of SMG fire as he switched off the flashlight.

Vince came to the open door onto the sundeck, where just now the only light was the moon. He put the flashlight on the floor and leaned out enough to see a Russian sentry, about ten yards forward, standing on a crate for rubber inflatable rafts as he fired down over the rail, at a lifeboat several decks below. Vince figured Hiya was hunkered in the lifeboat, unable to get on its roof because of the SMG fire. He had to get on the roof to release the lifeboat from the davit cables.

Vince brought the M110 up, tucked it into his shoulder, looked through the scope, and shot the sentry through the side of the head. But that wasn't going to deal with the problem; other gunshots hammered down from somewhere above, clanging into the deck, ricochets pinging from the metal outer walls of the cruise ship.

Vince could release the lifeboat into the water from up on the deck, using the emergency release button, but that would mean going onto the deck, exposing himself to fire.

He took out his satphone. "Hiya? I'm here. You hit?"

"No, but they're knocking holes in this boat."

"Is it taking on water?"

"Not yet. But they're going to hit the outboard... or me."

"I'm going onto the deck, try to hit some of the shooters with the sniper rifle, and hope it's too dark for them to get a shot. Then I'm going to go to the box and hit that release button. Brace yourself for that."

Vince cut the connection and called Morris on his satphone. "Hey man—can you count to sixty and turn on the power again?"

"Count to... yeah. If you want. I'm near the controls right now. But—"

"Turn it on for thirty seconds, then turn it off."

"Okay."

Two more bullets fired from the upper decks ricocheted and ricocheted again as Vince put the phone in his pocket. He looked for the darkest spot on the deck. There, a deeply shadowed position to aft behind the thin cover of the davit crane. He sprinted to the davit by the railing. A strafe of bullets impacted alongside him, striking bright sparks on the metal. He felt a searing jab along his ribs on the left side. Then he reached the partial cover of the davit crane, turned toward the shooters, tucked the rifle in place and scanned through the thermal imager for man-shaped signatures. A spray of bullets screamed as he spotted the probable shooter, seven decks up. Ignoring the pain in his left side Vince centered the crosshairs and fired and the thermal signature vanished as he was sweeping to the next one on that rail. He caught a target, fired again...

A third target, and he fired again, but not before the shooter had let loose a burst at him and a bullet cut into the meat of Vince's right hip.

Grunting with the impact, Vince squeezed off three shots, and a fourth target went down. A quick scan showed no other obvious shooters.

Vince ducked back, flattened behind the davit, gasping at the sudden, deeper pain in his hip. The power came on—lights flared around the ship. That would give him a moment as the shooters adjusted to the change.

He leaned the rifle against the railing and then ran to the control box for the lifeboat. He selected the emergency button for the boat and thumbed it.

Released, the boat crashed into the water and began to drift away. Then he heard the boat's outboard start up. Hiya was on his way to the load-in port.

Vince rushed to the M110, almost stumbling with the pain as he ran stiffly toward the hatch. Two bullets cracked by and when the sound of the shots carried to him, as he ducked through the door, he pegged the report as a Type 81 assault rifle, not a submachine gun. More accurate.

The power went off again, right on schedule. Shadows again draped over the deck. In the cover of the doorway Vince leaned the rifle on the wall, picked up his flashlight and used it to take a quick look at his wounds. One bullet had raked along his lower ribs—he could see bone exposed. The other had punched through the upper tensor on his right hip, right through the TFL, coming out the other side. The bullet would be somewhere on the deck. The wound was bleeding significantly but not copiously. No artery there. He reached inside his coveralls, tugged out emergency wound closure bandages, pressed them over the wounds and hoped they'd stick. The pain was manageable. He'd had far worse.

Vince grabbed the sniper rifle, and with the flashlight in his other hand he hurried through the lateral utility passages to the engine room, coming out on the cross-ship catwalk.

Muzzle flashes lit up the big room, bullets ricocheted, clattering around him, striking sparks. A squadron of Russians had entered the engine room and they'd seen his flashlight.

Vince threw himself flat on the catwalk; SMG rounds struck sparks and screamed around him. Muzzle flashes showed two—no, it was three, four, five and six Russians coming from the forward entrance, into the machinery aisle below him. He dug into his coveralls and got his flashbang loose. Vince tugged the pin out and tossed it over the railing down onto the men below.

He closed his eyes—and the second he heard the flashbang's detonation he got up, wincing with pain.

Vince turned, threw his lit flashlight back down the catwalk to the door he'd come through and then sprinted across the catwalk to starboard. Below, the Russians were blinded by the flashbang, shouting—but that wouldn't last.

He reached the stairway on the other side of the catwalk, crouched, and thought quickly about his options. He had a frag grenade with him, but the shrapnel might set off one of the plastic explosives he'd placed and that would be very, very bad timing. The rifle wasn't ideal in here.

The enemy made up his mind for him. Recovering, they spotted the flashlight at the other end of the catwalk and stepped out to open fire into the dark doorway. Bullets ricocheted screamingly around the room.

Vince stood up, looked through the scope and instantly got four targets standing close together. The image was a little blurred by their muzzle heat, but he squeezed the trigger four times, shifting aim minutely for each shot. Three men crumpled and jumped back under cover. The surviving Russians realized he'd decoyed them and drew back, shouting at one another. Lowering the rifle, Vince was in almost complete darkness.

By feel, Vince took the thermal imager off its track, laid the rifle down and drew the SIG Sauer. There was a sketchy smidge of illumination from his flashlight up on the catwalk.

Imager in one hand, pistol in the other, he clambered over the rail of the catwalk, braced on its frame and jumped into the near darkness, trusting to memory. He landed with a clank on top of the engine cowling.

Someone shouted in Russian from the inky darkness of a corner, which the flashlight glow couldn't reach. Vince moved in a crouch atop the cowling, then put the imager to his left eye, closed his right, and saw the thermal outline of the Russian. The shift of the man's arms told Vince the Russian was raising his SMG to fire his way.

Vince let his right hand go to an efficient kill positioning based on his experience and the information fed to him by his left eye. He squeezed off a shot with the automatic pistol; the man staggered. Vince fired twice more. The Russian went down.

Vince hunkered down and bullets coursed over his head. Crouching hurt like a bastard because of the wound in his right hip. Bullets ricocheted, once humming by his right ear.

Still crouching, he crept to the edge of the cowling and there was just enough light from the flashlight on the catwalk to show him the outline of two men turning his way.

Vince lowered the scope, opened both eyes, and fired twice. Then three times. Then four. A Russian fell, but one of the men had a Kevlar vest on and it needed a careful shot to place the bullet in the target's head at this awkward angle. But down he went.

Vince froze, listening. No noise… Just the creak of the ship, the distant slap of waves…

But another sense was picking up a scent of death. The Russians he'd left here earlier were beginning to smell. That rot joined with the smell of gun smoke and fresh blood and someone's feces—one of his bullets had smashed through a man's intestines. They were all smells he knew well, from the battlefield...

The darkness, the smell, triggered a flashback.

Syria. The night he'd escaped from the Islamic State terrorists who'd taken him prisoner.

No weapons in his hand, just the darkness as he slipped out the window. There were dead men nearby: Syrians sliced open by the Islamic State killers to make an example of those who did not swear fealty to the caliphate. The smell of feces and blood mixed sickeningly in the darkness.

Then a sentry in cammies and a headwrap had come by, his face catching the light from a post. So young. Not quite twenty years old. Looking scared and unsure. Vince felt raw pity for him. But the sentry had an AK47 in his hands, and on his hip was a combat knife.

Vince was crouching by a pile of bombing rubble. He took a brick from the rubble, crept up on the young soldier and hit him hard on the back of the head. The brick shattered, not doing as much damage as Vince had hoped. The sentry's knees buckled. He dropped the rifle. Vince clapped a hand over the young sentry's mouth, took the knife, and the light fell fully upon the young man's face again.

Fear. Despair.

Vince had a working use of Arabic in those days. "*Satajgydgyj allah 'iilaa aljana,*" Vince whispered into the boy's ear. *God will take you to paradise.* It was the least he could do.

Then he thrust the knife blade into the young sentry's heart.

And Vince had let a sob escape him, at that moment. The kid had just been doing what they'd conditioned him to do—maybe threatened his family to get him do it. And Vince had to kill him.

He could see the look in the young man's eyes, even now. His arms were still around the dying boy, and Vince could feel the life draining from him.

Vince felt a sick feeling, an anger at the whole world rising up in him. And then…

Flashback, he told himself. *PTSD. Don't go with it. Let it pass through you. You have a mission.*

He wrenched himself back into the present moment. Back into a new battlefield. With the same old smells.

Vince stood up, pocketed the Sig, climbed off the engine casing. Careful in the dark room, he made his way toward the loading port.

You have a mission…you have a mission…

You have a mission.

The women were waiting aboard the lifeboat. Despite being over-loaded, the craft was tossing in the waves, secured to the ship, bumping into the hull from time to time. Hiya and Morris hadn't boarded yet.

"Good luck out there," Vince told them. "Just keep heading west. Don't go directly to Macao. My people will find you—they're going to be looking for you due west from here."

Morris cleared his throat. "Hiya and I are thinking we ought to stay with you, mate. One of the women says she can run an outboard. You're wounded—you need backup, Vince!"

"The wounds are minor. I've got the bleeding stopped. I'm all good, brother."

"You have blood splashed all over your clothes!" Hiya pointed out.

"Most of it's not my blood."

"Vince," Morris said, "you're all alone against summat like sixty of the bastards. Me and Hiya figure we can do our part."

Vince was moved. He said, "Hiya, Morris—thanks. It's been an honor having you with me on this. But no. I need to know you guys get off this boat safely. See, I might have to blow it up at any time—with me aboard. I don't plan to. But it might be necessary."

"But if we are with you," Hiya began, "you won't have to—"

"Hiya—thanks, but no! Listen, we need to get you two out of here. The wind's rising. Best to get you on your way before it gets too choppy. I've got to go forward to the galley, find the kitchen staff, get them to the last lifeboat. And I've got to get the jump on Krupin and his men—so there's no time to argue about this."

Morris sighed and nodded. He handed Vince the oxy pill bottle. "Might need this."

Vince put it in his pocket. "Hold on, I'm thinking of sending treason boy with you. There's an FBI guy who can take charge of him." He turned away and went into the hold.

In the light of a Coleman electric lantern, Vince leaned against a crate next to Greenwald, who was sitting on the deck, his back to the crate, nodding from his second oxy. His wrists and ankles were tied up with old electrical cords.

"Greenwald!" Vince said sharply.

Greenwald snorted and sat up straight. "Ow!"

"That supposed to get you another oxy, Greenwald?" Vince asked wearily. His hip throbbed furiously and wished he could take a capsule himself. But any painkiller would slow his reactions, take the edge off his alertness.

"I'll make you a deal," Greenwald said. "I'll trade you the specs for Spring Glory for the rest of my oxy."

"What? Specs in what way?"

It's a flash drive with the codes, online location, passwords, launch programs, viral packages, everything, in both Russian and English.

They did the English part just for me. The password to get into the drive contents is *Mat Rossiya Amerikanskiy Syn Solzhenitsyn*. Also, there's one in Cyrillic but you won't need it."

"Let's see the drive."

"I'll tell you where to find it. If we have a deal. See, I thought maybe I might be able to use it to make a deal. Once the radio room and the bridge were blown up, I figured things were going to shit here, so... I was waiting for the moment. But I don't think any real deal is going to happen, except maybe right here with you and me."

"Okay, I'll give you the dope for this drive. Now where is it?"

"You seem like the kind of guy whose word is good. Do you give me your solemn word I get the oxy if I give you the flash drive?" He looked up at Vince.

"Yes," Vince said. "I give you my solemn word."

"Okay. I've got it on me. But I can't reach it, tied up like this."

"You've had it on you all this time?"

"Hence the need for you to give me your word."

"Please tell me you didn't keister it."

"Heavens no. It's in the sock, on my right foot."

Vince knelt and found the flash drive. "Okay. I'll take a chance this is the real thing."

"It is."

Vince put the pill bottle in his hands. "Don't overdose."

"No plans to, right away. But I'm not leaving this ship."

Vince raised his eyebrows, genuinely surprised. "Why not?"

"Because I can feel that I'm dying. I think I lost too much blood."

He shifted over a little, and blood oozed thickly out of a tear in his trouser leg. "The bandage came off a while ago. And I have a fever... and... I don't want to live out my life in some supermax. I was wrong, and I don't want to live in a box thinking about that till I die of old age. My whole vision was wrong. The world is too big and complex and dangerous for libertarianism. We need, I don't know, just a good government and a good democracy. Maybe we'll get it sometime. I won't live to see it. Just let me die here, please. That's justice enough—don't you think?"

Vince didn't trust Greenwald to give his word. He was, after all, treasonous. But he looked Greenwald in the eyes and asked, "Is that flash drive what you say it is?"

"Why else would I have it in my sock? It *is* Spring Glory. Give it to America with my blessing. Tell 'em I was sorry."

Vince had some expertise in recognizing truth in another man's face. He made up his mind. He unsheathed his knife and cut through the cords enough so Greenwald could take his pills. He stood up and found a receipt pad and pen on one of the crates. He brought it to Greenwald. "Write down that password."

Greenwald wrote it down.

Vince took the password and the drive out to where Morris and Hiya were waiting beside the ramp. "He's not coming," Vince said. "But..." He handed Morris the flash drive and the paper with the password. "That's supposed to have Operation Spring Drive all laid out and explained on it. The FBI's got a man in Manila, he'll be coming out to you. Name's Richard Chang. Give him the drive and that paper with the password to get into the files. Tell him what it is and where it came from."

Morris nodded. "You've got it." He put the items in his pocket and zippered it shut.

Hiya licked his lips, looked at the deck, then said, "One thing. Krupin has some new bodyguards. You ever hear of the Tortoise and the Hare?"

Vince shook his head. "That's someone's nickname? Never heard of 'em."

"The Spesky brothers. Russians. One very big, very slow, but very powerful: the Tortoise. The other is the Hare. Fast, very fast. Both very dangerous. Together—twice dangerous. You take special care, if you see them."

"I'll do that." He shook their hands. "Thanks fellas. I'll be in touch. Now go."

Hiya saluted and the two men went carefully down the ramp, then clambered onto the roof of the lifeboat. The pale hands of hectoring women tugged them into the craft. "Come on come on come *onnnnnn!*" Jill yelled at them, as they clambered into the crowded boat.

Vince used his combat knife to cut the ropes and the lifeboat drifted out into the moonlit waves. Jill stuck her head out of a hatch and waved at him. Vince grinned and waved back. The outboard started up and the boat veered toward shore. It soon vanished into the darkness.

Vince hit the button that closed the hatch of the loading port. The hatch rose and clicked into place, seawater running from it onto the deck.

Wincing with the pain in his side and hip, Vince went and leaned against a bulkhead and tapped a number into the satellite phone. Another memorized number…

The call went through a few moments of crackling but then he heard Richie Chang's voice. "Agent Chang."

"Richie, it's Bellator. I've got a satellite phone." Some part of Vince's mind, his senses, stilled assessing sounds, hints of any enemy approach, as he made the call.

"Vince! What's your situation?"

"Closing in on completing the mission. I've cut off their communications—as far as I know. Their transmitters, the radio room, and the ship's bridge is gone. The Russian captain and his two officers with it. Krupin was about to launch Operation Spring Glory from here: a cyberattack on America like you wouldn't believe. But that's been stopped, at least for now. You still in the Philippines?"

"I am."

"I got hold of Tighe—I told him he has to make sure everyone in the second lifeboat I sent in has a passport and airfare to wherever they want to go. There's a large group of women and two men. One of the guys is the ship's motorman, Morris. A good man. I got a flash drive from Jim Greenwald. It's supposed to have the specs for Operation Spring Glory, and I gave it, and the password to Morris. He'll give it to you for the cyber defense team, Homeland Security, the Bureau, the Agency, Defense Intelligence—-*everyone* should be copied on it."

"Holy crap, Vince…"

"Yeah. Now listen—everyone on lifeboat seventeen needs to go completely free, all of them. You have to *insist* on being there when Tighe sends his team out. You and Jerry. Maybe take a boat to meet the lifeboat part way. They'll need some money too. Dierdre can use my money—she can wire it to you. I think we can afford to donate four hundred bucks a person. These people helped me and the USA, they deserve appreciation. Only four of them have a clue what all this is really about, and they're sworn to secrecy. They get no debriefing. Remind Tighe I told him that—and that I'm *thinking* about him. He'll know what I mean."

"Sure thing, Vince but—there's someone here who needs to talk to you. In fact, she's about to snatch the phone from my—"

"Vince!"

It was Dierdre.

"What are you doing in Manila?" Vince demanded. "Who's watching the restaurant?"

"Our partners is who, and aren't you glad to hear from me?"

"Well of course! But what's going on?"

"Richie figured out Tighe didn't necessarily want you to make it out alive."

"Yeah, I suspected as much. You watching your back?"

"Yes. Yeah. I'm fine."

"You're not telling me something. I can tell, Dierdre. Come on."

"Ugh. Okay. Tighe hired a guy named Ramos to take you out when you leave the ship. And he sent Ramos after me and Richie and Jerry, to keep us quiet. Only that didn't work out. Ramos is in critical condition, and we got a statement from him. That Tighe hired him to kill us. If he screws with us again that statement's getting back to Langley. Tighe's scared for his job. He's denying everything, but he's playing nice with us now. We're coming to pick you up personally, Vince, when the ship goes down—"

"Don't do that, Dierdre! I'll get to shore on my own. I've got a plan. I've got all the non-combatants off but the kitchen staff. Eight people. I'll go with them on the last lifeboat."

"When?"

"Not sure, maybe tonight or tomorrow. I just know it has to be soon. I've got control of the remaining lifeboat, but they could find some other way to signal for help. This ship has to go, as soon as I get the last of the non-combatants on the lifeboat."

"Vince, don't sacrifice yourself for the likes of Tighe."

"I'm not here for Tighe." He heard distant voices echoing through one of the passageways. Getting closer. "I've got to go. Don't call me back, it might give away my position."

"Vince—wait!"

"Listen to me, Dierdre. "Whatever goes down—I love you."

Then Vince hung up. He let out a long, shaky breath. He realized that a certain fatalism had crept into his thinking. He had quietly, somewhere inside, figured he wasn't going to get out of this one alive. But now, more than ever, hearing Dierdre's voice made him want to live.

He was starting to feel worn down from fatigue. Blood loss, shock from the bullet impact, stress. But he had no time for rest. He had to stay a step ahead...

The job wasn't finished yet. Vince went to get his weapons—and the recharged pipe cutter.

CHAPTER FOURTEEN

In the light of the two electric lanterns on either side of his desk, Heggie Feske looked at the remaining staff of the disinformation and cyberattack team gathered around him in his stateroom. The blue-tinted lantern light threw deep shadows, and made them look ghostly, as if they were already dead.

There were nine of them total, counting Feske, now that Mojin was shark food and Greenwald had vanished. Feske presumed that Greenwald was dead, killed by the supposed pirate leader.

"You really think this man is a pirate?" asked Petrov, in Russian. A mousy, bearded little man with a bulbous head, Petrov was a brilliant coder but outside of that, always blinking cluelessly. Perhaps he is an *idiot savant*, Feske thought.

"No one believes that story about piracy," said Feske. They were all conversing in Russian. "Certainly not Krupin. Naturally this man is an operative for the Americans or the British; probably CIA or MI6."

"He can't be here alone," said Vasiliev. Luka Vasiliev was a man so tall he had to stoop a little in the stateroom. Hook-nosed and with arms as gangly as his legs, he was perpetually uncomfortable on the ship. Like most of the team, he was happiest sitting at the computer console.

"Presumably not," said Feske. "But who knows? Meanwhile we have been issued weapons. We are trained with these weapons and if he comes on this deck, we will use these weapons."

"The man blew up the bridge and the radio room—and the transmitters!" Vasiliev protested. "He has explosives! He is likely to sink the ship, too! Has no one a way to send for help, Feske? Surely Krupin has a satellite phone or a cell phone?"

Feske sighed. "He relied on the ship's radio room for messaging, because it was automatically encrypted. The satellite phones were kept locked away near the engine room. They're gone now, probably thrown overboard. Krupin and Lorvec had cell phones—both have been stolen by those whores!"

The men murmured at that, aghast.

"The boss is looking for a chance to signal some passing ships," Feske said. "There were a few signal flares up at the prow—we tried them. No one is responding. We suspect disinformation has led other ships to shun us."

"That is ironic," sighed Vasiliev. "What of our own cell phones? They were appropriated when we came aboard, they must be somewhere!"

"They are," said Feske dourly. "They're at the bottom of the sea."

The men groaned. One of the hackers, laughing bitterly, said, "Krupin's insistence on controlling every communication from the ship has led us to have none at all!"

"So," said Petrov, his copious brow wrinkling as he thought aloud, "we are expected to use the submachine guns. But the walls here are metal. Will not the bullets ricochet and kill us all?"

There was jeering at that. Feske sighed and said, "Well, of course, there's a certain risk, but if you aim carefully, hopefully you will kill the enemy before your ricochets kill you, yes? Now! While we are waiting for further orders, we must try to work on a transmission system for Spring Glory."

"How can we test such a thing without electrical power, Feske?" asked Petrov, innocently.

Feske nodded, "Yes, I know, but we will get the engines working again. That will restore power. That will mean recapturing the engine room. Two platoons are being readied for just that job. Meanwhile, we design the transmitters we will need…"

"What?" Vasiliev shook his head. "We are not those kinds of technicians! Does anyone here know how to do that?"

The men muttered a general reply in the negative. "We could look up how to do it on the internet," said Petrov. "But we do not have the internet."

"An astute observation," said Feske. "We do have some old radio manuals, which Boris found. We will see if we can come up with some way to build a transmitter, communicate with the satellites."

"They still hope to launch the operation?" Vasiliev said. "From here?"

"Yes, that is the plan," said Feske. He was dubious himself of its practicality.

"Does not the GUR have the Spring Glory files? Can they not send it from some other place?"

"I asked about that," Feske said. "Apparently, such arrangements have not been made." He knew that Krupin did not trust high-level men in the GUR, and thought they would take credit for the operation. He wanted complete control of it.

"We have guns," said Vasiliev, "but where are the bullet-proof vests?"

"There aren't enough," said Feske. "They're kept for officers."

176

"But we are the reason this ship is here!" Vasiliev averred. "We are the core of this ship's mission! We should have armor!"

"What is that buzzing noise?" Petrov said, goggling about. "Do you hear it?"

Feske did hear it, then. "It sounds like... some kind of saw cutting at metal... a power tool."

"It could be *him,*" said Vasiliev.

"Your weapons are leaning against the wall," Feske said, heading for the door. He had a strange, almost painful buzzing feeling that went with the buzzing of the distant metal saw, and realized that the feeling was naked fear. He had never felt fear so purely before.

Feske would not let it defeat him. He picked up a submachine gun and one of the lanterns. "The guns are loaded, so be careful. I'm going to ask the sentries at the passageway entrance about that noise."

"I'm coming with you!" Vasiliev called, snatching up a gun.

"There it is again!" called Petrov. "The sound is coming through the vent!"

Down the passageway toward the aft, Feske and Vasiliev discovered two sentries at the locked door, leaning against the bulkhead in the light of a lantern on the deck, and sharing a flask of vodka. "Drinking on duty!" Vasiliev said.

"Oh, shut your mouth, you! We put our lives on the line here—"

"You will be reported for this," Feske said. He snatched away the flash and threw it back down the passage. "We are investigating a sound—did you not hear it? Like a saw cutting metal?"

The two sentries looked at one another. "No!

"No!"

"Listen—I hear it again," Vasiliev said. "It's coming from the deck above."

The taller of the two guards opened the door a little, and listened. "Yes, I hear something... but I see no one..."

Feske looked past the sentry and saw a little light coming from a steep metal stairway to the right. The sound of the power tool ceased. A door creaked up above.

He raised his SMG and whispered to the sentry, "Go, look up those stairs! See if anyone is there!"

"No," the sentry demurred, "I think not."

Vasiliev put his own gun to the back of the sentry's neck. "Now, you drunken fool, do something useful. Go and look! If you see no one, go up the stairs, discover what it is! It could even be our people so stop being such a coward!" The intercom was no longer working, and all communication was done by runner. There could easily be a project being carried out that the cyberwar team hadn't heard about.

The sentry muttered a curse, but went slowly to the stairway, gun in his trembling hands. He peeked up the stairs, then drew back and looked at the others. He shook his head and shrugged.

"It must be our people," Feske said. "Go up and see!"

The sentry went up the stairs, ever so slowly, and out of sight. Feske heard a murmur of voices. Then a clattering sound.

The sentry came back down the stairs, with his hands up. Someone dropped from above onto a stair just behind the sentry; a dark figure hunched down, firing at them with an automatic pistol, using the guard as a shield.

The gun's muzzle flash was the last thing Feske ever saw.

The Russian in the doorway took a bullet in the head and fell, as Vince tossed a frag grenade through the open door into the passage of deck seven.

There was a shriek of fear—then the explosion. A burst of flame and smoke; a lantern's light vanishing. Semi-darkness. Shrapnel zipped through the doorway, ricocheted in the entry hall, and struck the guard that Vince was using as a shield. The man gasped and fell twitching. Vince stepped over him, pocketed the SIG Sauer, and unslung his HK416 from his shoulder.

He had the M110 with him too, strapped across his back. On his left shoulder he had the sling pack, now stuffed with loaded magazines, boxes of SIG ammo, bandages, the satellite phone, and, most important, the detonators.

Vince paced up to the smoking doorway and felt gnashing pain from his wounds as he leaned over just enough to look down the passage. There was a blackened but still glowing lantern overturned beside two dead men in the passageway. Up to the left, an open stateroom gave out a confusion of Russian voices. Sounded like there were six, or seven, maybe more men in there.

HK416 in his hands, two more frag grenades and one more flash-bang in his pocket, he was approaching the stateroom, when someone inside it stepped part way out and fired their weapon in his general direction. The bullets ricocheted off the wall close to his right, cutting past his back, as he returned fire more accurately. For a man of his experience, it was hard to miss from just thirty feet away, even firing from the hip.

The Russian spun with the impact of the bullets and fell back into the stateroom.

What do I do if they want to surrender? he wondered. *How would I take all those men prisoner and get the job done? Russians, please don't surrender.*

The muzzle of a gun was thrust out the door—Vince dodged left, flattened against the wall. He fired suppressively, aiming at the ceiling of the passage so the bullets would rebound down and away from him. One of the great dangers to him on this steel ship was ricochets.

Inside the stateroom, an argument was going on. The Russians seemed to be arguing about closing the door. The muzzle poking into the passageway fired, maybe trying to scare him off. Bullets clattered by.

The muzzle drew back. More tense Russian discussion.

Vince leaned a little to the right and aimed at the metal inside of the open door jamb, so that bullets deflected randomly into the stateroom. He squeezed off a burst. Someone screamed. He couldn't risk the endless ricochets from a group of soldiers. He had to use up another grenade. It was worth it—each of these men, using cyberattack and misinformation, could do more damage than a dozen soldiers. He took the HK assault rifle in his left hand, took the frag grenade out of his pocket with his right, pulled the pin with his teeth. Then he tossed the grenade into the room. The men in the room shouted in terror.

Someone came rushing out—Vince shot him with the HK416, and then threw himself flat so that he and the dying man fell onto the deck close to one another. The grenade blew, with a deep throated clangor, shrapnel whizzing over Vince's head. He felt a sharp sting on his upper right arm. As the smoke cleared, he looked through the dim light at the man lying on the deck. The man looked back with dead eyes.

Bits of metal pattered down, and men groaned inside the stateroom. Vince got to his feet, stepped into the doorway. A lantern behind a metal desk had survived the blast and gave him enough light to finish the job. Several men groaned and tried to crawl past dead comrades. Vince fired the HK in three-shot bursts into anything that could even possibly be alive. The bullets clanged and rattled. Bodies quivered.

Then all was still but for settling gun smoke. The grenade had shattered all the equipment in here too. That was good.

Now that was over, Vince noticed the stinging pain in his upper right arm more. He squinted at the arm in the murky light, and saw a twisted, bloody grenade frag sticking out through a slash in his clothing. He reached over, pulled it out, and tossed it away. *Not deep. Bandage that later.*

Vince checked the other berths—no one in them. They'd bunched together in the stateroom for a meeting. What he did see in the other berths was a lot of computer gear. There wasn't time to try to get hard drives out and collect them for US intelligence. But if Greenwald had been telling the truth, the flash drive would offer more than enough intel. Best make sure no one could put this equipment back in operation.

He turned to the man he'd shot in the passageway, found the submachine gun the soldier had dropped, and an extra clip for it. He put the HK over one shoulder and went from berth to berth, using the enemy's submachine gun to shoot through every piece of computer equipment he could find on deck seven. Best to conserve his own ammo. He would need every round, to get through to the galley workers. And to reach the lifeboat. That last lifeboat would be guarded, by now. Definitely: conserve ammunition.

Tossing the Chinese-made SMG aside, Vince took HK416 in hand and went looking for the enemy.

Sitting across from Pavel Krupin in the ocean view suite, Lorvec was nervous, tired—and also a little drunk. The only light was from the emergency lanterns. It made Krupin's face seem demonic to Lorvec, just then.

Krupin looked at him with disapproval. "You look disheveled," he said in Russian.

Lorvec responded in the same language. "It is late at night. I had a long workday."

"And you have been drinking!"

"I am Russian, and it is after supper time," Lorvec replied simply.

Krupin grunted. "You will get now sober! For it is now we make our move…"

"Ah, I have been waiting! We must find that bastard and kill him!"

"It seems he is no longer in the engine room. Unless he has gone back there. Devekov went to check on the hackers—all of them are dead. All their tech is destroyed."

"What! The German did all this? He seemed like such an imbecile!"

"As the Americans like to say, he played you like a fish. I doubt he is German. He is probably American. I have a suspicion…"

"Who do you think he is?"

"Never mind. But you notice something—this man has seen to it that all the women are off the ship. They are safe. And the Chinese are gone—Mun sounded like he was lying, to me. I suspect Mun made a deal."

"The treasonous scum!"

"Yes. Now, if this saboteur is the man I suspect, he may be concerned about the other civilians on board. The kitchen staff. So I want you to go there and take Spesky and his brother with you."

"The Tortoise and the Hare? Why take them to the galley?"

"Imbecile! This man may well go to rescue these people. That is his weakness. You and the Spesky brothers will be waiting for him. Take Garlisky and Alexeyev too, post them outside the dining room."

So, a posting to the galley. Lorvec liked that idea. He could find vodka in the kitchen. He doubted if this killer would bother to rescue a bunch of Chinese cooks. "I will do it, boss! But what about the engine room? We were preparing an attack."

"And it will happen. If he has gone back there, we will go in force and kill him. If not, we will take the engine room and restore power. I am going to meet with our officers and the platoons we are sending in the attack. I am elevating Artyom to lieutenant. He will command the engine room deployment, and he will see that anyone we find there, we kill."

Vince's hunch about a position above the lido deck paid off. He was now amidship, standing in deep shadow in a darkened media room, with a big, obsolete television screen taking up much of a wall behind him, and comfortable furniture set about the room.

He stood at a broad window overlooking the pool area, three decks below. Half a dozen lanterns had been set up around the lido recreational deck, and next to the pool, in a space that had been occupied by a trampoline, thirty-three armed men, now wearing cammie paramilitary togs, were lined up, submachine guns in hand and pistols holstered on their hips. Sentries stood around the corners of the Lido space, looking around.

Standing in front of assembled soldiers stood a Russian who seemed familiar to Vince. He removed the thermographic imager, and looked through the M110's scope. It was Lorvec's man, Artyom.

Across from Vince, also overlooking the lido deck, were other darkened windows. One of them had fronted a darkened discotheque. Another was a breakfast café. Cruise ships contained all manner of entertainment and dining venues. All deserted now, on *Cupid's Cruise*... or were they?

He could take out Artyom, weakening the enemy's leadership, or he could—

The window exploded in Vince's face. He felt broken glass slicing his left cheek and his chin.

He dropped to the carpeted floor, glass tinkling down around him.

A rifle shot. Someone in the discotheque across from me.

Russians shouted below, reacting to the gunshot.

Lying flat, Vince was in the cover of a section of wall holding the window. He took a few moments to feel gingerly at his face, carefully pulling out shards of glass. Blood seeped out.

I got sloppy, Vince thought. *Fatigue. Maybe blood loss. Got to tighten up.*

Vince rolled on his back, took a grenade from his pocket, pulled the pin, jumped up and pitched it hard through the shattered window. Snatching up the M110, he rushed to the wall on the right, as the grenade arced down.

The soldiers were still massed below, thinking he was dead. Artyom was shouting at them—too late. The grenade detonated. The lido space echoed with the blast.

Vince leaned out, chancing a glance out the window. Three decks below, a half dozen men lay dead or dying; several more were stumbling off, wounded. The others were charging for cover. Artyom was now nowhere to be seen.

That was my last frag grenade, Vince thought.

Three shots were quickly fired through the window, one nearly hitting him, the others smashing through the television screen on the back wall. He drew back, then slipped close along the wall to the back corner, away from the window. It was dark here, and he figured he could work his way over by the broken TV screen without being seen by the rifleman.

Vince edged over so he could see out the window, raising the M110 to set up a shot—and a bullet whined through the window and struck the scope of the M110, knocking the rifle hard against him. The enemy had seen the gleam of his telescopic lens.

He dropped flat on the carpet, wincing with pain from his wounds. Breathing hard, he took out his penlight and examined the M110. The telescopic sight was bent by the impact, its lenses broken. "Shit," Vince muttered.

He took off the intact thermographic scope, tucked it in a pocket. Then he picked up the sniper rifle and crept behind a settee. Keeping his head low, he set up the M110 so it seemed to be sighted over the top of the furniture, its muzzle out the window, pointing toward the disco. Almost immediately a bullet smacked through the settee.

Vince unslung his HK416, and crawled to the back of the room, dragging his assault rifle with him. He sat up, and looked through the red-dot scope at the disco's window. It had been pushed open, in one place. Taken in by the gleaming muzzle of the M110, the shooter fired once more at the settee, showing a muzzle flash.

Vince aimed just over the muzzle flash, sending a pair of quick three-shot bursts through the open section of window—and there was a flicker of spasmodic movement as the rounds caught the shooter.

No way to be sure, but Vince suspected he'd taken the Russian out of the fight.

Vince got up and hurried through the nearest door, into a passageway. He looked for moving lights, guessing most soldiers would be carrying flashlights or lanterns. None in here so far.

He turned at a cross-passage, heading along the beam of the ship, toward the starboard. He felt a stitch of pain from the gash in his right hip, another on the wound scoring across his ribs on his left side. Have to check the bandages soon. Blood was still running down from the cuts on his face.

I'm not going to be as pretty as I was.

It was close to pitch dark here, with just a little moonlight up ahead, spilling thinly through an open door onto the passageway.

Vince figured the soldiers who'd survived his attack on the lido would be spreading out, looking for him. He needed to get to higher decks and move past the Russians to the galley.

He hesitated at the door, leading into an open deck overlooking the sea. The deck ran to a set of stairs that rose to a promenade circling the superstructure. Vince heard voices from his left, below, and saw lights bobbing in windows one deck down. Across from him, something gave off a metallic gleam on the promenade, just below the charred ruin where his bombs had gone off. Moonlight on a rifle barrel?

He took a step back and took the thermographic scope out of his pocket and set it to his eye. Yes, there was a blob of lime there. He fixed its whereabouts—just below where the bridge had been, and under a warped light stanchion. But suppose it was someone from the forward galley, on some errand, or trying to hide from the soldiers? It wasn't that far from the galley.

Vince decided to take a shot, but not right at the target. He aimed, and fired a little to its left, to see how it reacted.

There was that rifle-shaped gleam again—and a muzzle flash. A rifle bullet zinged off the deck nearby. This time, Vince aimed at the dark place under the stanchion, and squeezed off three bursts. The gleam fell away. Then came a glimpse of the silhouette of the rifleman falling from his perch, slamming with a metallic *chunk* somewhere below.

Now, Vince had a choice. The gunfire must have alerted the Russians to his whereabouts. He could stay where he was and try to ambush them. Or he could sprint along the promenade, and to the next stairway leading to the galley deck.

186

Suddenly, a wave of dizziness went through him. His head throbbed. He flung a hand at the bulkhead and caught himself. He took a long, slow breath, and the dizziness passed. But it was clear—he was running out of time. Could be he'd lost more blood than he knew.

Better keep moving, or he'd simply fall over.

He took a deep breath, then ran through the door, along the deck as fast as he could manage it. He kept close to the rail overlooking the sea. A gunshot cut by from somewhere below.

Hip burning with pain, lungs aching, Vince kept running.

In the fading blue light of the lantern, Greenwald finally managed to get the tangled knots undone, and the cords off his ankles and wrists. His left leg was pretty much deadweight. It was still tied with a tourniquet. He couldn't feel much pain now, thanks to the lack of circulation and the drugs. But he felt unreal, and prodded, somewhere deep within, to get moving. He didn't want to die in this clammy freight hold.

So he began to crawl.

It was hard at first. He was stoned, and his numb left leg seemed heavier than all the rest of his body, as if he were pulling a big iron anvil as he squirmed along over the deck. But after a timeless time, he got a sort of rhythm and made substantial progress. He wanted to get to the deck for a specific purpose. He wanted a good view, to see the ship exploding.

Vince. That was the man's name. Morris had called him that. Surely a man like Vince could get the job done. He'd already blown up part of the ship. The others had been talking about it. More was to come. What a glorious thing! This hated ship—blown to pieces. Wonderful!

Greenwald was almost to the stairs up to the flush deck, when he heard the Russians approaching.

He heard a voice he knew. Greenwald had enough Russian to comprehend that Artyom was telling the men to break up into three search teams.

"Greenwald! You are alive!"

It was Artyom, walking up to him, carrying a flashlight in one hand, submachine gun in the other. He looked disheveled with the blouse of his paramilitary togs not tucked in, his face unshaven, two days' growth of beard.

Greenwald sighed. "Yes, Artyom, what do you want?"

"Why you don't tell us where you are?"

"How? I was shot in the leg, tied up, and the intercom is down. I don't have a phone. Krupin took them all away!"

"Who is this man, who kills so many?"

"I don't know. He's a plumber, I guess." Greenwald had no intention of telling Artyom anything about the man who called himself Vince. "He's a German guy named Graf."

"Graf is not real!"

"He was real enough to tie me up! I just got loose."

"But he is not real Graf! He is some American, maybe British. Do you know?"

"Sounded German to me. He's a big guy with a tattoo on his face. That's all I know."

"He shoots you in the leg but doesn't kill you?"

"He didn't shoot me—you did! Anyway, Krupin's men shot me. Trying to shoot Graf. This is all very tiresome. Do you have any water?"

"Yes, yes, *da*." He took a canteen from his belt and handed it over. Greenwald drank deeply. "Oh God, I didn't realize how thirsty I was."

"Where's this Graf now?"

"Why, I think he must have gone on the lifeboats. Two of them left, you know."

"No, no he is shoot someone, he is yet throwing grenades! Almost kill me! Still here!"

"I don't know where he's gone, Artyom. Where is Krupin?"

"He is making preparations."

"For what?"

"To take lifeboat!" Artyom glanced over his shoulder, then lowered his voice. "Only one boat left! Only some go—" He looked skeptically at Greenwald. "Maybe you go too. Important man. But..." He shook his head. "Why this Graf man did not kill you?"

"He doesn't kill just anybody. He even let the Chinese soldiers go. I was wounded. Maybe he thought he'd keep me as a hostage."

Artyom heard men calling for him. "I must go—no time to get you to doctor."

"We haven't got a doctor on board, anyway."

"Or... the medicine. No time. Maybe later. I ask Krupin."

"Good. I'll wait here. You go and hunt that guy down."

"We fix engines!"

Greenwald nodded. But he knew the engines were well and truly sabotaged.

"I go... Don't move!"

"I won't!"

"And don't speak of lifeboat to the other men!"

"Not a word!"

Artyom left the freight hold. Greenwald took out another capsule, broke it open, snorted some of the powder down, and then put the broken cap back in the bottle. *Whoa.* That was a strong hit. It made him feel like lying down, just dreaming. But that inner prod, that push to get up on the deck was still there.

Greenwald began to climb the stairs, crawling up them one at a time, grunting with the effort of dragging his dead leg up with him…It seemed to him that the wound on the leg was beginning to stink…

Two stairs. Three. *Rest now…*

It was going to take time. But he had to keep going. Death was coming, and Greenwald wanted to meet it on his own terms.

Breath rasping, Vince reached the deck with the galley, stepped out into a dark passageway. At the end of a passage was a door into the dining room by the galley. It was slightly ajar, letting through a little light. He'd almost reached his goal.

A click; a flashlight beam blazing in his eyes; a Russian voice calling an alarm.

Vince did two things at once—he threw himself flat and let go a full-auto burst from the HK416, up toward the middle of the passage. Someone grunted and the flashlight suddenly pointed upward as the sentry fell backwards, torso chewed up by the 556x45mm bullets. The flashlight clattered to the deck, shining on a spreading pool of blood.

Eyes still adjusting, Vince clicked the assault rifle over to triple-shot bursts. Heart pounding, he waited. The dying sentry groaned.

Someone opened the door wider, looked out—a light from behind limned the sentry, showing he was wearing Kevlar. Vince aimed from the floor, centered the red dot on the Russian's head, squeezed off a burst. The Russian spun and fell.

Grimacing from his wounds, Vince got up to one knee just as someone else fired through the doorway.

It was a giant of a man in armor—more armor than the other Russians had. He was clad almost like a hockey goalie, but in bullet-proof Kevlar and plates. Even his head was armored, in a full-face steel helmet. And he was about seven feet tall.

In his hands was a Russian RP-16 and he was leveling it right at Vince.

CHAPTER FIFTEEN

Still on one knee, Vince had no move to make against a man so heavily armored—except to center the HK416 in the armored giant's lower left leg. He squeezed off a long burst and the bullets struck just below the giant's knee—also armored. As he'd hoped, his burst knocked the enormous Russian off balance so he fell heavily on his face. Vince tried to fire at the top of the man's head, but his weapon was mute. He'd run through the clip.

The giant lifted up with one arm, raising the Russian assault rifle with the other.

With no time to reload, Vince ran toward his enemy and leapt, so that the Russian's bullets cut under him. Vince came down on the man's armored back, and stumbled past him through the door, fumbling in his sling pack for another clip.

As he ejected the empty clip, slapped in another, Vince found himself in a high ceiling dining room, with numerous large circular tables. On two of the tables, underneath an unpowered tiered chandelier, were two lanterns: the only light in the room except for a thin spill of glow from the galley doors beyond.

And sprinting from those doors came a small, armored man. Rushing toward him, flourishing a Grach pistol in each hand.

Vince swung the assault rifle and fired. But this smaller Russian whisked aside the instant Vince brought his weapon into play, so that only a few bullets from Vince's burst hit him, glancing off the armor over his hip, jolting the armored gunman enough so most of his shots at Vince went awry.

One of them connected. A slug from the Grach hit Vince in the left shoulder, knocking him onto his back between two tables. Grimacing with pain, Vince rolled to his left, under a table, narrowly avoiding more bullets fired from the little man's two guns. Vince reached up, pulled the table over to give him a semblance of cover.

Rounds spat from the door as the bigger man returned to the fight, firing the RP-16. They punched through the wooden tabletop over Vince, spraying splinters, ricocheted from the steel floor.

Hiya had warned him. *The Spesky brothers. Russians. One very big, very slow, but very powerful: the Tortoise. The other is the Hare. Fast, very fast. Both very dangerous.*

The murderous brothers, slow and fast, were moving in to finish Vince Bellator.

Gritting his teeth against the pain in his left shoulder, Vince dug in a pocket of his coveralls for his last flashbang. He pulled the pin with his teeth, and chucked the flashbang grenade over the table toward the tall, armored Russian. Vince closed his eyes as another bullet seared along his ribs on the left side—then came the bang and the flash, leaving the giant and his brother shouting in consternation.

Vince rolled from under the table, opening his eyes as he got to his knees and fired the HK416 at the armored men, spraying it so they staggered back—then he aimed into the lighting elements of the two lanterns.

The big room plunged into near darkness. The assault rifle fell silent, out of ammo. The enemy was recovering—no time to reload. Vince jumped up, dropping the assault rifle as he drew his combat knife and ran toward the Hare.

The Hare fired toward the sound of his coming, and a bullet chunked into Vince's upper chest just under the collarbone. He stumbled but kept going, tackling the Hare, plunging the knife through a thin opening in the armor between the assassin's neck and shoulder. The Hare screamed a Russian obscenity—and suddenly, Vince felt an iron-hard grip on his shoulders, enormous hands pulling him away from the Hare, dragging him backwards, slamming him down on his back. Vince felt like a small boy in the hands of a sadistic adult.

The Tortoise was looming over him, a dark silhouette lit scantly from the far side of the room. Gasping for breath, Vince reached into a pocket.

"American imbecile!" rumbled the Tortoise, drawing his Grach. "I shoot your belly and then I take your eyes with thumbs!"

Vince pulled out the .410 12-gauge pistol, and fired the incendiary round directly at the towering Russian's helmet.

The room lit up with the ghastly blue-white glow of the incendiary round, its pellets sizzling across the Tortoise's upper body, and helmet. One of them had gotten into an eye; it began to bubble out of its socket. The Tortoise cried out and clawed at himself.

Vince got on his feet and then a dark figure lunged from the darkness and tackled him around the middle. He fell heavily, once more on his back, as something clambered, snarling up Vince's body—it was the Hare, blood spurting from the knife wound, probably dying but still fighting, digging at Vince's eyes.

"You *are* a tough little fucker, aren't you?" Vince growled, tearing the Hare's helmet away, exposing his head and neck. Vince thrust fingers in the knife wound and ripped out the Russian's jugular.

Blood gushed and seemed to scream—no, the scream was from the Hare's mouth as he convulsed in death.

The Hare's blood coursed over Vince, hot and sticky.

Then the Tortoise was stomping up to them. wailing in grief, shouting, "*Ivaaaaan!*" at his brother.

Vince flailed for a weapon, found one of the Hare's guns on the floor, grabbed it and his fingers found the trigger. Fighting upstream against the pain, he yanked the Hare out of the way and fired the Grach into a crevice in the Tortoise's armor, pulling the trigger over and over to send bullets into the giant Russian's groin. The giant screamed like a little girl.

Vince got agonizingly to his feet and ducked a powerful swing from an armored fist, hearing it hiss by as he stepped around behind the big Russian and shoved the muzzle of the pistol under the back of the helmet.

Two bullets remained and they both went into the Tortoise's brain. The giant's remaining eye was blinded by splashes of his own brains.

The Russian giant swayed... and to Vince's amazement, turned sluggishly around and raised his own Grach...

And then went to his knees... and stayed there, quivering, head bowed. Vince backed away, stumbling into a table. Dizzy, he gasped for air, and looked for another weapon. There—he could see the Tortoise's RP-16, a shadowy outline on the floor. He walked unsteadily to it...

And then felt the room start to spin around him. He reached into his sling-pack and scrabbled with his fingers till he found an EWC bandage, got it in place over the bullet wound in his left shoulder. He took a deep breath, crouched down, picked up the Russian assault rifle, and stood...

Damn, it's a heavy rifle. Unnaturally heavy.

He glanced toward the Tortoise. The big Russian was lying face down, very still. Quite dead.

Vince took the RP-16 into ready position and forced himself to march stolidly toward the galley—trudge through the waves of pain in his hip, and his face and shoulder.

And then Boris Lorvec stepped out.

Lorvec was carrying his own RP-16. He blurred, smearing across Vince's eyesight.

Something going wrong with my eyes…

Lorvec swore in Russian and then added, "You! Graf!"

"You still think I'm Graf?" Vince asked hoarsely, trying to buy time to get closer. With his eyesight failing he had to get close enough to aim. He held the RP-16 pointed toward Lorvec from the hip.

"You… you have killed the brothers?"

"They weren't so hard to kill. Don't you know who I am, Lorvec?"

A little closer…

"You… you are…" Lorvec aimed his weapon.

Twenty feet away…

"I'm Vince Bellator, Lorvec. And I came here to kill you."

Then Vince threw himself to the right, firing at Lorvec's center of mass.

The gun spurted flame; Lorvec bellowed in pain and fired. Bullets scorched past Vince's left elbow, cutting graze marks.

Then his right shoulder hit the deck, and pain lanced through him.

There was a dark shimmering for a long moment. Vince's breath didn't seem to want to come.

At last, he sucked air in, and coughed, and took another breath. He turned over on his belly, used the rifle like a cane to stand.

Vince swayed and took three stumbling steps toward Lorvec, who was sitting on the floor, clutching his belly, trying to bring his rifle into action.

"Lorvec," Vince said hoarsely. "You remember… those professors in Russia… wanted to overthrow the… the regime… and you used an RP-16 to finish the job? You like the RP-16… right?" Vince wasn't choosing the words. They were just spilling out. It was like someone else was saying, "I've got this one here for you." He stepped closer and kicked the other assault rifle away from Lorvec.

"No…*nyet*…stop!" Lorvec said, blood bubbling out with the words.

"I'm not good for much in this world," Vince said. Was it really him speaking? "But I do have… a talent for revenge."

And with that, he shot Lorvec in the face with the RP-16.

He blinked at the other figure in the doorway… who was that? Familiar. Someone he knew, wasn't it? Wasn't that the man he'd called Uncle Jack, as a kid?

Wasn't that Jack Sullivan?

"Stand down, Vince…for now. You need to rest."

The dim room seemed to get darker, and darker yet, and then— nothing but dark.

Dierdre stepped out of the darkness, into the glow of the black Lincoln's headlights. A crew and a group of CIA operatives waited on the trawler, watching from the railing as she and Richie Chang approached.

Tighe stalked up from the gangway and blocked her way to the fishing trawler. "Where do you think *you're* going?"

"Get out of the way, Tighe," she said.

Tighe shook his head. "I've got the rescue party covered. You two buzz off!"

"I'm not going to trust you on this," Dierdre said flatly.

"More bullshit about how I'm compromising the extraction?"

"Compromising?" Richie laughed dryly. "Is that what it was when you sent Ramos to kill us?"

Tighe shrugged. "The two of you blundered around Manila, stepped on someone's toes. Ramos thought you were hunting him, so he went after you."

"That's not what Ramos says. We have it all on record."

"He's a wounded man in a hospital, lying to try to keep you from killing him."

Richie snorted. "As if we would kill a man in a hospital bed. That's more a CIA thing."

Dierdre said, "We're going aboard, Tighe."

"I can call people who will see to it you don't."

Diedre drew her .32. "Can they keep me from shooting you first?"

He stared. "You're insane. You'll go to prison for life!"

"If you don't plan to interfere with the rescue of Vince Bellator," Richie put in, "why stop us from coming along? It's a big vessel."

"You'll get in our way, and it's against extraction procedure." With sneering irony, he added, "The operative's wife doesn't usually get to be there, you know. And I'm not buying the bluff that you're going to shoot me with all these people around." Tighe took out his phone. "Goerig? Bring up your men. Couple of *problems* here to take into custody…"

Dierdre looked around. "Richie—are they coming or not?"

"Well—if the plane got here on time. They…"

Tighe glared at Richie. "Is *who* coming?"

"That would be me, I think," said the tall, Black FBI agent, striding up from the shadows. He wore the traditional FBI suit and tie.

Dierdre tucked her pistol away.

"Sorry I'm late," said the agent. "Paperwork took a minute." He showed his badge. "Agent Thomas Chesse, Federal Bureau of Investigation. This is Agent Lowell…" A husky blond woman joined them. Her shoulders were broader than those of any of the men here. Dierdre knew Myra Lowell a little—she'd gotten a silver medal at the Olympics in women's wrestling, before joining the Bureau. She was a foot taller than Tighe. She showed her badge, and her handcuffs, and before Tighe could stop sputtering she twisted his arms behind him and snapped on the cuffs.

"What the fuck!" Tighe blurted.

"Oscar Tighe, you are under arrest for attempting the contract killing of Dierdre Bellator and Jerry Timbol," Lowell said.

"I have the extradition papers all signed, right here," Chesse said, waving a sheaf of papers.

Jerry Timbol strolled over from the gangway. "I see you got here, Agent Chesse." He nodded to the woman clutching his boss's wrists. "Agent Lowell."

"You're part of this, Jerry?" Tighe said, aghast.

"I am a witness, for one thing," said Jerry. "The Director has approved this action—as of ten minutes ago."

"You were cutting this close," Diedre said.

"What about the Bellator woman?" Tighe demanded. "She just pulled a gun on me!"

"Gun?" Richie looked puzzled. "What gun? You haven't had enough sleep, Tighe."

"Right this way, Agent Tighe," said Lowell, hustling him to the rental sedan that would take them to the airport.

"We good to go aboard, Jerry?" Diedre asked.

Jerry nodded. "Yeah. And the doctor's there already. She's an off-duty

ER doctor and we're paying her big money for this. We've got to head out. *Cupid's Cruise* is a good distance offshore…"

"Let's do this." They walked briskly toward the trawler.

In a low voice, Riche said, "You know, I doubt the CIA's going to let the Justice Department prosecute Tighe. They'll invoke the Espionage Act, say too many secrets would come out, this can't be public, it's his word against a killer's. I figure the Director only agreed to the arrest to send a message to the Agency—don't endanger FBI agents."

"No doubt. But for now, he's out of the way. One less threat to Vince."

They boarded the trawler, but Diedre couldn't escape the dread that hovered over her, following her everywhere; the fear that they wouldn't even find Vince's body out there in the China Sea…

Vince woke to a blur of light and darkness. Was that a human shape, coming toward him?

He struggled to focus his eyes—and then the room snapped into view. Luke, the assistant cook, was there, smiling sadly down at him. There were lanterns somewhere, just out of sight.

Vince was lying on a long kitchen table. Felt like some blankets were laid out under him. His coveralls were missing. He had no shirt on. He was swathed in bandages. He wore only skivvies.

"You lost a good deal of blood, friend," said Luke. The head cook, the Chinese lady who'd tried to lure him to her berth, came and looked him over. She asked a question in Cantonese. Luke answered in the same language, shrugging.

"If she's wondering if I'm going to live, the answer is, I have to," Vince said. The pain started up in him then—it throbbed in his head, it radiated from the wound over his collarbone, it burned in the wounds on his hip and left shoulder. "I need to get up."

200

Luke shook his head. "You're hurt bad. You lost a lot of blood."

"You a doctor as well as a cook?"

"Some emergency medical training. I've worn a lot of hats, man. We've got a good medical kit here. Took your blood pressure. Chef even unlocked the infirmary, found two bags of plasma and the IV. We got some plasma into you. She…" he nodded toward the staring Chinese chef, "she dug some bullets out, too. Chef's good with a knife. Used to be a sushi cook."

"A Chinese sushi chef?" Vince murmured. "But then…" He dazedly remembered a Hispanic one in Los Angeles.

"You maybe have the inside bleeding," the chef said. "Clotting good. Don't know. Time for vitamins. Time for soup. Pain meds."

She disappeared from his line of sight.

"The Russians close by?" Vince asked.

"Beats me," Luke said. "You killed the ones that were hanging around here. I saw you kill Lorvec! I hated that prick. Glad to see him gone."

"They'll be here looking for me," Vince said. "I've got to get everyone in the kitchen to the lifeboat. That's why I came to the galley."

Luke looked interested and skeptical at once. "I'd love to get on a fucking lifeboat and get out of here. But they've got it guarded."

"Got to kill the guards. Those hats you wear include a military cap?"

"Hell no. I'm not crazy like you, man. Lorvec told us who he was waiting for."

"Great. Worst disguise ever."

"I thought something was up with you. That accent—"

"I know, I know. My name is Vince. I need some water, and then—"

"No!" The chef was back with a big cup of broth in one hand, vitamins and a meds bottle in the other. "Beef soup! Extra beef! Build up blood! First vitamins and meds—help him sit up, Luke!"

Vince struggled wincingly to a sitting position. "No pain meds. They'd fuzz me out. Won't be able to function."

"Don't you think you're done functioning today?" Luke asked.

"Wish I were, brother. I'm not. That's just a fact."

"Pain meds!" the chef snapped, scowling.

"Nope," Vince said firmly.

Grumbling, the chef put the meds bottle on the table. "Vitamins!" she said, holding a handful of pills under his mouth. "Open!"

"Take 'em," Luke said. "B complex, extra B12, multis, the whole shootin' match. It'll help with the blood loss."

"Okay, but just vitamins." Vince opened his mouth. She dumped the pills into it and held up the soup for him to drink. It was almost scalding, but he was grateful for the thick beef broth. It did make him feel stronger. "Got any coffee made?"

"Sure, strong as hell too," Luke said.

Three cups of soup and two cups of coffee with cream later, Vincent gently pressed the chef aside, so he could stand up.

"You lay down!" she said.

"Can't, ma'am," Vince said. "But I'm deeply grateful to you. Now let me help you in turn—I'm going to get you and the others safely off this ship. You see, the ship's going to sink."

Her eyes widened. "Sink? *This ship?*"

"Yes. Someone's going to blow it up. You need to get off. There's only one lifeboat left… We need to prevent Krupin from taking that boat. He's going to leave you here to die."

She nodded. "Yes. That is just what he would do."

"And that means you all have to accept I'm going to have to kill some more of the Russians."

The chef gave a broad shrug. "If you will get us off ship—you kill Russians!"

"Yeah, fuck those guys," Luke said. "They lied about our pay and shore leave, over and over. Them and some of the Chinese were the only ones that got shore leave."

Vince said, "Talk it over with the others. Maybe they want to stay here."

"I doubt it. But we'll see what they say."

Vince turned to Luke. "I need clothes. Something dark."

"You're a big son of a gun," Luke said. "Not sure if we have much that'll fit you. But when Sven deserted, he left some stuff here. Won't be needing it—they shot him. He was a big guy."

Something occurred to Vince. "How long was I out?"

"You were unconscious, oh, hours. Maybe six, or more."

Not good.

Krupin might have already taken the lifeboat and gone his way. Vince Bellator might have failed an important part of his mission.

Vince led the entire galley crew of eight down the passageway toward the portside of the ship. Luke was just behind him, with a flashlight, switched off, in one hand, and a switched-on lantern, partly covered over with cloth, in the other. They were using just enough light to find their way. Seven other galley workers followed Luke.

Vince's weapons had been restored to him. His sling pack was on his right shoulder. His HK416, with a fresh clip, was in his hands. The SIG Sauer was in his ammo belt next to the combat knife. The .410 was tucked in his waistband, loaded with a standard shotgun round. He had an incendiary round in a back pocket. He wore the dead Swede's jeans, which fit pretty well, and a black turtleneck sweater which was a bit tight across the chest.

He had enough strength back to be functional. And years of experience in the Rangers and Delta Force had taught him where to find reserves of strength and fortitude, deep inside. It had to do with conserving energy. Staying relaxed but alert.

His head was clear now. But it had been years since Vince had felt anything like this much pain. Being tortured in Syria—that had probably exceeded this. But maybe not.

He knew how to handle it. *One step at a time. One action at a time, eyes fully open. Don't get involved in the pain. Just let it be there. Focus on the mission, don't let your mind wander.*

Especially don't let it wander to Dierdre. Don't think about the strong possibility you'll never see her again.

But he kept picturing her all in black at a funeral.

A flashlight beam stabbed from a crossing passage ahead. Vince stopped, raising a hand, and everyone froze in place behind him. He raised the HK416 to his right shoulder; the wound in the other shoulder made his left arm tremble. He controlled it—just as two soldiers, both in Kevlar vests, came strolling, chatting in Russian, out into the passage, one a little ahead of the other.

Vince looked through the red dot scope and squeezed out a single-shot round, taking the first one in the side of the head. The other turned, mouth open wide to gasp as he raised his submachine gun. Vince shot him neatly through the forehead. The soldier went down before the signal could pass from his brain to his finger to squeeze a trigger.

"Whoa," Luke muttered. "Vince, you are a beast!"

Vince grimaced. "Hey, I *had* to shoot them—"

"No, man. It's a compliment."

"It is? I don't keep up."

"Listen Vince—you've got to take one of those bullet proof vests, man." He pointed at the dead Russians.

"Yes!" said the chef, behind Luke.

Vince said, "I try not to use them. They kind of muddle a full range of motion, slow me down. Just not my style."

"So basically, you're saying it's a miracle you're still alive?"

"That's a given. But yeah, take those vests off the dead men, and you and the lovely chef here put 'em on."

Luke grunted, and went for vests, handed one to the chef, and Vince helped her put it on. All the time his ears were attuned to sounds and his feelings, his sensations, alert for an approaching enemy. Then Luke held out the other one for Vince. "You're going... What do you guys call it? On point? You're out in front, man. You wear this vest."

"No, someone else..."

"You know, if you'd had one on, you wouldn't have a bullet hole right under your collarbone."

"Yeah." It was true. But Vince had always been stubborn about armor. His reluctance to wear it downrange in the Middle East had gotten him mocked; *"Oh look boys, here comes Superman!"* Maybe he'd have worn some if there'd been enough to go around for every service member downrange. But there wasn't. "But uh—no. One of you folks..." He turned to the others. "Step up and put the thing on. Bullets can ricochet like crazy in here. You need it."

But to his astonishment every other member of the galley team refused, one by one, to wear the vest. "You!" the chef said.

"Yes!" the others said.

"Put it on!"

"You wear it!"

"You!"

"All right, all *right*, keep your voices down!" Vince whispered, grudgingly putting on the Kevlar vest. "Okay, let's go. If anyone opens fire, flatten down—unless you can get under better cover fast."

They cut left at the passage, heading toward the portside stern, near the remaining lifeboat. If it was still there. If it wasn't, he'd have to find inflatable rafts to put the galley workers in. Morris had told him where he could find some. They were more dangerous than a real lifeboat but not as dangerous as staying on this boat.

"We're coming close to Krupin's suite," whispered Luke. "I used to deliver meals there."

"Yeah?" said Vince softly. Suppose Krupin was still there? He'd make a fine hostage, to get them to the lifeboat. "Point out the door…"

Luke pointed. "You see where the passage doglegs to port? First door on the portside, past there."

"Stay back here. If anyone comes along, act like Krupin ordered you to wait here."

Luke nodded. "Don't get killed, man."

"You know where the release for the lifeboats is?"

"I do."

"Can you run the outboard?"

"Definitely."

"If I go down, find a way to the lifeboat." With that, Vince turned away and walked to the dogleg in the passage.

CHAPTER SIXTEEN

A guard in paramilitary togs stood guard in the light from a lantern in front of the door to Krupin's ocean-view rooms. He was just thirty feet away from Vince.

Farther down the passage, past the guard, it was deep darkness. Vince stepped closer, raising his HP416, dropping the red dot to the guard's head—and realized that though the guard was facing forward, his eyes were turned to that deep darkness.

Realized it too late. Vince saw the muzzle flash, like a nova in that abyss, and was shot directly over his heart. It felt like someone hit him hard with a steel baseball bat. Knocked off balance, Vince stumbled back, grabbed a fire extinguisher case, used it to keep upright as he flattened against the wall, gritting his teeth with pain. He steadied himself on his feet, and a bullet cut past his face as he fired from the hip, a short burst into the darkness.

A man yelled something in Russian, fired wildly, ricocheting bullets ringing in the metal passage, as Vince fired again.

A thump in the darkness as the rifleman fell—but the door guard was stepping out, firing a burst toward Vince, which caught him across the belly section of his Kevlar. It was like a whole bunch of steel baseball bats slamming him at once.

Barely managing to stay on his feet, Vince fired back. The haphazard burst slammed into the guard's legs, knocking the Russian off his feet. He fell with a shriek of pain.

Groaning himself from the impacts to his chest, Vince took a deep, painful breath. The wound under his collarbone hurt like a bitch. But he was alive, thanks to the Kevlar. Krupin had set up a trap for him and only the vest had seen him through.

Vince stepped over and shot the guard in the head, almost as an afterthought, then reached for the door handle…

The door flew open—and there was Krupin, a Grach pistol in hand, and a smile fading from his face.

"It *almost* worked," Vince snapped, raising the assault rifle toward Krupin, who fired without aiming, the bullet striking Vince's armor near the wound under his collarbone. The pain of its impact there brought a convulsive judder to Vince's arms so the HP416 missed Krupin who slammed the door. Then came the click of a lock.

Vince tried the door handle. It wouldn't budge.

He stepped back, leaned against the steel wall, and put a fresh magazine in his assault rifle. And he waited, listening to the loud thump of his heart. Two minutes passed.

Can't wait long, he told himself. *You don't know if they're going to…*

Then the door opened—Artyom held it ajar, peeking out, eyes widening as Vince slammed his right shoulder into the door.

Artyom yelled, knocked over by the door as Vince pushed through into the lantern-lit suite. He immediately had to fire at a big Russian he hadn't seen before, coming at him from the bedroom on the right, snarling, teeth bared, firing a Grach. The shot cracked past as Vince blew the top of the Russian's head off.

The dying guard toppled as Vince turned to Artyom who was trying to get up—Vince was just in time to kick a pistol from Artyom's hand.

"Where's Krupin?" Vince shouted, pointing the assault rifle at Artyom.

"Gone, gone, he went—" He pointed toward the port side of the ship.

"Get up!" Vince snapped.

Artyom scrambled to his feet, hands raised, eyes wide in terror. "Please—I surrender! I do!"

"Shut up and show me where Krupin went! And keep your hands up and your mouth shut!"

Artyom nodded eagerly and led him through a door to a small, unoccupied living room. It opened onto a balcony with sun chairs. Beyond the railing, the sea was glimmering gold in the rising sun.

Jesus, Vince thought. *It's dawn.*

Artyom stopped at the door of the balcony and, sweating with fear, pointed at the orange Fibrelight emergency ladder hooked onto the railing. It drooped past the glass panes under the balustrade. Krupin had gotten away—at least from the ocean view suite.

"Where is he going, Artyom?" Vince growled.

"To the lifeboat! He has been getting everything ready! Please, let me go! We will bother you no more!"

"Krupin's got to die," Vince said, more to himself than to Artyom.

"Who are you?" Artyom asked, looking wildly about. "You are not Graf! Pavel said you are an American agent—is that so?"

"I am the guy who..." He disliked killing an unarmed man. "Is going to knock you cold."

Vince whipped the rifle butt to smack Artyom in the side of the head, in the "light's out spot" that usually worked...

Artyom's eyes crossed, and he folded up, falling to the floor, out cold.

A weariness came over Vince. He saw Diedre all in black at his fresh grave, numbly taking part in the age-old ritual, throwing a little dirt on his coffin.

Angry at himself for weakness, Vince turned away—and then stopped. He went back to the balcony and looked over the railing. On the deck below he saw four Russians in hot discussion.

He couldn't see Krupin. The deck had caught some rising sunlight, but it was still shadowed in places with deep darkness.

Vince took hold of the emergency ladder's hooks, and backed up, began pulling it up. No reaction from below. They assumed Artyom had done it.

He redoubled his efforts, and quickly got the ladder rolled up. Carrying it under his left arm, Vince hurried to the door of the suite. He leaned over enough to look down the passageway, saw no one, and decided to risk it.

He turned left, went around the dogleg in the passage, whispering, "Luke! You still there?"

"We're here!"

Luke turned up the light on a lantern. Vince strode over to him and handed him the emergency ladder. "Bring that and follow me. Couple of dead guys to step over down here. And by the way—that vest saved my life. Do not gloat." His chest still hurt like a bastard, though.

Vince decided they'd better risk a flashlight, used judiciously. He took one from a kitchen assistant and led the way, shining the light at the deck and little to the left, to diminish its glare.

They followed Vince past the suite, past the dead door guard, stepping over the pool of blood; past the dead man in the dark end of the passage, and to a stairway marked *Employees Only*. "Keep quiet, but be quick," he whispered.

They descended as quietly as they could, Vince hoping he correctly remembered the map of the ship's passages. The pain was rising in his chest. He suspected the blow to the Kevlar had broken up the clotting—he could feel blood oozing again. And there was a real possibility of internal bleeding.

Vince shifted his mental focus—something he'd trained for, with mindfulness meditation—so that he acknowledged the pain but didn't center his attention on it. Even so, the pain made him feel as if he was in a loud, old-fashioned metalworking factory. The pain was deafening bangs and the clanging of gigantic hammers, but Vince was still able to go about his business.

Now they entered a curving passage following the staterooms overlooking the stern, and Vince raised his hand for a stop. About four paces ahead, a blond, thick-bodied Russian officer a white uniform was taking out his keycard to open the stateroom. He was a little turned away and focused on the door. He had a lantern beside him on the floor.

Vince switched his assault rifle to his left hand, drew his combat knife and crept up with all the stealth his years in spec ops had taught him.

He got within reach as the officer, who had sensed Vince's loom, turned—in time to get a knife blade buried in his throat, shearing through his larynx so he couldn't call out. Eyes bulging, the Russian clutched at Vince's hand. Vince twisted the knife to cut through his carotid arteries.

Then he shoved with the cross-guard, holding onto the haft so the blade slid from the man's throat as the Russian pitched back, gushing blood. Glancing through the door, Vincent didn't see anyone inside.

He wiped his blade on the dying man's pants cuff, sheathed it, took the HK416 into both hands and checked out the stateroom.

It looked gloomy in the poor light of the lanterns. Must've been the officer's quarters. Dawn light slanted in through the sliding glass doors. Beyond it, he could see the distant horizon of the ocean, divided by light from the east, retreating darkness on the west.

He went to the sliding doors, quietly opened them and put his head out just enough to look around. There was a guard on a balcony about forty feet to starboard, a submachine gun over one shoulder. The guy was drinking coffee, staring out over the sea with a melancholy expression.

Vince ducked back, set his rifle aside and took out his SIG Sauer. He screwed the sound suppressor on it, and stepped part way onto the balcony, aimed carefully—and shot the guard through the side of the head, just an inch from the man's forehead. The sentry collapsed without a sound.

SIG still in hand, Vince returned to the passageway, looked carefully out and softly called for Luke and the others. Luke came trotting up, carrying the rolled-up emergency ladder. He stared at the dead man, still bleeding out. "Jesus Christ, Vince, you are a—"

"Don't say it," Vince said, as the others joined them. "Everyone, keep your voices down. Get that ladder in here, and hook it to the rails, Luke, on the starboard side, so it'll fall between the two balconies. Don't let it down yet. Be as quiet as you can. If anyone sees you up there and challenges you, act as if you were told to be there, wave at them and then calmly go back inside. You get me?"

"I do."

"You others come inside and wait out of sight. We're one deck above the stern, on the level with the last lifeboat. You're going to be climbing down a ladder onto the stern and if you're scared to do that, then you can stay here and go down with the ship or try to find some other way off. Now, be quiet and stay ready."

They filed past him. Vince considered dragging the body inside to hide it, but there was so much blood, it would be pointless. Dragging it, he'd leave a track of blood right to the stateroom.

He closed and locked the door and went to the small living room where the others were standing tensely about. "Sit on the floor for now, please," he said. "Be quiet. I'm going down first, to clear the way. Luke—you stay low and watch from the balcony. I might be able to signal you, but...use your own judgment. If it seems clear enough to get to the lifeboat, don't hesitate."

Luke swallowed hard, and nodded.

Vince took the satellite phone from his sling pack. He hefted it in his hand for a moment. Tempting to call Dierdre. But it didn't feel to him like he had time. And anyway—the emotional impact of talking to her would distract him. He was already functioning in a weakened condition.

He handed the phone to Luke. "If I can't join you once you get on the lifeboat, don't wait. Head out fast. Call for help after you're away from the ship."

He reached out and they shook hands. "Good luck, Vince."

"Thanks. You're a good hand, Luke."

Then Vince went to the balcony to recon for extraction.

He peeked out, saw no one else on the other balconies. He crouched in the doorway, found the detonator in his sling pack. He needed the detonator handy. He shoved it in his front pocket, on his left side. The wireless detonator was no bigger than a pack of cigarettes. It had a short antenna, and a little screen on it, the detonation button was under a flip-over cap.

Vince crept to the railing, looked down through the glass. The deck was on the port side. Deep shadow. He could see the aft part of the lifeboat, which had been winched up for Krupin, so that was good.

213

But Krupin could be already aboard it. They must be close to leaving.

He saw four armed men to portside; two stood with their backs to him, looking toward the lifeboat. The other two men were gazing toward the prow, maybe watching someone coming.

Vince decided he had to make his move right now.

CHAPTER SEVENTEEN

Kneeling, his SIG Sauer in his right-hand pocket, his HK416 lying beside him, Vince slowly let down the emergency rope. It dropped into the deep shadows between the balconies. No reaction from below. They hadn't spotted it. Not yet.

He slung his assault rifle over his back, glad he'd opted for a strap, and climbed over the rail and down the ladder. The Fibrelight ladder wobbled as he quickly felt his way down. He got to the bottom and found the ladder's lower end was hidden by a big white five-by-five bin marked *Emergency Life Jackets*. The top was unlocked. He lifted it up, took out a life jacket, and set it on the deck nearby. Then eight more, piled up. The galley staff would see them. Would be smart enough to put them on, in case the lifeboat didn't work out. And he might need one himself.

Holding the HK416 in combat ready position, Vince thought about tactics. If he went out farther on the deck, to see who was coming from forward, he could be exposed to fire from up the port deck, from the men by the lifeboat, and possibly from behind—there would likely be someone posted on the starboard, near the stern.

Optimal to fire from here, take down as many as you can, stir up the hornets' nest and see what you've got to deal with.

Vince felt a little dizzy; felt waves of physical weakness. Blood loss. He could feel it, sticky under his shirt, where it had leaked around the bandage. But he knew that the adrenaline rush of going into offense would brace him up.

He raised the HK416, switched to triple-shot burst, and sighted in on the two men standing near the raised lifeboat. They were clearly limned in the increasing dawn light. The sentry on the right had a Kevlar vest. Vince centered the red dot on the Kevlar sentry's head, squeezed off the shots, sending up the pink mist immediately. As the man's body jerked with the impacts Vince was already sighting on the other sentry, who was shouting an alarm and gaping around. Vince shot him the same way.

There were two Russians just out of his line of sight, toward the bow— and here they came, stepping into view, looking for the shooter. *Idiots.*

He shot them both through the torso, heart shots, then swung the rifle around toward starboard, and saw three men coming his way. One of them spotted him, yelled at the others, raised his submachine gun. Its burst ricocheted off the deck, strafing toward Vince. Vince moved out of direct fire and opened up on the Russian. The man went down. Bullets from the others clanged and banged into the bin beside him as he swept them with fire—and as one of their bullets struck Vince's Kevlar vest, so he was kicked back against the bin. The bin held him on his feet as he fired again and again at the oncoming men. Then they were all down.

He crouched—and pistol bullets cracked over his head, from the portside. There was the pounding of boots on the deck coming close and as Vince leaned out to fire, he was startled to see the man was far closer than he'd supposed. A massive officer was rushing him.

The big Russian officer was armed with a Grach and was wearing a Kevlar vest, and there was no room to bring the HK416 into action before the man was upon him. Vince let go of the assault rifle so he could grab at the SIG Sauer—then he was bowled over. The big Russian had hit Vince like a linebacker. The breath was knocked out of him, the stout officer on his knees straddling him, face contorted in a grimace of hatred, Grach about to centering on Vince's head—the Russian grinning in triumph-...

Vince jerked the .410 single-shot 12 gauge from his waistband and stuck it up under the officer's vest, pulled the trigger. The pistol recoiled viciously, stinging Vince's wrist—the Russian screamed and arched his back, as a full shotgun blast tore up his insides, sending blood and bits of bone out of his mouth.

Vince shoved the dying man off him, rolled over, and got to a crouch as bullets cracked by from the portside. Some of them smacked into the heap of life jackets, making them twitch.

He ducked behind the bin and snatched up his rifle, his heart thudding as he stood suddenly upright and fired recklessly over the bin toward the shooters: two Russians at the place where the superstructure cornered on the deck. One of them was hit, not lethally, and staggered out of sight. The other Russian returned fire with a CS/L57 and Vince felt a bullet dig along his right cheek, and a second round cut along his left jawbone—cold air and pain telling him it had exposed a patch of bone—a third thumped through the trapezius muscle between his neck and shoulder. Grunting with the shock of the bullet tearing through his flesh, Vince clenched his teeth as he fired two bursts, and the man went down.

He saw shadows coming along the deck from forward, cast from around the corner. Vince opened fire, emptying his gun at the deck

217

then at the rail to make a possibly effective ricochet, hoping to suppress the shouting men he could hear from around the corner.

Then Vince ducked down, making an involuntary hissing sound at the pain of the new wound as he reached over to tug out his other, loaded clip from the sling pack. An excruciating process with all the wounds, though brief. He ejected the empty magazine, plugged in the new one. Then he ejected the 12-gauge shell from the .410, hurriedly replaced it with an incendiary shell.

"Vince!"

It was Luke, crouching low as he came from the ladder. "We're coming down."

"Good a time as any," Vince said. He picked up the dead officer's Grach and handed it to Luke. "Use that if there's anyone waiting in the lifeboat. And put on one of those life jackets in case you don't get to the boat. The others, too."

They were dropping from the ladder, looking scared as they hurried toward Vince. "This bin is good cover," Vince went on. "I'll shout for you to run to the boat when I can. If I don't, go for it anyway. Watch out for shooters posted on higher decks."

"Vince—you're hit bad!"

"Don't wait for me," Vince said, switching his assault rifle to full auto. "If I get to the boat I get there. But just go."

Vince stepped around the bin, with the .410 in his left hand, the HK416 in his right, and ran as fast as he could to the curved corner of the superstructure. Stumbling a little. The pain seemed to be trying to trip him up. Leaning on the outer wall, he glanced at the bullet-hole in the trapezium. It was oozing thickly. His legs felt shaky.

Unlikely to get to that boat. Got to do what must be done.

Unconsciously, with the heel of his hand he felt the bulge of the detonator in his left front pocket.

He heard men getting closer… closer… Sounded like a fuck of a lot of them.

"*Go now, Luke!*" Vince bellowed.

Then he swiveled, deliberately exposing his head and left arm to draw fire. Saw well over a dozen men running his way, brandishing their submachines. Some of them fired. Bullets ricocheted from the metal near his head; his ears rang with the loudness of the impacts.

The nearest men were twenty feet away, the ones in the forefront aiming at him.

Vince pointed the .410 at them and fired it in their faces.

The incendiary pellets flared in the vision of the onrushing gunmen and smacked into their faces—this wasn't going to kill anyone, but they stumbled and blinked and fired wildly and some skidded to a stop causing others to bumble into them. Vince dropped the .410, at the same time stepping out enough to grab the handguard of the HK416 with his left hand—a lightning flash of brutal pain in the doubly wounded shoulder as he did that—his right bringing the weapon up to his shoulder. Bullets ricocheted from just over his head as, yelling in wordless pain and fury, he fired a long burst, raking the oncoming men to try and give sufficient cover to the galley crew running to the lifeboat.

"Vince!" Luke called. "Come on!"

"Go, just go!" Vince yelled, sending a second burst into a second wave of oncoming men. There were dead and dying all over the deck. Blood ran from the scuppers. He looked for Krupin, didn't see him. Was he coming from the starboard side?

Then, Vince saw the heli.

A dark gray Mil Mi8 helicopter, with the tricolor Russian flag on the side, was coming toward *Cupid's Cruise*. So, Krupin had found a way to send for help after all—maybe he'd sent men out on inflatables to get to ships in the area, from there call for help from the Russian navy. The lifeboat must be a backup plan. Krupin was hoping to get off the ship on that chopper…

"Fuck you, Krupin," Vince muttered, through clenched teeth. "Not going to happen."

He fired a third long burst at another wave of men, and some Russians beyond them—and then the rifle clicked on empty.

Vince drew back under cover, tossed the rifle away, drew his SIG Sauer—and his peripheral vision caught movement to his left. He turned to see three Russians coming from the starboard side. One of them was Krupin, wearing a Kevlar vest. They were going toward the pad on the stern, where the helicopter would be landing.

Vince smiled grimly. Hard to hit Krupin in the head from here, firing with shaky hands. He shot at the two men accompanying Krupin. One went down—the other fired a submachine gun burst as Vince staggered to the bin.

He got to its cover, hunkered down, leaned over for a firing angle and let loose with three rounds at Krupin. Vince gave a sickly grin as he saw Krupin clutch at his groin—that shot went right where he'd sent it.

But Krupin was still alive.

The still-standing soldier with Krupin fired and Vince ducked back, bullets strafing close.

He heard voices from the portside. More Russian soldiers coming.

He saw that the lifeboat was missing—the galley crew had gotten aboard and released it. Vince struggled painfully out of the Kevlar vest, grabbed the remaining lifejacket. He pulled it over his head and buckled it around his waist. The pain of those actions was almost paralyzing, but Vince managed it.

Then he dug the detonator from his pocket.

The helicopter was thumping the air overhead. It lowered into sight as if checking out for landing.

Vince leaned out from cover once more—saw Krupin with a hand on the guard's shoulder. They were about sixty feet away, moving unsteadily toward the landing area.

Vince glanced toward the sea—and saw the lifeboat tooling away, leaving a clear wake over the waves. He nodded to himself and looked back at Krupin.

"Hey Krupin, look!" Vince shouted.

Krupin looked. Vince waved the detonator. "You know what this is?"

Krupin stopped—put up a shaky hand. "No! You can come with us! You can take over! Come, come out! We won't shoot!"

Vince grinned at him. "Let's all take a swim in the lake of fire, Krupin!"

"No!" Krupin shrieked, "No! Bellatorrrrrr—!"

And with that, Vince flipped the button's cover back. And he pressed the button.

There was a five second wait, as Krupin turned to run toward the stern. Vince was afraid the transponder hadn't picked up the signal…

Greenwald was seated on the starboard deck, with Artyom, who was bleeding from a head contusion and cursing Krupin. When the ship tore itself in half.

Greenwald had taken two more OxyContin and now he witnessed the explosion through a veil of smooth, caressing detachment; watched in drug-induced slow-motion, as *Cupid's Cruise* erupted, the explosion roared from the engine room, up through deck after deck, followed by more explosions, lighting up everything all ghastly and glorious—it was like a giant metal flower opening, he thought. And here come the inner blossoms of red and blue fire, slowly expanding, reaching to the sky, and there went chunks of metal trailing lovely streams of smoke, and the deck tilted under them and giant scraps of bulkhead flew up and dropped toward them--each great ragged chunk of metal must weigh at least a ton!—

O, he thought, *what power! And I helped make it happen. What a splendid end!*

The shadow of the big slab of metal enveloped them.

"Nooooo!" screamed Artyom.

"*Yesssss!*" Greenwald yelled.

Artyom screamed as the gigantic, ragged chunk of bulkhead came down on him and Greenwald...

The whole ship bucked like an insane bronco and roared like a lunatic lion, and Vince struggled to his feet as the deck tilted with the first explosions. He was pitched back and forth, and clutched at the bin for support.

But then there came a final blast and Vince and the bin and sections of deck and Krupin were shot up into the air, as if flung by a giant catapult.

Vince's frenetic mind thinking, *I'm flying!*

Smoking metal slag flew by him, as well as cometing fragments of glass and the spinning slide from the swimming pool... and was that his SIG Sauer spinning by?

Then Vince reached the apex of his arc and his stomach seemed to come up in his throat as he plunged steeply toward the wrinkly, writhing mass of the waves.

Vince took a deep breath. He held onto it fiercely.

Then he smacked feet-first into the water, plunging down in a sheath of bubbles, the lifejacket shoving up against his armpits, spearing his left shoulder with pain. The water was cold.

He went deep enough that darkness closed around him, and then his descent slowed. He kicked his feet. A roaring, as the lifejacket buoyed him upward. His lungs ached. The pain at the wound under his collarbone expanded like an exploding grenade.

Then, Vince broke through the surface, rose a couple feet, and crashed down. More blinding pain, only mitigating when his lifejacket stabilized on the surface… Huge waves from the explosion shockwaves slapped over him, making him sputter and cough.

He dazedly noticed blood billowing velvety-red around him in the water. He was pretty sure it was his. And he was equally sure it would draw the sharks.

He heard a roaring, crackling. The ship had broken into several parts, all of them sinking, spinning, going down. The suction pulled him toward it. Maybe, he thought disinterestedly, he'd die before the sharks could get him. He'd die when he was pulled down by the ship's suction. He'd seen comrades burn to death, downrange. There were worse ways to die than in an undertow—one you had created to kill your enemies…

Flames gushed. A whirlpool caught at him. Barely conscious, Vince didn't fight it. Flames rose from burning oil on the water. He was suddenly sucked under water.

And Vince blacked out.

CHAPTER EIGHTEEN

Vince regretted waking up. It hurt too much. He was coughing up water, and his lungs ached. The waves weren't particularly large. Some of them were smoothed out by oil slicks. The *Cupid's Cruise* was gone. Sunk. There was a little debris, floating here and there. A Styrofoam cooler. A floating wooden box. Splintery deck chairs.

Apparently, he hadn't been close enough to the center of the whirlpool to go down far. And his lifejacket had brought him back up. *Too bad.*

He coughed again, and it hurt. Vince suspected the force of the explosion had cracked some ribs. He noticed a piece of shiny metal, shaped like the state of Montana, sticking out of the meat of his upper right arm. Blood was seeping up around it.

He felt sharp, brand-new pains in the back of his legs and lower back. More shrapnel.

Too much pain to keep track of. It all seemed to coalesce into one ache, with little glowing nodules in it.

May as well just go limp, let the lifejacket carry him. That would be less painful. Just let it all go and slide into death. No more pain, and no more...

No more what? Something was rising up into his mind from his subconscious.

No more surviving when he didn't deserve to. When his war brothers had died, and he hadn't...

He let out a long shaky breath, and just managed not to sob. *Don't turn into a little bitch at the end of your life,* he told himself. *Die with some goddamn dignity.*

What was it he'd said to Lorvec? *I'm not good for much.*

A few months ago, Vince had one drink too many after the restaurant closed in Harstine, and he'd said something of the kind to Dierdre: "I don't think I'm useful for much but... mayhem."

"You must be kidding," she said. "You saved so many lives at the Lincoln Memorial. You stopped an attempted coup. You ended a cartel. You—"

"But now... what am I good for? All I can do is kill people. I want to be good for more than that, Dierdre."

She took his hand and squeezed it. "You changed the lives of Lupe and Pascual and Diego. You gave them something wonderful, Vince. You're an *employer.* You *build* things! And you're the man I want to be with. Doesn't being my husband count for something?"

"It counts as an honor, darling. I just... maybe I just saw too many people die—at my hands. They were all rightful enemy combatants. Most of them were trying to kill me. But after it's all over you think, what were those people's lives really like? Those cartel thugs—did life offer much to them besides the cartel?"

"They had to be stopped, Vince. You did the right thing."

"I usually believe that. But sometimes lately... I guess it's catching up to me."

"It's PTSD, you know it is. It's dragging you down. You need to get back into meditation. You kind of let it slide. And I know you spec ops guys sneer at *therapy*, but—"

Vince laughed bitterly. "But we need it." He shrugged. "I'm an idiot talking about this to you. A man's wife doesn't want him to sound like he's doubting himself."

"I respect you for it! Because when you're needed, you always step up. Now step up to our bedroom, big guy. I'm going to show you just how much I appreciate you."

Now, he laughed softly at the memory—and coughed. The saltwater burned his throat. It burned in his wounds. The sea was tasting him before it ate him whole. He laughed again, and coughed.

What am I laughing at?

At myself. For not appreciating her enough. What a fool. What a punk to think you deserved her. Dierdre's better off without you. She's still young. She'll find someone.

Smoke drifted over him, and Vince realized he was drifting close to burning fuel. He had no wish to die by burning.

He kicked, and tried to use his arms to splash away from the fuel. He managed it, but just barely. His arms seemed to be going numb.

Then the sharks started for him. Had no wish to die piece by piece in the jaws of sharks, either. Did he still have his knife? He felt for it—it was still there, kind of stuck under his lifejacket. He forced his fingers to work, to press under the life jacket; to grip the knife.

Hold onto it. Don't fucking drop it.

Two sharks were cutting the water, coming at him, the larger one a little closer. Both were big enough to kill him.

They were just under the surface, so when the big one got near him, he jabbed at its sensitive snout with the knife. It struck home.

The shark writhed aside, trailing blood. Then the waves lifted him up, and the sharks were momentarily gone from sight. He found that he was encircled by burning oil slick. The air was fouled, his eyes burned with smoke, he could feel the heat of the blue flames flaring close by. Was he going to burn to death after all?

The sharks were gone—scared off by the burning diesel, more than by him.

But there was someone bobbing in the water about fifty feet away. It was Krupin, clutching a life jacket. And waving his arms at a helicopter...

A helicopter? Yes, there it was, the Russian heli. It was circling the wreckage, looking for survivors. But now--it was turning away.

"*Nyet!*" yelled Krupin, hoarsely. Then something else in Russian. But Vince and Krupin were ringed in by burning fuel—and the smoke had curtained them. They were hidden from the chopper. The pilot apparently made up his mind that there were no survivors.

The helicopter flew off toward Macao.

Krupin tried to shout Russian curses after it, but smoke wafted over him and he had a fit of coughing.

Vince laughed. It hurt. But he let himself laugh.

He took a deep breath. "Hey Krupin!" Yelling hurt, too. Then a wave rose and blocked Krupin from view.

But Krupin heard him and when the waves troughed Vince saw the Russian commandant looking his way. The waves shifted Krupin a little closer. His face showed dread—and then fury.

Vince chuckled a bit madly. He was sorry he wouldn't live long enough to tell this story to Diego. Man, he'd love it.

"Hey Krupin, how do you like the lake of fire!" Vince shouted, pointing at the flames.

"*You!* I will kill you!"

Krupin started splashing at the sea with one arm, and kicking, as if trying to get closer. Then he stopped, face twisted with pain.

"That's the bullets I put in your groin, Krupin! You're bleeding out down there! And you know who follows the smell of blood?"

Vince pointed at the sharks closing in on Krupin.

Krupin shrieked at the sharks and pummeled at them as they closed in. "*Nyet, derzhat'sya podal'she ot menya!*"

But then one of them had the good idea to go after Krupin from below. He jerked about in the water, flapping his arms—and then the sharks closed in.

One scream—interrupted by the water as they pulled him under and tore him apart, competing for the best bits.

"Couldn't happen to a nicer guy," said Vince. He laughed—and then he coughed, and he coughed again, and blood came up. He spat it out and thought, *this is it. Something just busted open in me…*

The sea looked strangely patchy now. Some of it was there and some wasn't. Same with the sky. Then the empty spaces took over completely, and nothing was there at all.

Shattering pain. Someone's hands pulling at his shoulders.

"Let me go…" Vince said. But he couldn't speak loud enough to be heard.

"Pull him in… carefully as you can manage," came a thin voice, rippling in and out of audibility. "I know it's… if we can…"

Was that Dierdre's voice?

Seemed he was hallucinating as he died. He wished the hallucination included a sight of her.

The pain was rippling and rolling now, shimmering through him. Something hard thumped his back. He tried to open his eyes, but the lids were just too heavy.

"Let's go, dammit…" Yes. Dierdre's voice.

A motor roared somewhere. Vibrations passed through from the hard surface he was on.

"Is he breathing?" A man's voice. Sounded familiar.

"He is." Diedre again. The Dierdre in his dying dream. "Let's get that piece of shrapnel out of his arm, dry the skin, press a bandage… and that wound there… and there's another…"

Vince groaned as someone prodded and pressed at one of his many little geysers of pain.

"He made a sound!" she said. "Vince! Can you hear me? We're here! Me and Richie and Jerry! And we're in a launch and we're going back to the… it's a fishing boat, a trawler…"

"If it waits for us," said the familiar male voice. Was that Richie? "I mean, after you pulled that damned gun on the trawler captain."

"He was being a big baby about the burning oil," Dierdre said. "He said he saw a Russian helicopter–he didn't want to come over here. It's not like the US government isn't paying him a big pile of money."

"Yeah, well they didn't mention that he'd have to sail into burning oil slicks—or that you would threaten to shoot him."

"Vince?" she whispered, close by. "Can you hear me? You have to hang on—we've got a doctor aboard the ship. She has transfusion blood, your blood type, and we're going to bring up your blood pressure and patch you up. I don't know how you let them talk you into those tattoos on your face…"

"They come off," said Richie.

"They better. Oh God, his face is all gashed… there's an exposed bone there, Richie. He's so…" Her voice broke into a sob.

Vince wanted to look at her. He wanted to talk to her, even though she was imaginary. He tried to speak. "Dierdre… you will find some… some…"

229

"Is he talking?"

"I think he said my name. Vince, we're almost at the boat…"

"He's shaking, maybe a seizure or…"

The voice faded out. The engine noise faded out. The sound of the sea was all that was left.

Then that was gone too.

"Vince!" Dierdre's voice.

He felt something crawling on him. Or off him. What was it? The pain came and went and came again, but it was like a fading anger, a peevishness.

"I think the pain meds are kicking in." A woman's voice, but not Dierdre's. A Filipino accent. "His heartbeat is quite arrhythmic. I am going to try some atropine… Erythropoietin is indicated as well, once we get him steadied…"

A flash of light. Then it was gone.

"I think I saw him open his eyes a little." Dierdre again. "Vince? Can you hear me?"

He felt so weak. It just seemed so very hard to talk. As if talking was as hard as pulling a wheeless car behind him with a chain. That was something he'd seen someone do, once. Or try to do. Some jarhead showing off at…

He lost the thread of thought. Was he really with Dierdre?

"Mr. Bellator?" The Filipino woman's voice. "Mr. Bellator, can you hear me? I'm going to take your hand, here. Can you feel it? Could you squeeze my hand if you can hear me?"

He experimented.

"He twitched his hand a bit there. Mr. Bellator, I'm Dr. Evangelista. I'm an emergency room doctor, from Manila. I am transfusing blood into you. You've had some internal bleeding and general blood loss.

230

We've cleaned your wounds and removed some shrapnel and closed everything up. You should feel encouraged. You mustn't give up! We're working very hard for you. We're on a fishing trawler. We're about to dock. I'm going to give you two more medications, and then we're going to consider some other options."

"How much blood infusion did he have?" Was that Richie?

The doctor didn't answer. "Okay there's the atropine and…" Then her voice faded. "We might need the… Yes, I think his heart is… we'll use this…"

A sizzling electrical shock at his chest.

"He's back." The doctor's voice. "But his heartbeat's still irregular."

Voice made a supreme effort. "Leave me 'lone. Let me go. Not much use to…"

"Vince!" Dierdre. "You're everything to me! Don't you dare give up!"

"Really, it's up to him, at this point." The doctor now. "I've seen this before, with severe blood loss, and trauma—the psychological side of it is very important. To come back from this, he has to want to live."

"Vince," Diedre whispering in his ear. He could feel her breath on his skin. He felt her warm hand on his.

She really was there. He was suddenly sure of it.

"Vince, listen to me—those women and those two men, Morris and Hiya—they made it to shore, and we saw they were taken care of. They're on their way to their homes now. That was *you* who did that, Vince. You set them free. The Chinese soldiers—they made it, too. That was your mercy, Vince. And we picked up the people from the galley. There's a man named Luke, right? He's here on this trawler! They're all here—you saved them! And now you have to save *me*, Vincent Bellator, and someone else too. Listen to me—I found something out the day after you left. I didn't want to tell you before, because I thought it might distract you on the mission. And I know distraction can kill out there. But Vince—listen… *I'm going to have a baby!* We both are, Vince! You and me! And me and the baby, we need you to be with us! You are going to be a father! You have to fight—you have to stay with us!"

A baby? He had to be there for the baby. For his child. For Dierdre.

A warmth was spreading through Vince. A little bit of strength was flowing into his arms.

Vince squeezed Dierdre's hand.

"He heard me! He understands!"

Vince felt the doctor's strong, probing fingers on his wrist.

The doctor said, "*Yes!* His pulse is steady. He's responding.! My prognosis is—I do believe that this man is going to live!"